The Elites

A Breakbattle Academy Novel

Ruby Vincent

Published by Ruby Vincent, 2020.

Prologue

"Excuse me." I raced up to them. "Excuse me, I'm one of the Elite students. Can you tell me who was hurt, please?"

"What's your name?" one of them asked.

"It's Zeke Manning."

"You're Zeke Manning?"

"Yes. Can you tell me who—"

"Zeke Manning." A rough hand seized me and spun me around. I cried out as my arms were twisted behind my back. "You're under arrest for the murder of Cameron Dupre. You have the right to remain—"

"What the fuck are you doing?!"

Derek rushed at them and one of the officers stepped out to meet him. I didn't see them clash. I didn't see anything. The world faded.

Faintly in the distance, I heard Christmas music.

Chapter One

The door opened behind me. I sat rigidly in the chair, my gaze pointed straight ahead at the neat, uniformed grooves of the cinderblock walls.

"Hello."

The cheerful voice reached me before the man stepped into my vision. My staredown with the wall ended as I met with a simple black suit and a surprisingly casual blue tie covered in cartoon ducks. He was a pleasant-looking guy. His beard sported flecks of gray and was trimmed neatly. His smile would be friendly if it wasn't for the fact that it didn't reach his eyes.

"Sorry for keeping you waiting, Zek— I mean... Zela." He pulled out the chair and sat. The smile still hung on his lips. "I'm Detective Langman. Did someone offer you something to drink?"

"Why am I here?" I asked bluntly.

I wasn't interested in the good-cop routine. My life had been turned upside down in the space of a weekend.

Langman cocked his head. "Were you not informed of the charges? Shit. That's an oversight."

I balled my fists. "No. I was told I was under arrest for Cameron's murder, but since that's complete nonsense, I want to know why you dragged me in here."

Langman's expression didn't change. "We'll get into all of that. You're underage so we've contacted your mother to be present during the interview. She should be here soon."

My muscles constricted even tighter. *Mom is coming? After lying to her, tricking her, and running away from her. The first time we'll see each other is in a police station.*

Might be a good thing, another voice spoke up. *There'll be cops here to save me when she loses her mind.*

"We don't have to wait for her," I said. "I didn't touch Cameron and you have no proof that I did."

"No?"

"No," I said firmly. "I wasn't even at school this weekend. I'm innocent."

He blew out a breath. "'I'm innocent. I have an alibi.' You won't believe how many times I've heard that."

"Can you just go?" I snapped. "If we have to wait for my mom, I'd rather wait alone."

"Of course, *Zela.*"

I pinched my lips at the way he kept saying my real name. Detective Langman might have worn a funny tie and a calm smile, but I knew when I was being mocked.

He patted my shoulder on the way out and I flinched. "I'll get that drink."

I resumed my staring contest with the wall after the door closed. My mind was a tangled mess. Every thought was whipping through my head too fast for me to grab one and make sense of it.

Jonathan Grayson wasn't my father. He wasn't *anyone's* father. My mother believed he was but she must have been with someone else around the time I was conceived. How would I find him? I wouldn't be stumbling over any more birth certificates and Mom went to school with hundreds of guys back then. How would I find my father in the midst of them eighteen years later?

And then there's Cameron...

Cameron Dupre was killed. Found dead in his own room. But why? Who would do that to him? And why in the hell did they think it was me? We've gotten into it over the years but I'd never hurt anyone.

He'd been going through something this year.

The whispered thought broke through the noise. I sat up straighter in my seat.

Cameron had been strange all year—quiet, head down, withdrawn. The lordly strolls through the cafeteria flaunting his status had stopped. He had given up torturing me like he forgot I existed except for—

"The party," I whispered. "He got into a fight at the party and then it sounded like he got into it with someone that day in the dorm."

I shook my head. I didn't know if it was the same person, or even who that person was. I had nothing to go on.

All I had was my innocence. That would have to be enough for Detective "Duck Tie" Langman.

The seconds ticked by in the chilly, concrete room as I waited. What felt like an hour but could have been minutes later, Langman returned and placed an unopened can of ginger soda on the table. I made no move to touch it.

He reclaimed his seat and we passed the time together—albeit in total silence.

"—is she?!"

I whipped around.

"How dare you bring her here without my permission! If I find out you've questioned her—"

"Please, ma'am!" The cry was laced with the special brand of exasperation my mother ignited in people. "Your daughter is in this interrogation room. You may go in. They're waiting for—"

The door flew open. Mom's growing hair was in the stage where it stuck out more than it lay flat. It could be why as she filled the doorway, radiating fury like I had never seen. The artificial lights caught her golden locks and made them look like they were aflame.

Sinking lower in my seat, I swallowed hard.

"Who are you?" she demanded.

"I'm Detective Langman." He rose and held out his hand. "You must be Miss Mann—"

She turned away from him, dismissing him outright. "Zela, get up. We're leaving."

I jumped up without question.

"No, you're not," Langman said. He smoothly stepped into the path of the doorway.

Mom kept coming until she was in his face. "You have no grounds to arrest my daughter."

Langman looked down on her impassively. "What I have are eyewitness accounts that your daughter got into an altercation with the victim more than once. What I have is a blackmail video hidden in the victim's room where Cameron Dupre has her stripped and threatens to reveal her identity as a girl to everyone."

"What? Cameron Dupre?" Mom turned to me. Her righteous fury melted away and was replaced by shock. "He did what to her?"

Langman's brows shot up. "You didn't know."

It wasn't a question.

"Then I also have a suspect with something to hide that she wouldn't report an assault to her mother. I also have a school with no cameras, an unlocked gate, and the only record of who comes and goes is one man and one sign-in sheet in the administration office. I think that's plenty, Miss Manning. What do you think?"

"I can explain all of that!" I cried.

"I would love to hear that explanation." He held out his hand. "Please, sit."

My mom's eyes remained on me as she slowly approached the table and pulled out her seat. I looked away. I couldn't stand the betrayal that shone in them.

Langman reclaimed his seat and gave me that smile once again. He took out a pad and pen from his breast pocket and flipped it to a blank page. "Okay, Zela. Tell me about that night in the woods."

"There's nothing more to tell. It's all on the video." I cut eyes to Mom. She was still looking at me, piercing me through with her gaze. I turned back to Langman. "Cameron agreed to keep my secret if I didn't get in the way of the expansion. I agreed and that was the end of it."

"I reviewed the tape and there was an interesting bit at the end when Cameron insinuates he'll reveal your secret if the attacks by this"—Langman flipped through his notebook—"For All don't cease. As we both know, the attacks did not stop and the principal tells me they have yet to identify the culprit."

I blinked at him. How is this guy so well-informed?

"Did you get panicky, Zela? Afraid that the next attack would be the outing of your secret."

"No. There was nothing for me to be panicked about. Cameron didn't know it but not long after that night in the woods, I accomplished what I came to Breakbattle to do. I had no reason to hurt him and if he revealed my secret, it wouldn't have changed anything."

I shook my head. "Not that he seemed interested. He's kept to himself for the last couple months. I barely remember the last time he looked in my direction. We didn't have a problem this year."

He nodded. "I see. And the night of the fundraiser?"

"I never touched him. Cameron got into a fight with someone else."

"Who?"

"I didn't see them."

His raised eyebrow told me what he thought of that. "How did you get blood on your clothes?"

"Cameron ran into me getting away from them. His forehead was bleeding and it got on me. I tried to ask him if he was okay and who hurt him, but he wouldn't talk to me."

"What about—"

"Listen." I cut my hand through the air. "None of this matters because I *wasn't on campus* this weekend. I was as shocked as everyone when I came back to school and found out he was hurt."

"Then—"

"Where were you?" Mom's sharp voice interrupted Langman. She grasped my chin between two fingers and made me face her. "Tell me."

"I was... with Derek," I whispered.

"Where?"

"His dad has a place near the studio. It sits empty when he's between movies, so Derek knew we'd be alone."

"What's the address?" asked Langman.

"It's—" I tried to look at him but Mom held me fast.

"Why would you go there with this Derek boy?" she asked. "Why didn't you answer my calls or tell me where you were?" Her hand shook my chin. "I was worried sick!"

"I'm sorry, Mom," I replied through trembling lips. "It was just too much. I didn't know what to do."

"You should have—"

Langman cleared his throat. "Excuse me. If I could conduct this interview, we can wrap this up much quicker. Cameron Dupre was seen at dinner last night, so we're estimating his death was between nine and midnight after he returned to his room. You're claiming you were off campus with someone?"

Mom let me go and I addressed Langman. "I was."

"Tell me the address and the full name of this person."

"I don't know the address. I wasn't paying attention to where we were going. You can ask Derek Grayson. That's his name."

He wrote something in his pad. "And your mother did not know where you were," he confirmed without looking up.

"No."

"Why is that?"

"None of your business," Mom said firmly. "It's a personal family matter and don't give me any nonsense about having a right to know everything in a murder investigation," she added when he opened his mouth. "She told you where she was when this Cameron was killed and that was nowhere near him. Derek Grayson will tell you the same thing. As I said, you have no grounds to hold my daughter, so unless you can provide concrete proof, we're leaving."

Mom and Langman stared at each other. The atmosphere was charged with two indomitable wills. I held my breath waiting to see what would happen.

Langman closed his notepad. "Actually, you can provide the concrete proof, Zela." He addressed me but didn't glance away from Mom.

"What does that mean?"

"I will speak to Derek Grayson of course and see if I can confirm this alibi, but we may be able to settle this conclusively if you provide a DNA sample."

"No," Mom said.

"There was blood on the victim that we assume is the killer's. If she—"

"No. She's given you her alibi and that is more than enough. I won't have you treat her like a criminal for a moment longer." She snagged the hem of my sleeve and stood us both up. "Goodbye, Detective. If you have any more questions, you can direct them to my lawyer."

"I just have one more."

His words stopped us at the door.

"What was it that made all of this worth it, Zela? The lying. The hiding. The blackmail. Why did you do it?"

I sensed Mom didn't want me to answer, but I did anyway. "I did it for my family."

"And you say you accomplished what you set out to do?"

A lump formed in my throat. I forced myself to reply. "Yes, I did. For better or worse, I did."

Langman's jovial smile returned. He rose from his seat and crossed over to me, making Mom put herself between us.

"That's good," he said over her shoulder. I could see his eyes clearly. "Because the academy has been informed of the truth. They know you're a girl... and I'm told they'll be in contact with you soon. Have a nice day, Zela." He stepped around Mom and grabbed the doorknob. "I'm sure we'll speak again soon."

Langman walked out, and then it was just me and Mom.

I couldn't lift my eyes higher than her knees. I steadied myself waiting for her to blow.

"Are you okay?"

"What?" I raised my head.

"He said that boy assaulted y-you." Her voice cracked.

I nodded slowly. "He and his friends tore my clothes off for the camera."

Her hand flew to her mouth.

"They left me in my bra and panties," I said quickly.

"That doesn't matter! How dare they touch you at all?! If they're in the video, then the detective can identify them. I'll let him know we intend to press charges."

Mom swept out of the room before I could stop her—not that I intended to. I didn't have a secret to keep anymore. It was past time they paid for what they did to me.

MOM WAS QUIET ON THE drive home. I was ready for her screaming, yelling, and raving but none came. Many times, I opened my mouth to apologize. Nothing I came up with was enough. I loved my mother. She was tough, unconventional, and hid more than she shared, but she was always there for me, and she did her best to raise me as a strong, healthy, smart, young woman. I lied to her and I would accept the anger I rightly deserved for it.

I peeked at Mom out of the corner of my eye. *If only it would come.*

Mom turned onto our driveway and killed the engine. She didn't look at me as she said, "It's been a long day. Go inside, get cleaned up, and I'll make lunch."

She grabbed the door handle.

"Mom, I'm sorry."

She stilled.

"I'm sorry I didn't tell you the real reason I wanted to become Zeke. I'm sorry about Jonathan. If I had known he couldn't have kids sooner, none of this would have happened."

"What does that mean, Zela? How would that excuse you tricking me?" Her voice was tight.

"It doesn't—"

"You're right!" She spun on me. "It doesn't excuse anything you've done for these last years, Zela. *Years!*" The calm mask cracked. Pain and anger leaked out of Mom's eyes as the first tear I've seen her shed in years ran down her cheek. "When did you find out about him?!"

"A... few days after we moved back to Chesterfield," I croaked. "I found my birth certificate."

"So you made up a story about wanting to help with my book and combat sexism to get close to that man. How could you do this, Zela?"

"I did it for Derek," I admitted. "I wanted to know my brother. I didn't see another way to be a part of his life without enrolling on the boys' campus. I won't pretend I didn't start this hoping one day I'd get close to Jonathan, but I wasn't going after him. I remember the last time I went after my father."

Mom's eyes flashed. "Do *not*, Zela. Don't blame me for what happened that day at the mall."

I pressed my lips together tight, holding in any reply that could make this worse. My love for Mom was always there through all of this. It tugged on my guilt even as my anger simmered beneath the surface. I didn't want to think it... but a part of me knew six-year-old Zela never would have ended up in the arms of a predator if my mother had told me the truth.

Maybe Mom saw that in my eyes because her jaw slackened. "Zela! I made up a name to protect you! How could I— How could I ever have predicted what happened?!"

She surged forward and took hold of me, cupping my face in her hands. "You're my daughter and all I've ever done is protect you. Jonathan Grayson was a name too well known. I couldn't have you track him down and be hurt the same way I was."

Tears ran freely down her cheeks. "He was awful to me when I told him I was pregnant. He called me a gold-digging slut and that I wasn't going to use my brat to trap him. He threatened me if I ever contacted him again." She shook me. "Do you see why I wanted you to have nothing to do with that man?!"

Mom blurred as wetness filled my eyes. "Yes," I rasped. "He was awful, but—"

"I know." She suddenly released me. "Jonathan and I had a long talk after you ran from me. He explained the difficult time he was going through with his wife and why. It wasn't possible for him to be your father and he came to the natural conclusion that I was with another man. He believed I was trying to trade in to get you a wealthier father."

She let out a long, soft breath. "I understand his anger now. I never knew he was sterile. I put his name on your birth certificate truly believing he was your father. We had been together many times and I slept with that other man only once." She stroked my cheek. "But once is all it took to give me you."

I swiped my eyes with the back of my palm and Mom came into better focus. "So you know who he was?"

"Of course I do."

"What's his name?" I asked. "Who is he? Where is he?"

"Oh, Zela." Mom pressed a kiss to my temple. "I'm not going to tell you."

I froze. "What?"

"I'm not telling you his name." She pulled back and looked me in the eyes. "We won't speak another word of this after today."

"B-but, Mom—"

"No." Before my eyes, she hardened into the mom I knew. "He does not matter. He never has. You've let this need to know your biological father define you. It's turned you into someone I don't believe you want to be. I don't blame you. It was my job to raise you to be an independent woman who didn't rely on a man for her identity."

My throat tightened as every horrible word fell from her lips.

"I've failed you in a lot of ways, Zela. I know that and I'm truly sorry, but I will not tell you who your father is."

"You h-have to."

She can't be serious. After everything I've done. Everything I've been through. How can she tell me no?

"He's my father," I rasped. "I have a right to know."

And then it broke through. The rage simmering beneath the surface roared up and spilled out.

"You have to tell me!" I screamed.

I punched the dash. Pain erupted in my hand but I barely noticed. "You've lied to me my whole life! You've let me be the kid who had to tell people I didn't know my own dad's name! How could I tell you the truth about why I wanted to go to Breakbattle? All you would have done is refused to let me enroll and fed me more lies! The person I've become is because of you!"

My chest heaved with hard pants. I'd never yelled at my mother like this before.

Her expression remained stony. "Let it go, Zela." She threw open her door and walked out, leaving me behind.

I gaped after her in complete disbelief. I couldn't breathe.

How could she say that to me? How can she just walk away from me?

I sprinted out of the car. "Mom!? Mom!"

She didn't look back. Mom stepped inside and shut the door behind her. I burst in, feet thudding on the hardwood floors as I chased after her. She slammed into her office. I rattled the knob.

Locked.

"Mom!? Mom, talk to me!"

Bang! Bang! Bang!

"Tell me his name! I have to know his name!" I screamed. Tears flowed hot and fast, soaking my cheeks and throat. "Tell me!"

Sinking to the floor, I twisted the knob until my palms cried out.

"Let me in!"

I pounded and screamed for hours. Mom never opened the door.

Chapter Two

"I see it's still World War III in here."

I looked up from my book as Jordan came into the room.

"Hey. Aunt Bev finally freed you."

My cousin climbed onto my bed and curled up at my side. "Temporary leave for good behavior," she replied. "Mom says I'm grounded for as long as it takes for you and Aunt Dronika to patch things up. It's my punishment for lying to both of them."

"I'm sorry." I rested my cheek on top of her head. "Especially because it's been weeks."

Yes, weeks.

After Mom refused to tell me the name of my true father, I returned to school in a cloud of pain, shame, and suspicion. Cameron's death hung heavy over the student body and everyone knew I was brought in for questioning. Their whispers and stares were unbearable... and still I preferred it to going home.

I refused to leave with Mom on the weekends and, eventually, she stopped coming to pick me up. I didn't speak to her for the rest of the semester until yesterday when the end of school brought us together. It had been a tense atmosphere in the Manning household since we came home.

"Don't worry about me," she said. "Mom eased up on the television privileges a couple of weeks ago. It's not so bad now but I miss Adam."

"He misses you too. The guy would not stop asking me how you were and when he'd get to see you again."

"What about you? How are you? To say things got crazy is an understatement."

I squeezed my eyes shut. The last several weeks had been the worst of my entire life. I cried almost every day. But I didn't want to do it any longer.

"Not so great," I admitted. "It's been hard but the boys have been amazing. I promised Cole I'd tell him the truth about what was going on with me and Derek. In the end, I told all of them. They understood, forgave me for lying about why I came, and they backed me up to Whittaker and Argyle."

"Did it help?"

I scoffed. "Not even a little."

Memories of sitting in Whittaker's office and going through my second interrogation in two days flashed through my mind.

"Having my boyfriends tell him they knew I was a girl all along didn't sway him that my presence on the boys' campus hasn't been a problem. He went on about flouting the rules on girls not being allowed in a boys' dorm and inappropriate relations until Miss Val stopped him."

"Ugh. So he made your search for your father about a nonstop sex parade?"

"Pretty much." I sighed. "There's so much I need to catch you up on, JoJo. From Mr. Sondheim being assigned to making sure I don't go into any other room but my own to the police tromping all over campus trying to find Cameron's killer."

"I still can't believe he was killed," she whispered. "Do the police have any idea who did it?"

"All I got from Langman is that their evidence is a few traces of blood, a blackmail video with me in it, eyewitnesses seeing me chasing after Cameron at the fundraiser, a bunch of people telling him that Cameron had it out for me, and my threats on the video to make him pay. They have an idea who did it and in Langman's head, it's solidly Zela Manning."

She shot up, gaping at me. "Are you kidding me? But you have an alibi."

"He said it's only Derek's and my word that we were there. He could be lying to protect me or I could have snuck away while he was sleeping. He knows it's not enough though or he'd force the blood test."

"Fuck," she cried. "And all this time he's wasting on you, he could be searching for the real killer."

"Seriously." I leaned against the board, gazing up at the ceiling. "I just wish I had a name to give him. Cameron was fighting with someone but I don't know who. None of his friends would talk to me, of course, because the world knows they've assaulted me. Now they've all graduated. It's a mess."

"I'm sorry, Zee." She squeezed my arm. "But you're not going down for this. This detective has nothing and that's not going to change. Soon, he'll move on to real suspects. In the meantime, you have your own shit to deal with."

I sighed. "Tell me about it. Mom and I are barely speaking to each other. I've gone from not knowing Derek existed, to believing he was my brother, to whatever we are now, and yesterday, Whittaker and Argyle gave me their decision about my final year at Breakbattle."

"Oh no, Zee. What did they say?"

I shook my head. "There was no way they were letting me stay even if they hadn't found out about the boys. Zeke is gone, Jordan. I think they went easier on me after finding out what the Network boys did to me in the woods, but all the same, if I want to go back to Breakbattle, I go as Zela. Whittaker says arrangements have already been made for the Elite girls' class to have their eleventh student."

"You're right," she breathed. "I've missed a lot."

"When is Aunt Warden coming to claim you? Because we still have a lot to talk about."

"Spill. I'm not going anywhere anytime soon."

Hours later, I walked Jordan to Aunt Bev's idling car and hugged her goodbye. Aunt Bev leaned out of the window.

"How are you, Zee? You and your mom still fighting?"

I let my silence be the answer.

She pinned me with a look. "Patch things up soon. I understand why you're upset, and you know I don't agree with Brenda on much, but I agree with her on this. Her first priority has always been to protect you. If she won't tell you his name, there is a good reason."

I heard her concern. It didn't penetrate. "I'll be eighteen in two weeks. At some point, you both have to stop treating me like that six-year-old girl who got lost in the mall."

"Zela, that's not what— Zela!"

I turned my back on her and went into the house.

"I do."

I paused with one foot on the steps.

Mom stepped out of the living room. "I have a good reason, Zela. You have to trust me."

"Okay, Mom."

"I don't want to fight anymore." She reached for me and I smoothly stepped out of reach. She slowly returned her hand to her side. "Dinner will be ready in a few minutes."

"Yes, Mom."

I continued upstairs without a backward glance.

"ARE YOU GROUNDED?"

"Not officially." I flipped over, cradling the phone in the crook of my neck. "Mom and I aren't talking much these days but I know her well enough not to ask to go anywhere."

"That's a shame," said Landon. "I was thinking I'd pick you up tomorrow and we'd watch another movie on the hill."

The beginnings of a smile tugged at my lips. It was the first in a while. "I wish I could."

"We have to get in all the quality time we can this summer. Senior year we'll be separated."

"It's better than being expelled. Still, I'll hate not seeing you guys except for breakfast and dinner."

"We're going to see each other a lot more than that. Moon and Melody make it work. We will too."

"Our matrons won't let us anywhere near each other's rooms."

"We both know you like getting it on outside."

I giggled. "Those were special circumstances."

"We're going to have a few more special circumstances."

Heat pooled in my lower belly just thinking about being with Landon. Mr. Sondheim put a serious kink in our sex life since I was outed on campus.

"About tomorrow, Zee," he continued. "We have to think of something. I can't not see you on your birthday."

"I don't know what we can do. My mom works from home, so I couldn't sneak out without her knowing. Plus, Jordan says they're coming over for the day. I can't get away right now, Landon, but as soon as I can, we'll celebrate to-gether."

"I miss you, baby. I hope things get better with you guys soon."

I dropped my head onto my pillow. "I don't see that hap-pening. This would all be over if she'd tell me who he is."

"It sounded like Jonathan Grayson was a total shit to her. What if this other guy was even worse? I mean, if he was a good guy that would have stepped up, why didn't she run to tell him the truth as soon as she knew it couldn't be Grayson?"

"Landon, not you too," I whispered. "Everyone is trying to convince me my biological father must be Satan to justify my mother refusing to tell me the truth. Why does no one get that isn't the point? I'm tired of her protecting me with silence and lies. He's my father. Knowing him should be my choice."

"I'm on your side, Zela. I promise you, I am, but..."

"But what?"

"It destroyed you when Jonathan rejected you and he wasn't even your father. What if your real dad does the same? What if your mom is sure that he will?"

Tears prickled at the back of my eyes. I pressed my palm into them, willing myself not to cry.

"I can handle it if he does. I just want to know who he is."

"Zee—"

"Can we stop talking about this? I was feeling better for a brief second there." I picked myself up and moved to my desk. "Tell me about your summer. Are you going to Europe again?"

"Um... yeah. Prague for a few weeks. I'll bring you back something."

It was slow but my smile was coming back. "Chocolates?"

"Definitely. Want anything else? The birthday girl gets whatever she wants."

"What she wants is to curl up with you in the back of a truck."

"I'll make that happen."

We talked for a little longer before saying goodbye. I went downstairs and found Mom in the kitchen.

"Mom?"

She jumped like someone who lived alone hearing a voice. I guess it felt like we both lived alone after the last few weeks.

"Yes?" She put the knife down on the cutting board. "What is it, Zela?"

"Argyle said she'd send forms to fill out for my new uniform and the rulebook for the girls' campus. Did you get them? I haven't seen them."

"Yes, I got them." She stepped away from the counter and pointed to the kitchen stool. "Sit down, Zela."

Unease crept into my bones as I took a seat. I did not like the serious look on her face. "What's wrong?"

"What's wrong?" she repeated. She claimed the seat next to me, and to my surprise, took my hand. "I don't like the way things have been between us the last few weeks, but in one thing I realize I was wrong. I did not ask you what you want to do going forward.

"A lot has happened at that school that I did not know about. You were held against your will, assaulted, and blackmailed. That is more than anyone should have to deal with." She sighed. "Despite what is going on with us, it's important that you know you don't have to return to that school if you don't want to. To be honest, I'm seriously considering pulling you out. You did not enter with a true desire to attend in the first place."

I quietly took in what she was saying. She had a point. I went to Breakbattle for Derek and we were closer than ever now. I didn't have to return to a place where I had been targeted, beaten, bullied, harassed, and forced to participate in the battle system. I didn't have to endure being looked at like I was a murderer.

My college applications were in. My grades and extracurriculars were perfect. I could ride out my last year at Chesterfield High with my cousin and for once not have a year filled with pain and drama.

There was only one problem.

"I don't want to leave, Mom. It's been tough, but I've made friends." Adam's grin popped into my head and I smiled. "The kind of friends that have your back through everything. I love my teachers. I love Archimedean Club. I love eating breakfast with Landon, running with Michael, and studying with Cole. I love being in one place for the first time in my life. If I let them drive me out, I'll lose everything good about Breakbattle along with the bad."

Mom listened to my speech with an expression I couldn't read. "All of that is wonderful, Zela, but your friends and boyfriends will always be there. I have to think of your safety."

"The boys who assaulted me have graduated and Zach, Rhys, Sullivan and his buddies can't do anything to me on the girls' side."

She released me and stood. "I will think about it. Get cleaned up and help me with dinner."

I hesitated. "You want me to help?"

"Yes. You can be angry with me but this silent treatment ends now. Tomorrow is your birthday. I won't spend it the way we have been the last few days."

I didn't know what to say. I was going to be angry with her. I'd be angry for as long as she refused to tell me my father's name, but I'd end the fight if it meant I'd no longer have to tiptoe around my house, be kept from my boys, and Jordan would be released from house arrest.

"Okay."

Mom kissed me on the forehead. If she lingered longer than normal, I didn't draw attention to it. She sent me off to get cleaned up and I came back to help her with dinner. While we cooked, we talked a little about what I wanted to do for my birthday. Neither one of us mentioned fathers or battle academies.

I WOKE THE NEXT MORNING to presents on my pillow. Three gifts and three texts to go along with them.

Landon: We drove down to leave these on your doorstep. I hope you like it. I love you. Happy Birthday.

Michael: Saw it and knew it would be perfect for you. Happy Birthday!

Cole: You've waited long enough. Happy birthday, Zela.

The last text was puzzling.

"Waited long enough," I read. "What does that mean?"

I tossed the phone aside and picked up a tiny box wrapped in gold paper. My face split in half as I laid eyes on the necklace. A butterfly hung on the silver chain by one blue wing. I put it on right away and then picked up a flat, rectangular gift. I tore it open and pulled out a blue dress covered in sequins.

Landon's gift.

I ran my fingers over the fine material. *This is the dress I wore the night of our first date. His original design.*

Getting out of bed, I held the dress up to me as I twirled in front of my mirror. Declan shouldn't have changed it. This dress was perfect.

I slipped out of my pajamas and pulled the dress over my head. It clung to my body in all the right places.

Last was a small red gift bag with pink tissue paper. I reached inside and took out a DVD. A note was taped over the front.

What would I do if I could do anything?
I'd be with you.

I removed the note and clutched it to my chest. Two sentences and one *Limitless* DVD and Cole kicked my heart up to maximum.

I picked up my phone and dialed him. He answered on the third ring.

"Do you mean it?" I asked. "We're done waiting? We're done hooking up?"

"I talked to Michael. We both want to be with you and you want to be with us. And it's good that we're best friends. We can trust each other to be good to you."

My heart was so full it might explode. "This is the best birthday present you could have given me. I want the real thing with you, Cole Reed. Even if you make the rest of my life a challenge."

"Guaranteed you'll do the same... for the rest of our lives."

I bit my lip. "I want to see you."

"I thought you were grounded?"

"I might not be. Mom and I called a sort of truce yesterday. But I want to see you no matter what. Come by tonight after she goes to sleep."

"I'll be there."

We said goodbye and I called Michael.

"Happy birthday, Zee."

"Thank you." I played with the butterfly charm. "Even though you're low-key making fun of me."

He chuckled. "I told you. I love it when you pretend you're flying around the track. It's cute as hell."

"That's me. Cute as hell." I settled back into my sheets. "I heard you and Cole talked."

"I'm sorry we made you wait. He's my best friend. I didn't want to lose him."

"I didn't want that either. I just want to know that you and I are okay."

"Of course we are."

I kept up my fiddling. "You said at the start you wanted to take things slow to make sure what we have is real. It's real for me, Michael. It's been real since Orlando. I don't want to hold back anymore, and I'm not talking about sex," I added quickly. "If you want to wait, then that's what I want too. Just tell me that we're both all in."

He replied a breath after me. "I'm all in, Zela, and I'm ready for what that means. I'm sick of slow and it was my idea."

I hid my smile in my pillow. "You know just what to give a girl on her birthday."

"I'll give you something else the next time I see you. I rewrote the letter you lost."

"You did?" Excitement filled and popped in my chest like bubbles. "What does it say? Read it to me."

"Can't." I picked up a teasing lilt to his tone. "But you can read it yourself when I give it to you."

Groaning, I said, "I thought you were done making me wait."

"Apparently, I got one more in me. I can't wait to see you. Enjoy your day."

"Bye."

I hung up. I held my phone in one hand and my charm in the other. It's amazing how they did it. They washed away the torment of the last few weeks of my life and made me feel like I would never be happier. All it took were three little presents on my doorstep.

I had one more call to make but my stomach was rumbling. Stepping into the hall, I sniffed the heavenly scent of sizzling bacon and roasting butternut squash.

"It smells great, Mom," I called. "Did you make your famous guacamo—"

"Surprise!"

I shot back and almost tripped over my feet. I fell against the banister with a hard smack.

"Ow."

Adam and Jordan rushed out of the kitchen.

"Are you okay, Zee?" Jordan helped me up. "How sad would it be if you broke something on your birthday?"

"Incredibly," I muttered. I rubbed my bruised tailbone. "No harm done though."

I scooped her and Adam in for a hug. "I'm so glad you're here."

"I wasn't missing your birthday," Adam whispered in my ear. "Your mom said it was family only at first, so I got my mom to talk to her. She went full therapist and filled her head with stuff about your 'emotional development' and 'the calming influence of a friend being important during hard times.' I wanted to get Michael, Cole, and Landon an invite too, but Mom said we shouldn't push it."

I squeezed him tighter. "Thank you for trying. I'm just glad I can celebrate with you."

"One more thing." He pulled back. "About Derek…"

I stiffened. "What's wrong? I've been calling him but he doesn't answer. And I can't bring myself to call his parents."

"He's on major house arrest. They took his phone away and everything. I found out when I tried to visit him yesterday. He probably won't be able to talk to you for a while."

My heart sank. It shouldn't have surprised me he'd be in trouble after hiding his father's supposed love child and then running away with me after the truth came out. Still, Derek and I had a lot to figure out. Also, I missed him. I wanted to talk to him. Especially today.

"Happy birthday, Zee," Aunt Bev called. "Come, come. We've made breakfast but we can skip ahead to cake."

"Sounds good to me."

My party was low-key but I enjoyed every minute. Jordan baked me a chocolate ganache cake and she, Adam, and I ate in front of the television watching videos Mom made of our travels.

"I can't believe you took a mud bath with elephants," said Adam.

Ten-year-old Zela beamed at the camera as she skipped through the mud in her bathing suit. Surrounding her were creatures fifty times her size. Our whole life felt like a vacation, but that trip to Thailand was a proper one. Mom and I took two weeks off, eating and taking pictures around the country. My dignified mom even got in the mud with us.

There was no one to hold the camera, so there was no proof. Aunt Bev still didn't believe me.

"And people tell me I've lived a charmed life," Adam went on.

"It was incredible," I replied. "Elephants love mud. You should see the big guys rolling around in it like kids at a waterpark. I got to rub them down and then wash off with them in the river."

"We should travel together," he said. "After we graduate, we can go backpacking around Europe or someplace like that."

I paused with my fork halfway to my mouth. "Are you serious? Don't tempt me, Moon. Because I would love that. We'd have so much fun."

Adam cracked a grin. "Completely serious. We can do the whole thing. Oversized packs. Hostels. Crowded tourist sites. My mom would be cool." He made a face. "But she'd have to convince my dads. You wouldn't believe they're the overprotective ones."

I squealed. "Yes, let's do it! I've been dying to go back to Europe. I'll take you to all my favorite places in France. We can—"

"Ahem."

Jordan gave us a look from Adam's right. "Am I invited on this best friend adventure? Or do we not care about girl-friends and favorite cousins anymore?"

Adam kissed her. "Course you're invited, Jo. We wouldn't want to go without you."

"How nice."

Our heads snapped up. Mom and Aunt Bev came into the living room carrying their plates. It was a proper breakfast of avocado, bacon, and butternut squash wraps for them.

"We'd love to go on a trip around Europe," said Aunt Bev. "Wouldn't we love that, sis?"

"It's been too long since I've been," Mom echoed. "The five of us would have a great time."

"On second thought," Jordan muttered. "I should spend the summer getting ready for college."

"What's that supposed to mean?" Aunt Bev moved fast. She caught her daughter's face and peppered it with kisses as she cried out. "You don't want your old mom on your big trip with your boyfriend?"

"Mom, stop!" she squealed. Laughing, Jordan tried to get away. Aunt Bev put her plate down and chased after her.

I smiled watching them mess around. Amazing that after everything—Aunt Bev snooping in her phone, violating her privacy, and grounding her—they were able to patch things up quickly.

I glanced at Mom and found her looking at me. I dropped my gaze quickly. Mom and I had never been in a fight like this, but either way, I knew we wouldn't resolve this as quickly.

Adam nudged me. "I'll talk to my parents about it tonight and let you know."

I nodded. "Okay. Make sure they know I'm quite the wrestler now. I'll protect you if anything goes down."

He laughed. "I'll start with that."

We finished up our cake and then they brought out the presents. Jordan, Mom, and Aunt Bev carried one gift each into the living room. Adam had three on each arm.

I gaped at him. "Did you do something you're making up for?"

"Nope." Adam dumped the lot in my lap. "They're from all of us. Esme even threw something in there for you. The gifts are all for *Zela*," he admitted. "Since the secret is out."

I looked away. "They aren't mad that we lied to them? You shared a dorm with a girl for two years. I've stayed at your house so many times."

He sat next to me. "They aren't mad. Especially after I explained about you, Derek, and your dad. Mom said she understood."

She would understand. She'd understand more than most.

Aunt Bev brushed the hair back from my cheek. "It must be a relief to not have to lie anymore. You can be yourself from now on."

"In a way, it is," I said softly. "But this year will be hard for different reasons. I didn't like Cameron but... he didn't deserve that."

"Hey." Jordan knelt in front of me. "Don't think about this stuff on your birthday. Come on. Open your gifts. Mine first."

She shoved hers on me. I ripped the paper off the small box and revealed a silver bracelet. Aunt Bev's gift of a baby blue jewelry box was the perfect companion. Next, I tackled the mountain of presents Adam's family sent me.

From Jaxson, I got a record of an obscure South African artist that I swore no one knew of except for him and me.

Maverick gifted me a new tablet. From Ezra, I got a bunch of goodies such as a new travel mug, travel purse, and a passport holder. He didn't know how soon I would be using this.

Esme drew me a pretty picture of me and Jordan together. She had never seen my real hair before, so she guessed and made it the same shade as Jordan's. We looked like sisters and I loved it so much I forgave her for years of abuse.

"And this is from my mom and Ryder." Adam placed the last gift on my lap. "They said it's tradition to give this to a young woman on her eighteenth birthday."

"Tradition?" Mom asked. "What is it?"

I revealed my gift and gasped. A beautiful, shining string of pearls lay on top of an ivory bed.

"Oh my gosh," I cried. "What would they have gotten me if I was Zeke?"

He shrugged. "I don't know. Socks."

I laughed. "Lucky I'm a girl, then."

"This is too extravagant a gift," said Aunt Bev.

"It is."

I made a choked noise when Mom's hand flashed across my vision and took the pearls. "Tell your mom and dad we appreciate the thought, Adam, but Zela cannot accept this. Save it for Esme's eighteenth birthday."

Mom's tone brokered no argument. I watched in disappointment as Adam put the gift back in the bag.

I guess I knew Mom wouldn't let me keep it. At least I got to hold it for all of a minute.

"Alright, my only one." Mom stepped around the couch and moved in front of me. In her hands, was a present no bigger than her palm. "Today is the day that marks you as a woman and quite a woman you've become. You're a strong, intelligent, *defiant*, and beautiful young lady."

Every word was a dagger to my anger. It slipped further away as Mom gazed at me with a tender look that was made more special for being rare.

"This is my gift to you."

I took the small, wrapped box from her outstretched hand. I peeked at Jordan as I tore off the paper. She was smiling ear to ear like she was in on the secret.

I lifted the lid to a folded piece of paper.

Frowning, I pulled it out. My eyes grew huge as I flipped it open.

"Mom," I whispered. "But— But— Why?"

A check for one thousand dollars lay nestled in my hand.

"My life changed for the better the day I packed up my baby and we set off across the world together. I discovered who I was and the woman I hoped to one day be. Use this to buy your own plane ticket. Anywhere you want to go." Her voice took on a knowing tint. "Maybe to Europe with your friends."

Tears stung my eyes. It wasn't fair her doing this. I wanted to be mad at her. I had a *right* to be mad at her.

I dropped the check and ran into Mom's arms. I hugged her so tight she grunted.

"I'm sorry, Mom," I whispered. "I love you."

The next thing I knew she was squeezing me back even harder. "I love you too. Please remember that no matter what, I love you. You're my only one."

"Damn." Jordan's voice broke in. "I'm going to start crying."

I gave a sob-choked laugh. "No tears. Let's start planning our trip instead."

"Hell, yes."

I gave Mom one last squeeze. She kissed the top of my head and then sent us upstairs. Adam, Jordan, and I had a blast looking up the places we wanted to go and what we'd do. The only thing that could have made this birthday better was spending it with my boys. I just hoped I'd get to see one of them that night.

Adam's phone went off in the middle of plotting how to tackle Austria.

"Hello? Yeah," he said. "No, her mom said it was too much. Okay. I'm coming."

Adam hung up. "My mom is outside. I'll let you know what she says about the trip tomorrow." He kissed me on the cheek. "Happy birthday, Zee."

"Bye, Adam. Thanks for coming."

Adam pulled Jordan off to a corner and gave her a longer and much more intimate goodbye. I averted my eyes when their hands snuck beneath their clothes.

Jordan skipped to my side after he left. "Best birthday ever."

Aunt Bev and Jordan stuck around for a few more hours and joined us for dinner. Jordan and I cooked and presented them with chicken stir-fry and fresh, tossed salad. As we laughed around the table, it was almost like the last few months never happened. We were the Manning women once again. Four strong personalities that fit just right together.

Mom and I waved Aunt Bev and Jordan out of the driveway.

"Did you have a good day?" Mom asked.

"It was perfect."

"Good." She brushed my cheek with a kiss. "I'm going to write for a little bit and then head to bed. Good night, Zela."

"Night."

I stood motionless in the hallway until I heard the telltale click of her office lock. I pulled out my phone.

Me: My mom will be passed out in an hour. Two tops. Start driving now.

He came back right away.

Cole: Going with the sneaking-in option.

Me: No choice. I wasn't getting a yes for what we're really going to do tonight.

Cole: Hmm. I thought we said no more hooking up. I'm more than just a piece of meat, Zela Rae.

I stifled a laugh.

Me: We can always stay up late and talk. I like you for your conversation too.

Cole: Wanna bet how long we can last without putting our hands on each other?

Me: Make it a bet I want to lose.

Cole: If I win, I'll swallow needles.

I didn't hold my laugh this time.

Me: So your hands will be on me the minute you come through the door?

Cole: Pretty much.

My heart fluttered in my chest like it was trying to escape. I had no delusions about what we were going to do tonight and it wasn't talking. After a year of dancing around it, I was ready to be with Cole in every way.

The nerves set in as I stepped into my room. It might have been my ascent to womanhood that flipped the switch. I looked around my room at the pink, floral bedspread. The childhood photos of me buck-toothed and cheesing at the camera, and the clincher, my teddy bears decorating my desk.

I snatched them up and tossed them in the ottoman before my bed.

This place is a freaking kid's room! Why did no one tell me?

I raced around, picking up stray clothes, hiding the most embarrassing stuff, and fixing my sheets. I put the last pillow in place and then took off my dress. Jordan gave me sexy underwear as a joke when Landon and I started having sex.

My face burst into flames when she gave me the lacy, see-through bra and thong. They did the same the second time around. I was too embarrassed to wear this before but something about Cole made me want to do things that scared me.

I changed my underwear and put my dress back on. Breathing slow, I lay across my silk sheets and willed my pulse to calm.

There is no reason to be nervous. Cole and I have done almost everything there is to do. We're just taking it to the level we've been waiting for.

My phone buzzed.

Cole: I'm outside.

I glanced at the clock.

Me: How? I texted you twenty-five minutes ago. You didn't speed, did you?

Cole: I was already in the car by the time you texted me. I was seeing you whether your mom said yes or no.

My smile split my cheeks.

Me: Hold on. I have to check my mom is in bed first.

Silently, I slipped out of the door. A soft hum spread through the top floor, signaling the air conditioner was doing its job. I heard nothing else.

My footfalls were soundless on the carpeted steps. Reaching the bottom floor, I peeked around the banister and saw the lights on in Mom's bedroom. She was awake but wouldn't be for much longer.

I crept to the front door and pulled it open, revealing Cole obscured in shadows. He stepped closer and the moonlight fell across his face. My breath caught.

The light played in his silver-blue eyes, reflecting within them as they glowed. They held the same promise I knew was in mine.

"Happy birthday."

I pressed my finger to my lips. With the other hand, I snagged his sleeve and led him inside. I pointed at the light shining beneath my mom's door and he nodded. Together, we tiptoed upstairs. I didn't breathe until we got into my room.

"We have to be careful," I whispered. "Mom will go insane if she finds—"

Cole spun me around. I didn't get my "eep" out before his lips were on mine. I melted into him, opening my mouth and tangling our tongues. All sense of caution blew out of my head like a gum wrapper in a tornado.

"Ready for your present?"

The lust in his voice was a straight hit to my core. I nodded hard.

Cole took my hands and backed toward my bed. My anticipation mounted as a grin spread across his face. It was an intoxicating feeling of nerves and anticipation—like the one that mounted as you climbed to the top of a roller coaster. What was coming next would thrill me in all the right ways.

Cole gently grasped my waist and pushed me back. I looked at him in confusion.

"Strip for me, birthday girl."

Heat surged through my body. This was new.

"Strip?" I squeaked.

He leaned back, propped up on his elbow. His legs fell open and Cole gazed at me through hooded eyes as he rubbed himself through his pants.

"Yes."

My breathing picked up speed at the look in his eyes. Cole tracked me like a hunter watches his prey. It pulled goose bumps to my skin as I reached around and undid the clasp one-handed. The dress slid off my body and pooled at my feet. Cole pressed harder, taking in my new underwear.

"Your turn," I whispered.

We broke eye contact for the barest moment as he pulled his shirt over his head. He didn't need to tell me to keep going. I was enjoying this game immensely.

I slipped one strap over my shoulder, then another. Pulling the sheer fabric down, I hissed as it rubbed over my pebbled nipples.

I grinned as I played with the hardened nubs. "Your turn."

Cole didn't need more encouragement to unzip his pants and free his straining member. Wetness soaked my panties as he gripped his length and stroked.

I turned away with difficulty. Cole was a mesmerizing sight.

Hooking my thumbs through, I bent over and slowly pulled my thong down. I threw in a little wiggle as I slipped my panties to my ankles.

Cole hissed. "Fuck, Zela."

He pumped harder and it was ridiculously hot, even up-side down. Cole leaned forward and nipped my bare ass.

I almost let a gasp escape. I had to be careful. Now that this had started, I would die if we were forced to stop.

"Come here," he growled.

"No." I turned around and got on my knees. "You come."

Clutching his thighs, my tongue darted out and licked the tip.

A groan ripped from his throat. "No, Zee. I've come on you many, *many* times. Tonight, I'm only doing it inside of you."

I shivered. "That's okay with me."

Cole pushed down his pants as I climbed on top of him, straddling his waist. I got to enjoy my position for all of two seconds. He gripped my hips and threw me over. I clapped my hand over my mouth, covering my laugh.

Cole kissed the back of my hand and then the tip of my nose. I moved my hand so he could claim my lips. My skin rippled with heat as we kissed slow and deep. I wanted him in every cell of my being.

We broke apart panting.

"I've waited so long to be with you," he breathed. "Part of me can't believe this is really happening."

I playfully nipped his lip. "Can I just say this would have happened a *long* time ago if you and Michael talked about your feelings sooner."

His laugh was warm air on my cheek. "Fair enough."

My fingers skated up his back and tangled in his hair. I loved threading my hands through his silken locks. I'd tug on them while Cole gave me head and he'd swat my ass if I got too rough—which motivated me to pull a little harder.

I bit my lip. *Thinking of which, we should— No, we can't. Can't risk making that much noise.*

Sighing, I pulled him down so I could nuzzle his neck. "I'm sorry we have to be careful. Next time, we won't hold back."

"I'm just happy I get to be with you now."

Cole gripped my thighs and wrapped them around his waist. My pulse quickened, feeling him brush against my opening.

"Can I tell you a secret?" he whispered. Cole moved—slowly, deliberately—rubbing his length against my clit. It was suddenly too warm in this room. Beads of sweat collected on my chest, slicking our bodies as he moved against me.

I pressed my lips together hard. I'd let out a moan if I tried to speak, so I nodded instead.

He placed a light peck on my lips. "This is my first time." *What did he just say?*

"Your first time? Your first time doing what?"

"Having sex," he said with a chuckle.

I blinked. "But you— I thought— You seem so experienced. You do things to me that make my eyes cross."

He shook his head. "I've done stuff but I've never done that. I'm guessing you and Landon..."

"Yeah," I said softly.

"It's okay. I couldn't be your first but I'm glad you'll be mine."

I traced his jaw, grinning into his eyes. "I wish I knew I was deflowering you tonight. I would have had candles and flower petals and jazz."

"Fuck you."

Giggling, I draped my arms around his shoulders. "That's what I'm trying to get you to do."

His grin was wicked. "You're going to have to wait a little longer for that crack." He slipped out from under my arms.

"Are you serious?" I hissed. "What is with you guys? You never miss a chance to mess with me even when sex is on the table."

I snapped my mouth shut.

Cole took my nipple into his mouth. He flicked and teased it with his tongue and I quickly forgave him for making me wait. My heels dug into the mattress as electricity zipped through my nerve endings—bringing them to life. Cole's hot, wet mouth on my breast. The silk sheets beneath me. My fingers tangled in his hair. The sensations overwhelmed me and I felt my orgasm cresting fast.

I reached between us but Cole was already there. He rolled my sensitive nub beneath the rough pad of his thumb and I choked, holding in a moan.

"Please," I gasped. "Don't make me wait any more."

Cole released my nipple from his exquisite torture only to flash me a grin that could be considered evil under different circumstances.

"I like you begging, birthday girl. Keep it up and I'll give you your present."

I almost came right there. Cole was playing all kinds of new games with me. It was insanely fucking sexy.

"Please, Cole," I rasped.

"Please what?" Cole moved to the other breast. He kept his eyes on me as he licked the tiny, pink pebble.

"Please fuck me. Fuck me, Cole." Now that I started, I couldn't stop. "I want you inside of me. That's what I want for my birthday."

"Can't say no to that."

Cole rose up. He gazed down at me as he moved my hips and got me just where he wanted me. My heart rocketed in my chest as he positioned himself against my entrance.

"I have one more present for you," he said.

Growling low in my throat, I smacked his ass with my foot. "Give it to me later."

He chuckled. "Yes, ma'am."

Cole pushed in before the final word left his lips. A moan escaped me and I hurried to grab a pillow. Cole ripped it off my face.

"Uh-uh. I don't think so."

I bit my lip hard as he continued pumping. Still, soft sounds slipped through. The bed took up his rhythm and faint squeaks filled the room.

My eyes fluttered shut. *We are so going to get caught. Just don't let it happen before I come.*

I felt him shift and then his lips brushed against mine. "Don't hold back," he whispered. "I want them all."

He kissed me and I gave him what he wanted. I moaned, letting him swallow every one as he brought me closer and closer. The faint squeaks picked up in sound and speed. Pleasure wracked my body, washing away my fear of getting caught. All that mattered was Cole.

The pressure built in my lower belly, and just when I couldn't take it anymore, Cole hit that spot and explosions went off in my mind.

I came down panting. The room spun as I fought to catch my breath.

"You are in... so much trouble for lying to me," I breathed.

"What did I lie about?"

I let him see my smile. "There's no way you haven't done that before."

He chuckled. "Guess that means it was good."

"Better than good."

Cole lifted a brow. "Better than Landon?"

I swatted his backside.

"Ouch. You really like smacking my ass."

"You really like getting smacked," I said, giggling. "That was amazing. Definitely worth the wait." I kissed him. "I wish we could do it again, but we shouldn't tempt fate. I want you to stay the night."

"Then I will."

Cole lay down next to me. He kept me pressed firmly against his body as we gazed at each other across the pillow.

"Will your parents notice you're gone?"

He shook his head. "I told them I was sleeping at Michael's place. I'll sneak out early in the morning and be back by breakfast."

"Good."

Smiling, Cole brushed the hair away from my damp forehead. "Can I give you your other present now?"

"I got you and your virginity today," I teased. "What else can you give me?"

"I can tell you that I love you."

My grin melted away. "What?"

"I love you, Zela." His hand was still on my head. He traced small circles on my temple as emotion welled up in me. "I've loved you since sophomore year."

"But you were so mean to me then," I blurted.

Wow, Zela. Not the time.

"Because deep down I wanted you but I knew I couldn't have you," he said. "I've never handled that well—not being able to get something I want. Thankfully... *you* get everything you want."

I laughed—a light, joyful sound fed by bubbles of happiness growing and spreading throughout.

"I love you too," I said.

He tipped forward and kissed me until my lungs cried out for breath.

"I know you don't want to get caught, but I'm willing to risk one more time if you are."

I held up a finger between us. "Maybe one more time."

"Yes." He jerked his head. "Get up and wriggle that ass for me again."

I rolled my eyes even as I got up. "Didn't take long for my asshole to put sweet, sensitive Cole to bed."

"*Your* asshole is right."

Yes. Mine.

Chapter Three

"I can't believe you have to go back to school tomorrow."

"You can't believe it? I don't know exactly what I'm in for tomorrow," I said, "but it can't be good."

I set down my cup and pushed it across the table. Jordan and I were spending our last day of freedom wandering through Chesterfield. We made a pit stop for ice cream but my second favorite flavor wasn't doing a great job of cheering me up.

Jordan dug into my gummy bear cookie dough treat without hesitation. "Why did you convince your mom to let you stay if you feel that way?" she asked between bites.

"Because," I said. "I may have been kicked off the boys' campus and accused of murder, but every time I think of leaving, I remember the boys, Adam, Derek, and my friends. I know they have my back through this."

She gave me a knowing look. "How are things with the guys?"

My grin was all kinds of goofy and I didn't care. "They're great. Landon and Michael were in Europe over the summer but we talked every day. Cole and I saw a lot more of each other." I flushed just thinking of the things we got up to. "I've never felt so close to him. There will always be a little asshole in him, but now that he's not holding back, I love seeing this side of Cole."

Talking about Cole buoyed my mood enough to reach for my ice cream again. "What about you and Adam?"

Jordan ducked her head. "It's been amazing. Adam is seeing another girl but somehow he makes me feel like I'm the only one. Last week, he took me to the next town over and we watched fireworks, kissed, and talked about all the amazing things we'd do in Europe."

"Did he get his parents to say yes?"

Jordan's smile fled beneath her groan. "He wasn't lying about them being overprotective. Val thinks it's a great idea. Jaxson says it'll only happen if we stay with friends of his in Europe—forget hostels. Maverick wants him to carry a tracker in his bag, wallet, *and* on his phone. Ezra thinks going for the whole summer is too long, and Ryder said no. That's it. No."

"Oh boy."

She blew out a breath. "Val promised to work on them but who knows. I hope he can come. The whole thing was his idea."

"Val got all four of those guys to love, adore, and worship her. I think she can get them on board."

Jordan laughed. "I should get me a stable of guys like you and Val, but honestly, I'd totally play favorites. No one else can possibly be as good as Adam." She winked. "Especially in bed."

I cleared my throat. "Time for a subject change."

"Yes, it is," she cut in, "but not a good one. We need to talk about school, Zela." She rested her hand on mine. "Are you going to be okay? It's been months and the police haven't found the real killer. What if people still believe it's you?"

"I'm the best suspect," I confessed. "I can't deny it. Cameron was blackmailing me. We have a rough history. Witnesses thought we got into a fight. And the campus isn't Fort Knox. If I wanted to sneak into the dorms, it wouldn't have been hard. When you think about it, I make sense, but I think deep down people know I wouldn't do this. They just can't think of who would."

She inclined her head. "I get you, but it makes me worry more. The boys know you. The girls don't. What if they believe you did this?"

"Melody knows me. She'd vouch for me no matter what." I slumped in my seat. "But I hope it doesn't come to that. Life on the girls' side is going to be hard enough. Things are finally going well with the boys and I get kicked out of my room. My sex life takes a hit just when it's getting good."

She snorted a laugh. "It can't be that hard to sneak a guy into your room."

"Adam explained just how hard it is. They lock the doors to the girls' campus at night and it can only be opened on their side with a code until five in the morning. The girls know the code because it's dangerous if something happens and they couldn't get out, but it means they have to risk sneaking past Matron to let their guy in.

"It doesn't sound so bad until you find out their side is more hi-tech than the boys'. Their dorm doors record every time it opens and closes in the middle of the night. Matron will know if she needs to do some interrogating.

"Adam told me Melody gets up early for 'training' and they meet in a secluded spot in the woods. It's better than trying to bring her back to his dorm. If she's caught over there, she'll be expelled." I gestured to myself. "Like I almost was."

"Harsh."

"Very." I sighed. "We'll make it work. Other couples at school do. I'm just stressing because Derek will be set free tomorrow."

"You're finally going to talk to him. Are you worried things have changed?"

I dropped my eyes at the pang that struck me. "We said we loved each other but everything got so crazy. We never really talked about what it meant."

"Can I ask?" Jordan plucked a cherry out of her melted, strawberry soup and curled her tongue around it. "Sleeping with your brother isn't allowed, but what's the rule on getting with the guy you thought was your brother?"

A flush crept up my neck. "Do you have to?"

She grinned. "You've thought about it. That's why you want to have this big talk. To figure out how wrong this relationship is going to be. If you ask me, the only ick factor is his dad and your mom have seen each other naked. Other than that, you're good to go."

"Thanks for the vote," I deadpanned. "Trust me, I know it's weird. Derek once said I was too possessive of him for it to be anything but love. It was proof I knew deep down we weren't related. But I don't know. All I knew then is what I know now. I have to be with him."

She gripped my hand. "So, don't let him get away. Find him tomorrow and sort it out."

"I will. I want to. I miss him." A thought occurred to me. "Maybe that's the point. He could have been forbidden from seeing or talking to me this summer. That's why I haven't heard a word." I bolted upright. "They punished him because of me. I doubt they want us together."

"They punished him because he lied, ran away, and worried them sick," Jordan said. "To be fair, Jonathan might not be eager for his son to date the daughter of the woman he had an affair with, but he and your mother talked. They cleared the air and he must understand that you did what you did to find your father. I'm sure it's not about you."

I hung on to Jordan's reassurances as I packed the car the next morning. Sunday dawned in defiance of my wishes and it was time to return to Breakbattle Academy... as Zela Rae Manning.

I smoothed down my sapphire dress for the zillionth fidgety time. It fell on the other side of casual, but by now I considered it my lucky dress. Landon made it for me. I wore it for Cole the night we made love. It matched Michael's blue butterfly necklace like they were made for each other. This was the dress I would brave Breakbattle in.

"Are you ready?"

I pulled myself out of my thoughts as Mom came around the car. She put the last of my bags in the trunk.

"Remember, you don't have to do this," she said. "I admit I still have doubts about sending you to that place."

"I have doubts too but it feels like the right decision."

She leveled a finger. "What did we agree on?"

"I will report it immediately if anyone tries to harass or assault me. If the police try to speak to me again, I refuse, call you, and wait for you and our lawyer. I'll keep my head down and focus on finishing my final year."

Mom nodded sharply. "Yes. If there is any trouble at all. If you so much as get a papercut, I will transfer you out of that school and I'll hear no argument about it."

"Yes, Mom."

"Alright. Let's go."

We piled into the car and set off to the academy. We didn't speak much on the drive. Things were still a bit strange between us but the truce held through the end of summer and I didn't want to break it now. Eventually, I would. My search for my father wouldn't end until I found him, but that search had lasted eighteen years, it could wait a little while longer while I sorted out my life at Breakbattle.

"I'm going to pick you up on Friday."

"Hmm?" I turned away from the window. "Friday?"

She kept her attention fixed on the road. "I'm picking you up this Friday and every Friday after. You will come home on the weekends."

I was silent for a moment, thinking of last semester. "Okay," I said. "But..."

"But what?"

"I was thinking that some weekends I might go to Evergreen."

"And spend time with your boyfriends."

"Is that okay?"

"You can go for the day, but you sleep at home."

Honestly, that was more than I thought I would get. "Thanks, Mom."

Soon, the gates of Breakbattle loomed on the horizon. The iron glinted in the sun, drawing the eye to the BB emblazoned in gold on the gates. It was clear to see because the gates were closed.

I sat up straighter. "Why are the gates closed? The senior packet said move-in started for the Elites early as usual."

"There are cars here. We must have gotten the time right."

It seemed like we did. We rolled into the parking lot and students streamed around us. They rolled heavy suitcases and hugged parents and younger siblings goodbye. Then they joined a growing line.

Mom parked and got out to help me unload my things. I hitched my duffel on my shoulder and leaned in to kiss her cheek.

"Bye, Mom. See you Friday."

"Why are you saying bye? I'm going in to help you get settled. Also, I intend to have another discussion with your principal."

"You are? But I'm sure he's busy—"

"He won't be too busy to speak with me." She grabbed my suitcase handle and walked off.

I followed at a slower pace. The line of students and parents led to the closed gates. Looking closer, I spotted Argyle walking down the pavement. She stopped to say something to each family individually. Mom and I were waiting awhile before she reached us.

"Good morning, Miss Manning. Morning, Zela."

She said my real name as though she's been using it for years. Argyle's reaction to my big reveal was nothing like Whittaker's. She was calm, but her disappointment leaked from her pores. She spoke of expulsion like it was inevitable. I was lucky it turned out a different way.

"Morning," I replied.

"Forgive us for keeping you out here in the heat. In the wake of Cameron Dupre's death, we instituted changes to ensure the safety of our students." She gestured behind her. "One of those changes were new automatic locks on the gates. These were not supposed to go into effect until tomorrow morning, but there was a miscommunication. They will unlock on their own in"—she glanced at her watch—"twenty minutes. Please bear with us."

"I understand," Mom said. "I'm pleased to hear you made changes. While I have you here, I'd like to know what you'll be doing to keep my daughter safe."

Argyle shifted away like she was thinking of the rest of the people she needed to speak to. "Of course," she said instead. "We've hired more security to monitor the halls and cafeteria following certain... incidents last year. The locks for the students' rooms have been upgraded. Also, the door between campuses have been fitted with the same automatic locks. There is no danger of anyone crossing from one to the other in the night."

My ears perked up at the last statement.

"We can't leave campus?" I repeated. "I thought girls had the code to open the door."

"Not anymore."

"But isn't it dangerous for us to be trapped inside like that?"

She shook her head. "You will not be trapped. If you press on the handle and hold, it will set off the emergency release. This, of course, triggers an alarm."

"But—"

Argyle held up a hand. "I'm sorry, Miss Manning. I need to speak to the other parents. All of this will be explained further during the assembly tomorrow."

I let her go without a fight. I was busy thinking of what this meant for me and the boys. They were a huge part of why I wanted to come back and now it was going to be even harder for us to see each other.

I can't blame Argyle and Whittaker though. A student was murdered on campus and they still haven't found the killer. They have to do something to protect us and making it harder for people to roam about in the dark makes sense.

My sigh rattled my depths and pinched my heart. How could this be our reality? A person dead. A killer on the loose. A fog of suspicion blanketed the school. I remember when my biggest worry was juggling battles. A few extra tests and running around a field is not so bad in comparison.

Eventually, the gates clicked open and we were allowed inside. Mom trailed me up the stairs and into the main entrance. I paused just before the threshold.

Two doors. Two campuses. One I had never set foot on.

"Cooeee. Over here, Miss Manning."

A chirpy voice drew our attention. A woman in an ankle-length brown dress, sensible shoes, and cat-eye glasses emerged from the crowd.

"Good morning." She grasped my hand in a surprisingly strong grip and shook warmly. "I knew it was you. I know all my girls and you're the first fresh face." She tittered.

"Hi," I said slowly.

"I'm Matron West," she announced. "I look after the girls in the dorm and I'm going to start by taking you up to your new room." She turned to Mom. "Miss Manning, I'm sure you have a lot of questions for me in the wake of our recent tragedy and I'm happy to answer them all. Your daughter's safety is my first priority."

"Thank you. Please lead the way." Mom handed me the suitcase and fell in step with Matron West. "I'd like to start with the new locks on the doors. How do we know these are any safer?"

"Great question. These locks..."

I trailed them in silence, listening with only half an ear. Matron opened the door to the girls' campus and together we stepped inside.

Wow. I don't know what I was expecting... but this should have been it.

The hallway we walked into was identical to the boys' side in almost every way except for one. The portraits of famous alumni were all women.

Mom and Matron chattered the whole way through the main building and into the dorms. Girls passed us up and down the stairs. I knew most of them by sight after years of sharing a cafeteria with them, but the girls who passed me looked at me like they had never seen me before.

We topped the sixth-floor landing. "Zela is still an Elite student, so this will be her floor. I'm sorry, Zela, but you won't have your own room. There are exactly forty Elite dorms and exactly forty Elite girls. Thankfully, one of the girls was happy to share."

I nodded. "I understand. It was cool having my own room for a while but I don't mind sharing. I just feel bad someone has to give up their space."

She waved that away. "Don't feel bad. She was truly happy to do it."

There was only one person I could think of who would be happy to have me as their surprise roommate. My suspicions were confirmed when we knocked on the third door on the right of the entrance. Melody burst out of the room and seized me in a hug.

"Can I just say you're a legend?"

I grunted in her hold. Melody wasn't the touchy type. The male and female masses fawned all over her, and she didn't give the satisfaction of rewarding their sycophancy with attention. She liked me, and I liked her, but she never hugged me before.

Turns out I was lucky for it. This girl is about to break my ribs.

"Why am I legendary?"

She freed me. "Are you kidding? Sneaking in undercover, flouting this school's sexist rules, rising to the highest class, turning the system on its head, getting the lower classes to fight back, and then revealing all the time you were a girl. Was this your plan the whole time?" She shook her head in amazement. "You're incredible, Zee."

"*Was* this your plan the whole time?" asked Mom.

I flicked from her to Melody. I wasn't entirely sure what the correct answer was here. Mom was spitting mad about my lies and what I kept from her over the years, I had no delusions about that. Even so, she was an activist at heart and knowing I did this for a cause might set me a few notches higher in her esteem.

Or it might get me grounded every weekend until I graduated.

"I wasn't planning on revealing myself," I finally replied. "The police did it for me. I do want people to see the system for what it really is. I've always wanted that. My motives for becoming Zeke were..." I trailed off as I caught Mom's look.

"They were my own, but if any part of it made people see we have to merge the campuses, end the targeting, and change the system, then I'm glad of it."

Melody shook her head. "I've been working to prove this school is wrong for how they treat and separate us, and all this time, you were the one truly getting something done. You've shaken things up, Zela. Whittaker can't ignore it any longer."

"There is a lot that man will no longer be able to ignore from this point," my mom cut in. "Go in and get settled, Zela. He'll be expecting me." She snagged my collar and pressed a kiss to my cheek. "Goodbye. Call if you need anything."

"I will."

Mom and Matron left and it was just me and Melody. I looked around my new home. The room was big enough to fit two Elite/queen-sized beds. It meant the couches had to be moved to beneath the windows and the television pushed to the space between my new desk and the wall. It was a tight fit but we'd hardly be uncomfortable.

Melody tossed my suitcase on my bare mattress and dragged me over to the couch.

"What do you have planned for this year? I want to know everything."

I shook my head. "If I had a plan, it'd be tossed in the air now that I'm on the girls' side. I knew the boys. I knew playing the Battle Doctor would get them riled up." I looked away. "And in a lot of ways, it went too far. It got violent last year and Cameron's response to me becoming Elite and threatening the expansion landed me as a murder suspect."

Melody put her arm around me. "None of that was your fault. You couldn't have predicted they'd start a schoolwide fight, and no one believes you hurt Cameron. Anyone could have done it. I dated the guy and he was far from a good person. His list of enemies must wrap around the entire campus." She gave me a supportive squeeze. "Don't stress about any of that. The police will find the true killer."

A knot of tension began to ease. Everyone might not feel the way she did. All the same, it was nice to have Melody's support.

"As for the girls' side," she continued, "you have the right idea for how to push buttons. They are crazy competitive over here and pretty much no one is friends with anyone outside their class. If you played Battle Doctor over here, the upper classes would lose their shit. The problem is getting the lower classes to trust that we want to help."

I nodded. "After last year, I can't play innocent like I don't know it'll piss the upper classes off. Whittaker praised me before. Now he won't look so kindly if I stir up more trouble."

Melody looked me right in the eyes and said, "Screw him. We're in our final year and I'm done playing nice. Right now, the classes are on the edge. Stopping you from helping other students says to everyone that the administration wants to keep the lower classes in their place, and letting you go ahead rattles the upper classes' sense of entitlement. It's a win-win either way because it exposes the problems with the battle system."

She leaned in, getting in my face. "This is the time to do something big and you can help me. They can't ignore us right now. No one can."

"Happy to help. Just tell me how."

Melody beamed and it was a sharp reminder of why Adam couldn't quit her. She was beautiful in every sense of the word, but her passion made her otherworldly. It was hard to believe this goddess walked among us mere mortals, determined to right the wrongs we made for ourselves.

"We need to make a move that won't get us suspended or Stand Up shut down." Melody hopped up and grabbed a notebook off her desk. She was scribbling in it before she sat back down. "Another silent protest obviously, but with a bigger impact than the flyers."

"What if we got people outside of school involved? I told the school board how I felt about the battle system. We could spread the message to parents, government, and the media. The world thinks Breakbattle is this amazing place because we let them."

Melody bobbed her head, writing everything down. "You're right, we do let them think it. We could organize a walkout or a sit-in."

I snapped my fingers, warming to the idea. "What if we all went down to breakfast and refused to leave the cafeteria until Whittaker and Argyle say they'll sit with us and discuss how to improve the battle system?"

"I love it. Do you think we can get enough people on board?"

My pocket vibrated.

"Definitely among the lower classes," I replied as I pulled it out. "The boys are spoiling for a fight. Let's channel it into protests that won't get us all suspended and our privileges taken away."

Melody shook her head. "Would it be so bad if they were taken away again? The Elites and As bitched themselves sick over losing their precious televisions and all-access passes, but, for once, we were all treated the same. It should be like that all of the time. Above all, I believe our end game should be getting rid of the battle system entirely. Without it, there is no reason to separate the genders. Targeting won't be a problem and students can't treat others like shit because of the letter on their chest."

"We might be able to get them to listen to changes, but getting rid of the system entirely? Whittaker would never go for it." I glanced at my phone. "And the school board..." I trailed off.

On my screen were five letters I'd been waiting months to see.

Derek.

"It'd be a disaster if the school board voted to adopt the system." Melody's voice sounded far off. "We can't stop fighting though."

"You're right," I whispered. "We can't stop."

Derek: I'm sorry it's been so long. I wanted to see you every single day of summer. I'm at the place where we first became friends. Come to me.

I rose as though I'd been lassoed and Derek was on the other end, pulling me to where I belonged.

"I have to go, Melody," I said. "We'll talk more when I come back."

"Oh. Okay." Surprise colored her response. "I'll think of ways to get the media to take notice while you're gone."

"Sounds good."

My feet carried me downstairs and through the halls without a thought. I knew exactly where he was. Every single moment I spent with Derek Grayson was burned into my brain. Every word he spoke, every laugh, every moment, every time he touched me.

Maybe Derek was right. My obsession with him was always more than it should have been.

I stepped into the clearing. Derek leaned against the boulder. Wind played with his hair, flitting in from his eyes, but yet we stayed locked on one another. He appeared wholly at peace in the place where he faced off with Cameron and lay at his behest in a pool of blood. The memories that clung to this clearing were more awful than the last, but one thing was true, this is where we were bound—for better or worse.

Derek's lips quirked up in a grin and I swallowed hard. I once thought of his smiles as gifts bestowed on the younger sister he let into his heart. *Why didn't I see the fierce need behind them?*

Pressure built between my legs. I clenched my thighs as I neared him. The same need was pulsing through my veins, wild and untamed. Not for a second did I think sexually about him when I believed he was my brother, but the thoughts going through my head now...

We're the most screwed-up couple on the planet, and I'm in love with three other guys who had me beaten into a bloody heap on a locker room floor.

I stopped a few feet from him. "Derek—"

"No. Come to me."

I couldn't have fought the command even if I wanted to. I molded my body to his, burying my face in his chest. The last of my pain, tension, and stress leaked away as he enfolded me in his arms.

"Did you miss me?"

"You know I did. I can't stay away from you, remember?"

I felt his chuckle against my cheek. "You wouldn't have been away from me if there was anything I could have done about it."

"Adam said they put you on lockdown."

"Dad was actually understanding about us running away." Derek's hand slipped under my dress. My eyes fluttered shut as he gently stroked the soft, tender skin of my thighs. There was no hesitation. Derek knew I was his as assuredly as I did. "He said he got that I needed space after having a bomb dropped on me. Mom not so much.

"They never planned to tell me Dad wasn't my father or about that horrible period of their marriage. Coming home to find out I not only knew everything but I ran away put Mom in a spiral. She was a mess by the time I came back. I think part of her feared I wasn't going to."

"I'm sorry, Derek." I widened my stance, pressing his leg against my middle and his against mine. The acts of our bodies were at odds with the seriousness of our conversation. "None of this would have happened if I didn't force myself into your lives."

Derek found his way under my panties and dug his fingers into my ass. I hissed as he moved my hips, rubbing me against him. "Mom said that many times but she's wrong and so are you. It's no good playing happy family when the root is a lie. I won't pretend it didn't mess me up at first, but now I'm glad to know the truth.

"Jonathan Grayson could have rejected us both. Instead, he's been nothing but the best fucking dad since the nurse put another man's kid in his arms. This changes nothing for me, but Mom had trouble believing I was fine. She says I don't tell people what I truly feel. Wonder where she got that from."

I threw my head back, letting out a moan. The friction on my clit was sending shockwaves through my body. This was tame compared to the things I'd gotten up to with Cole and Landon, and yet I was trembling in his hold like a virgin.

"They grounded me for lying and running off," he continued.

I lifted my foot as I ground against the bulge poking my thigh. My mouth dried just hearing his breath grow labored.

"But they were on me the whole time," Derek forced out. "Mom canceled filming and stayed home. Every day checking on me, making me spend quality time with them, only letting me off the p-property for family counseling."

How can he talk right now? I was barely hanging on to my name and the ability to stay upright.

Tugging my dress down, I popped one breast free.

"Fuck, Zela." Derek immediately tweaked the innocent little pebble until my core wept. I bit my lip hard but my moans hissed through my teeth.

"After all that, they still didn't want me to come back to Breakbattle."

I shook loose of my fog. "What? You weren't going to come back?"

He shook his head. "No, and damn, we went at it. They both want me to forget all of this happened and go back to the way things were... hard to do when I go to school with you."

My grip tightened. "So they do want us apart."

"Of course they do. You're a reminder of the worst time of their lives. But we have to be together, Zela." He released my nipple and took hold of my chin. "I belong to you."

Derek slipped inside of me. I arched my back as I cried out, "Yes. You belong to me. You always have. You always will."

"We've wasted so much time."

Derek's words whispered around me, filling me, enveloping me. I picked up speed, rubbing against him as I sensed our orgasms coming.

"We should have been together years ago. Instead, Landon, Cole, and Michael got there first. Your first kiss should have been mine. Your virginity should have been mine. Your first 'I love you' should have been mine."

"They would have been."

I loved Michael, Cole, and Landon absolutely, and I wouldn't have changed a thing that happened between us, but deep down I knew, if I had walked into orientation week thinking Derek was just another guy instead of my brother, he would have claimed all of my firsts.

"But it had to happen this way," I said. "Or we wouldn't have gotten to this."

"I know... but it doesn't change what I have to do now."

"What does that m-mean?" I was practically bouncing on his thigh. He crooked his finger, hitting the right spot while I rubbed against his length.

"I said I would share you," he replied with a guttural groan, "and I will. But it's important that you know you belong to me just as much as I belong to you."

His nails dug into me, marking half-moons on my ass, and the pain was the final push over the edge. I came violently, body convulsing as a small scream ripped from my throat.

I slumped against him. The only thing keeping me up was Derek. He tilted my head up. His hair was dark where it stuck to beads of sweat on his forehead. It thrilled me seeing the glassy sheen over his eyes—he was no less affected than me.

"We're making up for lost time."

He bent and I parted my lips for a kiss. Derek's hand left my middle. He held my gaze as he curled his tongue around his finger.

"Now I know how you taste," he said softly. "I'm going to know everything else about you."

Desire pooled in my lower belly. We just rutted against each other like wild animals and I was already hot enough to go again. I did not understand the hold he had on me. I don't believe I ever would.

"I've never been able to hide myself from you," I said. "Not even when I was Zeke. All that's left to know is sexual."

"I'm not hearing a problem with that."

Derek lifted me up and gave me the kiss I'd been waiting for. I melted into him, pouring two months of agonizing separation into a hungry, almost brutal kiss.

"You're going to come to me every day," he growled against my lips. "Here. Where we can be alone."

"Yes." It didn't occur to me to disagree. I'd go wherever Derek wanted me to go. School rules be damned.

"We'll start now."

Derek stepped out of my grasp and pulled his shirt over his head. I watched in equal parts bewilderment and excitement as he balled it up and set it on the ground. "The least I can do is make you comfortable."

We shed our clothes in the clearing with feverish hands. Derek guided me down, resting my head on his shirt, and then proceeded to kiss and lick every inch of my body, starting from my toes. He took his time, not letting me rush him on his ventures along my pale, quivering thighs. It was the most intimate experience of my life and I orgasmed two more times on the tickling bed of grass.

"I'm on the pill," I rasped.

Derek found his way to my nipples. He flicked them with his tongue, undoing me molecule by molecule.

"Make love to me."

"Not now."

My nails dug into the dirt. "Why? We're alone. We have all day."

He dropped kisses down the valley of my breasts to continue his torture on the other one. "We're not doing it here."

I bit out a groan. "How in the hell did I end up with the only four guys on the planet who turn down sex when it's offered up on a silver platter?"

His chuckle vibrated my nipple. "Can't you tell how much I want you?" He pressed his length against my sex to drive home his point. "There's nothing more I want than to make love to you, but we're going to do this the way we would have if we had known the truth back then."

"But—"

"Shh." Derek kissed me—long and slow, weakening my muscles and my resolve.

I'd give him whatever he wanted. When had I ever said no to Derek Grayson?

Chapter Four

We walked back to school hand in hand. I leaned against him, so happy I could bust. The trick was keeping it off my face. Derek's smirk every time he looked at me told me how good a job I was doing.

"This really is my lucky dress."

"What?"

"Nothing." I draped his arm around my shoulder and burrowed in his side. "I wish I was still on the boys' side," I said. "Being Zeke for another year is a small price to pay to read books in your room, talk all night, and fall asleep on your bed."

He kissed the top of my head. "We couldn't do that anyway thanks to Sondheim. Gotta get creative with places to meet up." Derek traced a pattern on my collarbone. "You'll come to me tomorrow and every day after. On the weekends, I'll pick you up."

I shivered under his touch. "What about your parents? My mom?"

"No one is going to keep us apart. It tore me up believing I couldn't be with you." He put his finger under my chin and raised me to meet his lips. "We will be together, Zela." He kissed me. "Zela," he whispered. "Have I ever told you how much I love your name?"

"No one loves my name."

"Everyone else are idiots. Your name is perfect. Unique, strong, fierce. No other girl could have stormed into my life and made me fall in love with her. Only Zela could."

Warmth spread through my body like sunlight dancing on my bare skin. "I love you," I said softly.

"I love you too."

Together, we passed through the trees onto the soccer field. The grounds were mostly empty. Only the Elite roamed the school, prepping for another year of being on top. Somewhere on the boys' side were Michael, Cole, and Landon. Close and at the same time farther from me than they'd ever been. I would have to carve time to be with all of them this year. Derek may have claimed my mornings, but those three belonged to me too.

Derek walked me to the side entrance and kissed me over the threshold.

"Tomorrow. Seven o'clock. Come to the clearing."

"I'll be there."

I went upstairs floating on a high. The only thing that would have made this day more perfect was making love to him. He wanted us to take it slow—to make each moment last and infuse it with meaning like it would have been if we had fallen in love at the right time and in the right way.

I loved him for that. Derek reminded me at the perfect moments that underneath he was the sweetest guy.

But months of teasing like he put me through today will unravel my mind like soldiers hooked on LSD. I couldn't resist giving him what he wanted. Let's see if I have the same power over him.

I walked onto the Elite floor and made for the third door on the right.

"So, it's true."

Three girls emerged from the room two doors down. I recognized the girl leading the pack immediately. She was the one who bumped me down the table at the Graysons' reception last year, crowing about Fs sitting at the end.

Copper strands flowed out of a black beret. Few people pulled off the look, but taking in her cornflower blue eyes, bow-shaped lips, and narrow nose, I had an inkling she pulled off everything. The face of a goddess. The cruel twist to her lips that said she knew she was one.

"Whittaker didn't kick you out."

"Looks like it," I said simply.

The girls fanned out around me. I moved with them, keeping their leader in my sights.

Everly, Isla, and Adeline if I remember Melody correctly. She told me there was a group of girls in her class who loved being Elite a little too much.

"Seems like there's nothing you can do wrong, F," said Everly. "Cheat your way to the top, sleep with half the Elite boys—"

"Not half," I broke in. I flashed her a grin. "I'm sleeping with forty percent of the Elite Boy Class. Adam and I are just friends."

She bared her teeth. "Thanks for clearing that up. I'll give you this much, whatever you're putting out has those boys hooked. Landon, Cole, Michael, and Derek have closed up shop since you spun them into your androgynous web. It's a shame because Isla and Cole really had something."

Everly jerked her chin to the girl on her right with long, brown hair and sable skin. Isla sniffed. "I'm not jealous. I'm with Lars now. It's just a shame because he doesn't give head nearly as well as Cole did."

My stomach twisted. Of course the boys had a past, but I wasn't fond of said past walking up and throwing it in my face.

"Do you need something?" I asked.

Everly closed the distance between us. "We just want to make sure you understand something. You got away with shit because you had your boyfriends watching your back. That's over. You're on our campus now, *Zela*, and if you pull that Battle Doctor shit, we'll make sure the expulsion sticks."

I raised a brow. "Wow. Threatening to get me kicked out for giving a couple of kids tips and tutoring sessions? You'd think the top students in the school wouldn't be so intimidated."

"We're not intimidated," she snapped. "The Failures and Dumbshits couldn't hope to beat us if they went back in time and made better choices. Either way, you're one of us, so you need to act like it."

Standing up straight, I saluted her. "Message received."

Everly scoffed. "Whatever. Just don't think we're playing around."

"Oh no. Sadly, I know you're serious."

The girls strode off, missing my eye roll. I left the boys' side only to run into the female Sullivan. It wasn't enough for them to have all the privileges, parties, recognition, and fawning. They had to lord it over everyone else too.

"Zela, there you are." Melody popped off the couch and snagged my arm. "Your suggestions were gold. I've been planning since you left. What I'm thinking is..."

I let her words wash over me.

New year. Same problems. Welcome to Breakbattle.

DEREK DID UP THE BUTTONS of my blazer. I was still a little shaky following the last orgasm. I woke up early and met him in the clearing as instructed. Derek was waiting for me with a blanket. He stripped me, laid me down, and buried his head between my legs. I came with body-wracking, throat-strangling cries.

I caught his hand and threaded our fingers. "Tomorrow," I said, "we'll have sex."

He grinned. "Is that an order?"

"Yes."

"Can't." I felt his smile as he pecked me on the lips. "We haven't had our first date yet."

"Yes, we have," I protested. "The late nights—"

"Not a date."

"Practicing together—"

"Not a date."

"Spending time at your place—"

"Definitely not a date."

"Hiding away at the cabin."

He brushed his lips against mine, soft and addictive. "Simultaneously the worst and best weekend of my life... but not a date. I want to do this right."

"But we love each other and we want to be together. It is right."

Derek cupped my cheek. "You want us to move faster because you're already on that level with Landon, Michael, and Cole. You're not in one relationship with four guys, Zela. You're in four relationships. Ours has to move at the right pace."

I pressed my face into his neck, breathing him in. He was right and I knew it. This was the same situation with Michael. He needed to know what we had was real and our own. My relationship with Derek was a roller coaster that shot off track and fell plunging toward a screaming, fiery explosion more than once. He had to trust that we were on the right path now.

"I understand," I said. "I really do, but weeks and months of these morning meetings are going to reduce me to a quivering mound of goo."

"You do quiver. Especially when I kiss you here." He caressed the base of my spine. "Or lick you here." Derek lazily moved up and stroked my breast through my clothes.

I bit back a moan. "You're doing this to me on purpose, aren't you? It's payback for believing you were my brother."

"Fuck. You caught me."

"Derek!"

He laughed. "I'm kidding. No revenge plot here. And trust me, it won't be months or even weeks. I couldn't hold out for that long."

A smile spread across my lips. "Yeah?"

"Yes." He stood us up and pulled me to his chest. "What are you doing this weekend, Manning?"

I threw my arms around his neck. "Going on a date with you."

"Correct answer."

We walked back to school with grins that read like signs over our heads. All the crap coming my way once school officially started couldn't dent my delirious happiness. Returning to Breakbattle was the right choice.

Derek and I parted before the main doors. He went upstairs to put away the blanket and I continued on to the cafeteria. The place was an Elite-only zone since move-in didn't start for the rest of the school until after breakfast. I walked in and had no trouble finding Landon.

Smirking that smirk, he pushed back his chair and patted his lap. I all but ran to him.

Squealing, I hopped on top of him, straddling his waist, and pulled him in for a passionate, tongue-clashing kiss.

"I missed you so much." I peppered his face, chin, nose, and mouth with kisses. "Don't ever leave again."

"Yes, ma'am." He grasped my hips, holding me firm. "I missed you too. I'm going to show you how much tonight."

I shivered. I was rife with sexual frustration. A night with Landon was the perfect cure.

"I know where we can go," I said into his ear. "We'll sneak away after dinner."

"Perfect."

Something caught my eye. I looked up and made eye contact just as the girl whipped around. It was obvious she had been staring and the side glances the rest of her table were giving me backed it up. I didn't recognize them, which meant they were freshmen.

If they are, how do they know I'm an object of fascination? Am I being stared at for pretending to be Zeke, dating four guys, or being accused of murder?

The girl inched back around and found me looking right at her. Her freckled cheeks flushed red but embarrassment didn't stop her from sneering. Whatever she knew, her feelings about me were clear.

The sound of a tray hitting the table made me look up. Cole pushed the food in front of us.

"For you," he said simply and went off to get his own.

"Aw. Cole can be so sweet when he's ready."

Landon plucked a sausage off my plate and tore off a bite. "He better be sweet to you. He told me you guys made it official over the summer."

I peeked at Cole. *What else did he tell you we did over the summer? Not that I'm under any delusions that the guys don't talk about me. I wonder if that extends to our sexual escapades.*

Thinking of sexual escapades...

Leaning back, I took a deep breath and held it. I owed it to Landon to have this conversation, but even the thought of hurting him made me sick. Derek wanted to be my first, but Landon actually was. I wanted my first love to be happy.

"Landon, I need to tell you something."

"What?" His smile was soft as he stroked my hair. "Is it about Cole? I know you guys took it to the next level. I'm glad for you guys."

"You are?"

He nodded. "Even though I think you're perfect in every way, I want you to have all of your pieces back."

My lips trembled, sensing an onslaught of tears. *My good-ness, this boy is incredible. Every time I think I couldn't love him more, he proves me wrong.*

"Thank you," I replied, "but it's not just Cole. I told you things changed between me and Derek after we found out the truth from Jonathan. I want to say yesterday we made it official but... we always were." I shook my head. "We've been together from the start. We just didn't know it yet."

"I knew it." Landon pulled me closer, bringing our fore-heads together. "I saw you two had a connection and as much as I bitched about Moon, Derek was the one I feared would steal you away." His voice shook. "Is that what you have to tell me?"

"No," I cried. I made him look me in the eyes. "No, Lan-don Foster. I love you and I'm not going anywhere. It's you I was worried would leave. I promised you one or two guys and I've given my heart to three. Can you be okay with this?"

"I can be okay with any future that has you in it. You can give your heart to fifty more guys as long as I always have a piece."

"You do... and you will."

We froze with our lips just touching when someone cleared their throat.

"Miss Manning, I presume. I've heard about you."

A woman I'd never seen before towered over us. Brightly painted toes stuck out of plain, boring brown sandals. She kept up the confusing look with bland khaki pants and a matching polo shirt to go with short, spiky electric blue hair. It wasn't the uniform or the hair that told me not to mess with her. It was the toned, muscled body her simple clothes couldn't conceal.

"There are nine empty seats, Miss Manning. Hop in one."

"Who are you?" I blurted.

"Welsh. I'm security and the cafeteria monitor. Last year you guys proved you're not capable of eating in here without a problem. I'm here to make sure we don't have any more." She yanked out the chair next to Landon. "Sit."

I sat.

Welsh nodded sharply and strode off. Landon turned to me when she was gone.

"Don't worry, baby. You can ride my lap tonight."

I swatted him upside the head and he fell over laughing. I had every intention of doing so, but that wasn't the point.

Cole returned with his breakfast and claimed the seat on my other side.

"Where's Michael?" I asked.

He leaned over and gave me a quick kiss. "Went for a run. He said he'd catch us up at the assembly."

"The assembly. Argyle spilled some of the changes they're going to announce. There's no question they need to step up security after what happened to Cameron, but I have a feeling it will make it harder to see each other outside of meals."

"We'll make it work," he replied. "And even if I can't spend time with you during the week, I'll be with you on the weekends."

I rested my head on his shoulder. "That's true. Mom said I could come up to Evergreen for the day. How about next weekend we take Toby out to the park and have a picnic?"

"My parents are going out of town and Christina is up at college. I'll be bending you over in the shower next weekend, but sure, we can do the picnic too."

I heaved a sigh. *I also ended up with four guys with absolutely no filter.*

Landon spoke up, "Speaking of bending Zela over—"

"We're not speaking about that!"

"—did she tell you she's with Derek now?"

"Really?" Cole snaked his arm around my waist. "It's about time. It would have happened sooner if his parents hadn't locked them in their gilded prison." He shrugged. "I guess I understand them freaking out, but I hope they don't blame you."

I blinked at him in surprise. "You're okay with this too?"

"Course I am. We all called it."

I smiled. "I admit I was worried. You guys are weird about Adam."

"Because we know that if anyone could steal you away for good, it's Adam Moon. The guy has some devil charm hiding behind that innocent smile. He could make Argyle leave her husband and run away with him."

My mouth dropped open seeing Landon nodding along.

"We like him too," said Landon. "Adam doesn't leave us much choice, but still, we know the truth about him. He better always see you as a friend."

"I love you both, but you're certifiable. Besides, he wants Jordan and, let me tell you, my cousin isn't one to mess with."

"Then we're good," Landon replied.

Adam slid into his seat, shooting us all a bright smile. "Good about what?"

Cole and Landon took one look at him and burst out laughing.

"What? What is it?"

We finished up our breakfast and headed over to the auditorium. Students were trickling in from all classes. We spotted Michael toward the front and I sat next to him and accepted a sweet, lingering kiss.

"I believe you have something for me," I said under my breath.

"I do. You'll get it later."

"Okay. On to other things I'm no longer waiting for..." I let my grin finish the sentence.

Michael's chuckle filled my ears. "How much do you trust me?"

"Absolutely."

"Good because we're not doing it in the woods, behind the gym, or fumbling one out between classes. I'm going to take my time."

I clenched my knees together. Pressure built between my thighs. "So what does that mean?"

"It means I'm making love to you in my bed. Upstairs. I've thought of a way that we won't get caught."

"Yes," I said before he finished the sentence. "Let's do it."

He winked. "I'll tell you when."

We spent the rest of the assembly flirting and hinting at what we'd do when we were finally alone. Argyle and Whittaker went through the new safety measures and it was essentially everything she told my mom. New locks, more security, and harsher punishments for students being unsafe.

Afterward, I said bye to the boys and walked with Melody to the girls' campus. As we passed students on the way up to the dorm, I didn't have to question it. People were definitely staring at me.

"WHERE DID YOU GO LAST night?" Melody picked up her brush and fussed with her flawless hair in the vanity mirror. "And this morning."

Heat licked at my cheeks. Last night I proved Landon right about my love of having sex outside and rolled around with him in the woods. Afterward, he fed me the chocolates he brought from Europe and held me until I almost fell asleep. I snuck back in before the locks clicked on by the skin of my teeth.

This morning, Derek texted me to meet him in the basketball gym and we fooled around in the boys' locker room. There was little chance of us getting caught. Singh gave his star player keys to the gym and we went there for early morning practices all the time. Now we had another reason.

"I met up with the boys," I replied. "Did I wake you leaving this morning?"

"No, I was out. I didn't notice you were gone until my alarm went off." Melody picked up her curling iron. "How is that going? Dating four guys at once. Adam and I are technically in the multiple-partner situation but it doesn't feel like it sometimes because I never see Jordan. All five of you go to the same school and they're in the same class."

I took a minute, considering her questions. "It's not as hard as people might think. Jordan once said she couldn't date more than one guy because she'd play favorites, but it's not like that with us. I'm their favorite girl, of course, but they're each my favorite guy in different ways. I love how Michael supports me, Cole challenges me, Landon inspires me, and Derek... Well, Derek infuriates me most of the time but I love that too."

Melody giggled. "You're so lucky. It's hard to find one decent guy—let alone four of them."

I gazed at her in the vanity. "Can I ask you something?"

"Sure."

"You have a decent guy. You have an *amazing* guy. So... why are you breaking up with him?"

Her hand stilled. "Adam told you about that?"

I nodded.

Melody lowered her head. Her hair fell over her face, obscuring her expression so I couldn't see if my question angered her.

"I'm sorry, Melody. It's none of my—"

"I don't want to." Her voice was small. I almost didn't hear her. "He's the kind of guy you could have forever with, and if I let myself, I could picture staying here, going to Somerset, getting engaged, and building a life with him. But that's not my plan.

"I've been accepted to the Sarbonne and my parents are making their move to Paris permanent after I graduate. I'm going to be top of my class, learn at least half as many languages as you, and then come back and work my way up the government. *That* is the plan. It's always been the plan. But since I fell in love with Adam, I've been thinking of a new one... and that's why we have to break up when senior year is over.

"He makes me want to give up everything for him, but it's not who I am, and he's so amazing that he understands." She lifted her head. Her reflection smiled at me, tears dripping onto her makeup. "I am giving up a great guy. I'm a fucking idiot."

"No, you're not." I rushed over and enfolded her in a hug. "If anything, you're strong for knowing who you are. Adam wants to stay in Evergreen, be close to his family, and run Shea Industries. He won't give that up either. It wouldn't be better for one or both of you to end up resenting each other."

She cried harder. I rubbed soothing circles on her back.

"You're both going on to an incredible life," I said. "You'll meet some scorching hot French guy who respects your mind and treats you like a queen. Or maybe you'll meet a string of hot French guys and pass it around like a day-old baguette."

A rough snort broke through her cries. Melody giggled into my chest.

"The point is," I continued, "you'll have a great career *and* a great guy. I promise."

"Thanks, Zee. I see why you're Adam's best friend."

Melody untangled herself from me and reached for tissues. Twenty minutes later, she was perfection once again and we left for class. Along the way, girls attached themselves to us like barnacles on a passing boat.

"How was your summer, Melody?"

"Did you get into your top choice, Melody?"

"Melody, are you seriously hanging with her?"

We paused on the second-floor landing. Everly and her crew were posted against the wall, passing a box of chocolate croissants back and forth. Adeline actually offered one to Melody. She accepted it.

"Thanks," Melody said, "and to answer your question, yes. I am hanging with her. Why? You don't believe that shit about her attacking Cameron, do you?"

Sensing a presence at my back, I turned and saw we were attracting a crowd. Girls stopped dead on the staircase, clogging up the path for the rest of the classes.

To my surprise, Everly snorted. "No. Grayson backs up her alibi and the police say Cameron was beaten. I don't see this one taking him in a fight." Everly looked at me as she said, "She may not have killed him but she has been stirring shit up since she got here."

"Zee is cool and she's my friend." Melody took another croissant and pointedly handed it to me. "We Elites have to stick together, right?"

"That's right. Don't you agree, Manning?"

I bit off a piece and moaned. "I agree these are delicious. Keep 'em coming and we can all be friends."

She sniffed. "We'll see."

Melody snagged my sleeve and continued on. I waited until we were out of earshot.

"Is she always like that?"

"Yes."

I peered over my shoulder. "Why is she cool with you, then? You fight back against the system."

"She doesn't believe I can do it, or that I truly want to. Most of the girls are convinced it's all a show to look good for colleges and something I can point to when I'm running for president. You know, proof that I was always socially conscious. She doesn't see me as a threat"—she pulled me up short—"but she does see you as one. You've proven you're for real and you're dating Landon Foster, who she had a massive crush on in middle school." She cracked a smile. "They almost hooked up freshman year, but *Zeke* got there first."

"For the love of— Do all of those girls have a history with my boyfriends?"

"We come from a small town and we've been going to school together since preschool. We don't have a lot of options."

"I'm really missing the boys' side right now."

"Don't." Melody squeezed my hand. "Everly is all bark and you won't have to deal with her for long. In the meantime, think of the good we can do on this campus. The boys have been shaken up but the girls are still trying to go along like everything is fine. We'll wake them up."

"I can't think of a better way to spend my senior year."

We polished off our chocolate croissants and continued up to the top floor. It struck me how similar this space was to the boys' campus, right down to the popcorn ceiling and letters stamped on the entrances.

I consulted my schedule. Our classroom was at the very end of the hall. Room 404. Mrs. Munoz's class.

We walked past the club sign-up sheet and a twinge of regret slowed me down. Archimedean Club shown proudly on the bright yellow butcher paper.

But it won't be my Archimedean Club and it won't be Mrs. Peterson. I told Mom I wanted to stay so things wouldn't change, but everything is different now.

"Zee? Are you okay?"

I shook myself. "Yeah. I'm fine. Let's go."

Room 404 was much like I expected. The only difference was the desk and chair shoved in the corner in the back by the bookshelves. I didn't bother to ask the diminutive older woman shuffling in front of the board if it was mine.

Melody placed her things on a seat at the front and gave me a supportive wink. It made me really want to speak to my guys and I slipped my phone out beneath my desk.

Me: I miss you. Love you. Have a good first day.

Their replies came back one after the other.

Michael: I miss you too. It's not the same without you.

Landon: Love you too, baby. Let's meet up after dinner again.

Cole: Good news is I'll be valedictorian and captain of Archimedean Club this year. Winning because your opponent is out of the game still counts.

Why am I in love with this asshole?

The feeling only compounded when I read Derek's text.

Derek: You saw me literally an hour ago. Why is your clingy ass missing me already?

Pinching the bridge of my nose, I stifled a groan. Someone really needs to talk to me about my taste in guys. I'd say it should be my therapist, but Val and I have gotten too close and too real. She let me know all about her past with her men and she was the queen of taming assholes.

I have a feeling Derek Grayson cannot be tamed.

My phone vibrated again.

Derek: I love you too.

My smile made my cheeks hurt. Okay. Maybe I could soothe this savage beast.

"Miss Manning?"

I jumped. The diminutive woman was suddenly in front of me.

"There are no cell phones in my classroom. I'll take that. You can have it back by the end of the day."

I passed it over to hushed snickers. At some point, the class had filled up. Everly, Adeline, Isla, Shannon, and Melody took the desks one after the other in front of me. The girls on the other side of the room I knew only by sight.

"Good morning, everyone. I am your new teacher, Mrs. Munoz." She set my phone down and turned to face us. "As we have a new addition, we'll begin the day with introductions. Miss Hamilton, if you'll start."

A girl with a multitude of colorful braids stood and waved to me. "Hey, Zela. I'm May Hamilton. I'm the girls' wrestling champion and on track to be salutatorian after Melody. Can I just say, I'm super impressed with how you pretended to be a boy so you could hook up with every hot guy in our school. I respect a woman who goes after what she wants."

"Yeah!"

The whoop was followed by applause from half of the class. A flush traveled up my neck. *Please tell me people don't honestly believe I went through the trouble of being Zeke to get guys.*

Well, you did do it for a guy, a voice reminded me.

But it definitely wasn't to have sex with him!

No wonder people kept giving me strange looks.

"That's enough of that," Mrs. Munoz snapped. "We do not cheer or encourage rule-breaking in this school. I expect better of young Elite ladies."

Her reprimand was supposed to be directed at May and the clappers, but Mrs. Munoz looked directly at me.

"Next."

The girl behind May got to her feet. "I'm Jade. My sport is soccer. I just found out I won a full ride to Somerset University and a spot on their team."

The class clapped again and Munoz allowed it. Jade bowed and waved like this was all about her.

"I'm Lauren. I'm also on the soccer team, but I'm getting my MBA from *Har-vard*!"

"Congrats, Lauren."

The girls whooped and cheered for her and the introductions continued in much the same way. It was less about me and more about announcing their college acceptances and accomplishments. That was fine with me. I cheered them on same as everyone else.

"Alright, alright," Mrs. Munoz called. "Settle down. We have a lot to get into today, so let's jump right in. The rules for my class are simple. Do not speak when I am speaking. Do not attempt to hand me late or incomplete work. Respect your fellow classmates. Respect the patch you wear on your chest. Is that clear?"

"Yes, Mrs. Munoz," we chorused.

"Good. As for the schedule, this semester you'll take World Literature, Calculus II, Physics, and Psychology in that order. The final period of the day will be self-study. Any questions?"

We shook our heads.

"Turn on your computers and open your notes. We'll do a review and then there will be a test after lunch."

I bent and pressed the on button.

Nothing happened.

I tried again.

Must not be plugged in.

Leaning over, I followed the snaking cord to where it stuck firmly into the outlet.

"Mrs. Munoz, my computer won't turn on," said Lauren.

"Mine too."

"Mine either."

"Me too," I spoke up.

Frowning, Munoz went to her desk and jiggled the mouse. "Hmm. There must be a power outage."

We tilted our heads back to the steadily shining overhead lights.

"They could be doing maintenance on the system and forgot to tell us," Munoz tried instead. "It's been hectic around here with the new security measures. We can—"

"Oh. There it is," May broke in. "It's working now."

The screen warmed up and treated us to synchronized dots chasing each other around.

"Excellent. As I was saying, the review test will cover topics from last year to ensure we're all on the same page. Zela, if there is anything you don't know or if you need more clarity, don't hesitate to speak up."

I barely heard her. Gasps spread through the room. Glaring on my screen—on all of our screens—were four bold scarlet words on a pitch-black canvas:

END THE BATTLE SYSTEM

Mrs. Munoz ran to her computer and banged on the keyboard. When that predictably did nothing, she tried shutting off the computer.

The words blinked out and were replaced by a math symbol I saw more than + or – these days. The upside-down A spun three-sixty in a mocking, animated dance.

"More pranks," she cried. "Clearly the actions of that troublemaker on the boys' campus. There goes our hope he graduated." She stabbed the monitor off with a huff. "Pull out your notebooks. We'll make do without our computers until this is fixed."

It took all day. At the end of class, the IT guy was still huddled over my computer, muttering to himself. I got my phone back to a bunch of texts from the guys and Adam.

Adam: For All shut down the Elite and the A computers. I guess we should feel lucky this message wasn't written in blood.

Me: I still think this is about Becca Taylor. Who else could "she" be?

Adam's reply hit me when we entered our room.

Adam: If it is about her, why now? Breakbattle made changes since then. The last person to be targeted was you and that was because of Cameron. For All has no reason

to defend you and Cameron's gone. What are they trying to prove?

Me: They've made changes but things are far from perfect. There's also the well-known fact that they're pushing to spread this nonsense statewide.

Adam: You don't think For All killed Cameron, do you? Cameron pushed for the expansion harder than anyone and For All has escalated.

Me: I've thought about it. Trust me, I've considered every possibility since the cops slapped cuffs on me. I can't say for sure For All isn't involved, but it's quite a step up from greasing floors and bloody messages to cold-blooded murder. There's also whoever Cameron was fighting with the night of the fundraiser and the argument I overheard in his room. A real person hit him and he knew who they were. Why would he protect For All by not coming forward?

Adam: Why would he protect anyone by not coming forward? He must not have seen them as a threat.

A thought occurred to me.

Me: Or he couldn't explain why they were. What if this has something to do with the Network and Cameron couldn't say anything because it meant revealing a problem among his underground boys' club?

Adam: If that's what it is, Michael, Cole, Landon, and Derek would be the ones to ask about it. But wouldn't they tell you if there was?

Me: We kind of have a silent agreement not to talk about Network stuff. It might be time to break it.

Adam: Good idea.

"Who are you texting?" asked Melody.

"Your main squeeze."

She wrinkled her nose. "That was such a weird thing to say."

"I know. It felt weird even as it was coming out of my mouth."

We burst into giggles. One good thing about all of this was Melody and me getting closer.

Back in our room, I changed into my gym clothes, my mind whirling.

For All was clearly through messing around. I wondered how long it would take before they moved from pranks to demands and the answer was now. The issue was what would happen when he inevitably did not get what he wanted.

The chances of Whittaker doing away with the system this academy was famous for was slim to none. The only course of action I could see for Whittaker was to search out For All and levy the torrent of punishments he promised, or do like Mrs. Munoz suggested and wait for him to graduate. Unless For All was a teacher or part of the staff, that wouldn't be long.

For All must know that as well as anyone. It has to be why he's escalating. Time is running out for him to be heard and he will make sure he's recognized. But at what cost?

"Zee, are you ready?"

"Yes, let's go."

I picked up my water bottle and trailed Melody to the wrestling gym. Breakbattle didn't go so far as to have separate gyms and swimming pools for the genders, but we did have different coaches. I could admit it. I would miss Singh and Nelson and the rest of them. They were good coaches who treated me fairly and lifted me to the standard of Elite.

"I miss the boys' side," I spoke up. The two of us walked side by side across the quad. "Is that strange?"

"No. Someone who moved around as much as you did must cling to familiarity stronger than most. You made friends, had your favorite teachers, and learned how to navigate life over there. This year you're starting over again and it wasn't your choice." She looped her arm around mine. "You don't have to like it, but for what it's worth, I'm glad you're here. No one in my class really gets me. It's why I spend so much time hanging with Adam and your friends."

I put my head on her shoulder. "I'm glad you do. And I'm happy I was outed if only because I don't have to lie to my friends anymore. You can get to know the real me."

"What have you been holding back, Manning? Been to over thirty countries instead of over twenty? Did you pick up some ancient ancestral magic on your travels that grants you power over hot guys?"

"No... and yes."

We walked into the gym cracking up. Most of the class was already there, tossing their things on the bleachers or getting into their warm-ups.

A woman in baggy shorts and a loose Breakbattle polo shirt stood at the top of the mat, speaking to someone I knew.

"Coach?"

As if she heard me, the woman turned and latched on to me. She had a face I could only describe as severe, and it wasn't just because her glare looked permanent. Sharp cheekbones, an upturned nose, and hair wrangled into such a tight ponytail it pulled the corner of her eyes up.

"Manning, front and center!"

Snapping to, I scurried over to the person I safely assumed was Coach Webb and her companion, Coach Franklin.

She looked me up and down like a puzzle box that was stubbornly holding out. "I've heard all about you from my counterpart, Manning. Let me tell you right now, I don't stand for nonsense."

"I don't—"

"A lot of rumors going around about you. That you rose to Elite by becoming the personal projects of Landon Foster, Michael Young, and Derek Grayson."

She pierced me with a look and I took a step back. "I say that's bullshit. Not just anyone can become Elite and you have to have talent to exploit it in the first place. Franklin says the same, telling me that you're small, but scrappy," she continued, "and you read your opponent's weaknesses like no one he's ever seen."

My former coach inclined his head. He was a man of few words, so to hear he used so many to praise me was hard to believe.

Webb scoffed. "Now that people know the truth about you, they want to put your success on the shoulders of boys. Typical." She thumped my arm. "I have high expectations of you, Manning. I want to see what you can do."

"I won't let you down, Coach."

"Alright. Get going. Start your warm-ups."

Melody found a spot near the locker rooms to roll through her stretches. Unfortunately, she wasn't alone.

Everly, Adeline, and Isla parked themselves next to her like that was their spot.

"Zela, over here."

I veered off without much thought and went over to the girls beckoning me. May and Lauren patted the floor. They were beautiful—proving that some people got it all in life. Wealth, intelligence, athletic ability, and great looks. May's waterfall of rainbow braids was as gorgeous as Lauren's conventional bob. Their smiles were open and kind.

"Sit with us. We were just talking about For All's latest prank. Crazy, right?"

"Crazy." I stretched out and reached for my toes. "Do you guys have any idea who For All could be?"

"We were going to ask you that," said May. "Everyone says he's got to be on the boy campus. That's where he hits the most."

"It makes sense," I said, "but I don't have a clue who it could be. Although, I think I have a reason why. Last year, he left a message saying her blood was on our hands. The only death I know that's connected to this school is Rebecca Taylor's." I glanced at both of them. "You grew up here. You know everyone. Any idea who could do this? Or why they'd do it in her name?"

May shrugged. "Rebecca Taylor was way before our time. Super sad story, but we didn't know her."

"We know what happened of course," Lauren added. "Her parents moved out of Evergreen after she killed herself. They tried to get the school to do something when the boys started targeting her, and it wasn't enough. A cautionary tale to all the Breakbattle parents. Mom's been on me since freshman year, making sure I'm not under too much pressure."

"Exactly," May said. "Our parents have our backs. Breakbattle made changes and split the classes. It's so much better now. What more does For All want because they can't seriously think the battle system is going anywhere?"

I twisted my torso and bent into a deep side stretch. "It's not that much better. There are still a lot of problems with the battle system."

Lauren copied my movements. Her confused look was even more comical upside down.

"What do you mean? What problems?"

I forgot who I was talking to for a moment. Life is pretty rosy at the top of the food chain. Why would Lauren and May know what the Fs have to go through just to get the education they're entitled to?

"Never mind," I replied.

May piped up. "I still say it's an F. Or maybe a D."

"If it was just stink bombs and breaking into storerooms, sure," said Lauren. "But hacking into the school's computers are beyond the capabilities of an F."

"Not if they hired someone."

"Like an F could afford to. They're all from Chesterfield." Lauren cut eyes to me. "No offense."

"None taken," I said.

A sharp whistle interrupted the conversation. "Ladies, I hope you're warm. I want the first pair on the mat now."

"That's us," said Lauren. She and May clambered to their feet. "Let's hang out after practice, Zela. We'll study in my room."

"Okay."

Coach got wrestling practice underway. As the odd girl out, I didn't have a partner. I watched the girls go through their practice from the bleachers, and at the end, Melody offered to partner with me. Melody was good. She was *very* good, and yet my opponents for the last three years had been taller, heavier, and quite a few fought dirtier. I took her down after a prolonged match and Coach Webb gave me a smile like I met those expectations.

"That's what I want to see, Manning," she told me. "Keep your head on the mat and not the boys, and you might just claim a late spot on the team."

I flushed hot—and I was hot enough from grappling with Melody. Is this who I am now? I've got to shake this boy-crazy reputation.

Melody and I trudged to the locker room. With my secret revealed, I couldn't use my made-up excuse for not wanting to be naked in front of other people. Although, that excuse earned me points when Whittaker and Argyle were tossing around my expulsion.

"One thing we should note," Miss Val said, "is that Zela did not attempt to take advantage or violate the boys' privacy."

"No. She just made nightly jaunts to her boyfriends' dorm rooms," Whittaker shot back.

I shook the memory away with the same blush on my face I had when he said it. I couldn't deny I took advantage of my proximity to Landon, Michael, and Cole. It was a miracle my birth control held up with the number of times Landon and I got naked in his sheets.

"Possessive type."

I jumped. A finger caressed my spine.

"Which one of them left you these?"

The locker mirror reflected my cherry-red cheeks. I was down to my panties. My back was to the room, giving them all a peek of the love bites decorating my body. Derek's thorough exploration of my body left a few marks.

Which was the point I bet. 'Cause when Landon saw them, he left a few of his own.

Adeline leaned against the locker next to me, completely naked and not that bothered.

"Was it Michael?" she asked, smirking away. "The guy spends every moment on the track. You can't catch up with him long enough to hook up, but you know what they say about those silent types. He must be wild in bed."

"I say it was Cole," Everly put in. She threw her towel over her shoulder instead of wrapping it around her. In one afternoon, the count of people I'd seen naked tripled. "Sharing you with all of those guys, I bet he likes to claim his territory."

"Ohh, Zela." May ran up to Everly and hugged her from behind. She beamed at me from her shoulder. "Which one of them is better in bed?"

"How do I make this stop?" I asked.

The girls laughed.

"By spilling *all* the dirty details," May cried.

"Ladies never tell."

Shannon snorted. "Ladies also aren't so desperate for dick that they pretend to be a boy to get some."

"Shannon," snapped Melody.

I slammed my locker shut. I faced them all with my bare chest on display. "Here's what I have to say. I became Zeke because I wanted to get closer to my father. It wasn't the smartest move, but it was the only one a fifteen-year-old could come up with. While on the boys' campus, I got to know Michael, Cole, Derek, and Landon, and we fell in love.

"It wasn't planned but I'm grateful three years as Zeke gave me them. What we have is real and it's not gossip. I won't give you details about my sex life or my relationships. We're not close like that."

"But we will be," May said, sounding far from put out. She tugged me toward the shower. "You can at least tell us the falling in love stories. Where did you go on your first dates?"

Sighing, I gave in to my fate.

"WHAT'S IT LIKE ON THE girls' campus?" asked Tanner.

Wednesday afternoon, Tanner, Nico, Justin, Owen, Derek, Cole, Landon, Michael, Adam, and I were sitting on the grass in the middle of the track.

"It's odd," I replied from the circle of Michael's arms. "The other classes give me strange looks and stop whispering when I pass them in the halls. As for the girls in my class, they're the perfect blend of sweetness and cruelty us women have perfected."

"You're not cruel." Michael rubbed his stubbly cheek against mine the way he knew I loved. "It's all sweetness over here."

Contentment spread through my body like his warmth. I had seen a lot of Derek since I returned to school. I even managed to sneak away with Cole and Landon to the clearing, but outdoor romps weren't Michael's thing. Being in his arms was everything I wanted.

"The guy is far gone," Cole muttered.

I nudged him with my foot. "Aren't you far gone too?"

He grinned. "Only you know how much."

We shared a smile. I knew we were both thinking of the night before. Cole loved me to distraction. I didn't question it.

"I still don't get how this... works." Nico glanced between the five of us. "I thought you guys were experimenting or something before, but now that I know Zee is a she, I get it even less."

The guys replied before I opened my mouth.

"You don't need to get it, Kazan," said Derek.

"Mind your fucking business," came from Cole.

"Guys hooking up are just *experimenting*?" Landon challenged.

"Watch yourself," Michael threw in.

Nico shrunk back, looking instantly regretful.

"Easy, guys." I soothingly rubbed Michael's forearms. "It's okay, Nico. Our relationship is different and it's not for everyone, but it works for us."

"Sorry," he mumbled.

I pulled away from Michael to hug Nico.

"Are you going to get all huggy now that you're a girl?" asked Tanner.

"I was always a girl," I quipped, "and yes."

I tackled him and peppered his face with kisses. "Love you, T."

"Ah!" Tanner flipped me. He pinned me to the grass and skittered his fingers on my sides.

Shrieking, I was breathless trying to get away.

"That's enough."

The next thing I knew Tanner was gone. Michael, Cole, and Derek lifted him up and deposited him on the other side of Owen. Landon picked me up and put me in his lap.

I should have told the girls in the locker room that they were all possessive.

"Don't feel bad, man," Owen said. "You're going to want to see this anyway."

"What's going on?" Justin asked.

The three of them huddled over Owen's phone. I watched Tanner and Justin adopt Owen's slack-jawed expression.

"You guys aren't going to believe this," Justin breathed. "They said no."

"What?" asked Michael. "Who said no?"

"The school board. They voted no." He gazed at us, wide-eyed. "The battle system isn't taking over the schools."

We descended on him. Our heads knocked together attempting to see his phone. Derek tore it out of his hands.

"In a historic vote that had the potential to revolutionize the school system of our state," he read, "the school board voted unanimously to not integrate the Breakbattle system into the public schools. They cited many reasons for their decisions. Chief among them were budget issues, accusations of discrimination among the classes, and fear that it would foster disharmony among students. They feel..." Derek trailed off. His incredibly handsome face was still handsome, even as it paled.

"They feel what? Come on, man." Tanner took it and read it himself.

I didn't hear the rest. "Derek, are you okay?"

He shot up as I reached for him. "I have to go."

"What? Bu— Derek!"

Derek charged off across the lawn.

"We have to go too."

Landon kissed me and then took off after Derek with Michael and Cole. Elation and guilt battled inside of me. The expansion was important for the Network and the Network is important to my guys. This was a blow to them too and I wasn't indifferent. I wanted them to succeed and I'd support them if they felt the Network was the best way to do it. Even so, deep down there was something wrong with the expansion.

Nico shook me. "Isn't this great?!"

"It is," I said softly. "It's for the best."

I WOKE BEFORE MY ALARM the next morning. My body clock responded to the time and the promise of Derek. Silently, I slipped out of my sheets and padded to the bathroom.

I wonder what we'll do this morning.

So far, every day had brought something new. The day before, Derek taught me what he liked. I explored his body to my heart's content on a blanket slightly damp from morning dew. Those delicious memories played through my mind on a loop as I tiptoed through the halls.

I wouldn't get in trouble if Matron found me now. Everything was locked down during the night, but students like Michael required early morning access to the tracks and fields. The doors opened early to let them—and me—out.

Derek was waiting exactly where I expected him. Only one thing was missing.

"You didn't bring our blanket."

His response was to hold out his arms.

I ran to him and he held me tight.

"We won't need the blanket today." He pressed his lips to my forehead. "I came because I wanted to see you."

"What's wrong? Why won't we need the blanket?"

"Sadly, your clothes are staying on this morning." Derek sounded truly regretful. "I was planning on counting the freckles on your back while I played with you from behind."

My knees went weak. "We can still do that," I said hoarsely. "We don't need a blanket."

He tangled his fingers in my hair and brought it to his lips. "It has to be this weekend. My dad is going to call in a few minutes. Shit's hit the fan since the board made their announcement. I'll be dealing with this today and tomorrow."

"Why do you have to? Because of your dad's position in the Network?"

"No," he replied, "because of mine. I took Cameron's place when he lost his authority in the Network."

I stepped back, gaping at him. "You did? But... you never told me."

"I haven't told you a lot of things, Zee. I promise you, I'll change that."

"Will you?"

"Yes." He grasped my hands and pulled me back. I let him. "We'll talk this weekend. If you still want to go on a date with me?"

Derek sounded unsure like he was certain he ruined everything.

I tried for a joke. "The date was in exchange for daily orgasms. If I'm not getting my satisfaction today, then I don't know about this."

I laughed but it rang false to my own ears. Pressing my lips together, I swallowed hard. A thick, sludgy feeling crept through my bones.

I hated this. I hated feeling like I didn't know the man I loved. I hated that I let him—all of them—keep me in the dark about the Network.

"I'll tell you everything, Zela. No more secrets. Just give me some time."

He raised my chin and kissed me. His tongue swirled with mine, enticing a soft sigh as my tension ebbed away.

His phone went off but he took his time pulling away.

"I love you. I'll make up for those missed orgasms Saturday night."

"Looking forward to it," I whispered.

I left him in our spot.

"Hey, Dad," I heard. "I spoke to them but..."

I trudged through the woods and into the main building. The school was beginning to stir. Students passed me in their gym clothes, bright-eyed and alert for their morning workouts. I walked around a clump of girls.

"Murderer."

I jerked to a stop.

"Can't believe they let her come back after what she did."

Spinning around, I found them facing me head-on. They wanted me to hear and they were ready for my reaction. I zeroed in on the girl in front.

I know her. She was the one staring at me and Landon in the cafeteria. My eyes raked over her. She had a plain, smooth face and the knobby knees of a kid. *She has to be a freshman. What I didn't notice before was the E on her chest.*

"Well," she snapped. "Nothing to say for yourself?"

"Yeah, I got something to say." I jerked my chin at the door. "Bundle up. It's chilly outside." With that, I turned to go.

"We were friends," she cried. "Cameron was a good guy and you—"

"—didn't touch him. I wasn't on campus and I told the same to the police, the principal, and the rest of the school when they accused me. Cameron may have been your friend, and I'm sorry for your loss, but you know nothing about me. I'd never hurt anyone."

Her snarl twisted further. "I know plenty about you. You're the freak who pretended to be a guy to sleep and cheat your way into the Elite Class. What happened? Did Cameron threaten to reveal your secret?"

"Many times," I replied, "but like I said, I was nowhere near him when he died."

"They never should have let you back in here." It was like she hadn't heard me. "Innocent until proven guilty my ass. All the shit you've pulled since you've been here. There's obviously something wrong with your head. How are we supposed to feel safe with a murderer in our dorms?"

Her friends nodded along.

Irritation and sympathy niggled me. I felt for this kid who lost a friend. I truly did, but it didn't mean I was cool with being called a murderer.

"You don't honestly believe I did it," I said.

"Yes, I do!"

My tone was calm. "No, you don't. If you really thought I snuck into dorm rooms and killed people, you wouldn't be trying to make an enemy of me now."

Her friends gasped. The eyes of the girl I still didn't know bugged out.

"Are you threatening me?" she screeched.

"Nope. Just pointing out that this is the act of someone who is hurting, lashing out at the only person they can blame. I understand, but you need to listen to me. I didn't kill Cameron."

"You—"

"She may not be threatening you, but I am."

Footfalls sounded behind me. Everly, Adeline, and Isla fanned out around me.

"You're new here, so I'll give you a pass just this once," Everly continued. "Elite stick together. We don't accuse each other. We don't put on shows for the lower classes to gawk at."

I peered over my shoulder. Girls had gathered behind us—our disturbingly silent audience.

"She has an alibi and Whittaker wouldn't have let her back in here if he thought she was dangerous. Don't pull this shit again, Beth."

Beth's face reddened. She glared at me through furious tears. "She's their only suspect."

"Put that down to crappy Chesterfield cops. And you know what, I heard from my mom a few days ago that Mr. Dupre has private investigators on his case now. We're all on the same side, Beth. Everyone wants Cameron's killer caught."

Beth held my gaze for a few more seconds, then she burst into tears.

Everly snapped her fingers. "Guys, get her to the bathroom, clean her up, and then tell Ethel to make her some tea from my stash."

Beth's friend stared at her like they were trying to figure out who this beautiful stranger was that was giving them orders.

"Are you waiting for something?" asked Everly. "Go now."

They hopped to it and led their sobbing friend away.

"Thanks for stepping in," I said to Everly.

She gave me a look. "Like I keep saying, Elites stick together. I hope you got the message too."

Her group marched off.

"What did I do now?" I muttered at their backs.

Shaking my head, I returned to my dorm to get ready for the day.

"HOW WAS YOUR FIRST week?"

"Fine."

"Fine won't cut it, Zela." Mom stepped in front of me, pulling me up short on the sidewalk. "Did you have any problems? Did anyone bother you?"

"No. Some of the freshmen don't know what to make of me and what they've heard. Otherwise, life on the girls' side isn't so bad."

She leveled me with a shrewd look. "Are you certain?"

"Yes, Mom. If anything, they're singularly focused on me being their friend whether I like it or not."

Mom studied my expression, looking for a hint of deceit. I couldn't blame her. I kept a lot of secrets over the years.

"Okay," she relented. "Let's get going. I'm making garlic butter steak with zucchini noodles tonight and I still have to stop by the grocery store."

"Why don't I cook dinner tonight? You can take it easy."

"Is there a reason I should be taking it easy?"

We started off for the car.

"Because you're my beautiful, wonderful, radiant mother and you do so much."

She laughed. "I see. And what else?"

"And I wanted Jordan to come for dinner tonight, so I'll make extra."

"And...?" My beautiful, wonderful, radiant mother was not a dummy.

"And I was hoping to go to Evergreen tomorrow. Derek is going to pick me up."

"Is he," she stated.

Mom picked up the pace, rounding the car for the driver's seat. I tossed my things in the back and climbed in as she started the car.

"Is that okay?" I asked. "You said I could spend the day in Evergreen."

"To see your boyfriends, Zela. Not to see the son of my ex who kidnapped my daughter."

She stepped on the gas with more force than needed. We peeled out of the spot and roared through the parking lot.

"He didn't kidnap me. I wanted to go with him and it was me who didn't return your calls." I placed my hand over her whitening knuckles. "That was on me and I'm sorry, Mom, but please don't blame Derek. He's been there for me through all of this and... I love him."

She whipped around, eyes wide. "Love him? Zela, he's not your brother."

"I don't love him as a brother. I just love him. We're dating now. Or we will tomorrow. He's taking me out for our first one."

Mom gaped at me for so long the person behind us blared his horn. She jerked to attention and turned onto the road.

"I don't understand. Why him?"

I shook my head. "Has anyone ever been able to answer that? It's him because it is. I've wanted to be near him since I found out he existed. My feelings have changed and grown stronger since we learned the truth about Jonathan."

"Jonathan has made it extremely clear that he doesn't want us disrupting his family and their lives any longer."

I stiffened. "Are you going to forbid me from seeing him?"

"Would you obey me if I did?"

I didn't reply.

"Jonathan Grayson does not make rules for my child," she said. "You're eighteen now. You can decide who you want to date, but let me be clear, I will not be forced into contact with Jonathan again. He's a part of my past I want to stay in the past. Only Derek comes to our door. He drops you home *on time* and you stay off their property. Understood?"

"Yes," I replied without hesitation. I was too ecstatic at her agreeing to think about arguing with her.

"Good." She released the dash and claimed the hand over hers. "And are you sure about this? The relationship you're entering into will be far from uncomplicated."

"I'm dating three other guys. Two of them are best friends and the other couldn't stand the rest up to a little while ago. All of my relationships are complicated, but being with them is worth it."

"Alright, my only one. Tonight, you are making dinner and you can invite Jordan."

Mom swung by the store and we bought the steak and zucchini noodles on tonight's menu. I was prepping the steak marinade when Jordan blew inside.

"Hello, cousin." She hugged me from behind. "What are you making me?"

"Your second favorite."

"Sweet. Never tell Mom how much I like your body power food. She'll get it into her head to do something about all the takeout she feeds me."

"Your secret is safe with me."

She let me go and I heard the kitchen stool scrape across the floor. "Spill. I know I'm not here just for your cooking."

I jumped right in it. "Derek is taking me on our first date tomorrow and I need something to wear. He's already seen me in my lucky dress, and as you've pointed out, nothing else in my closet is in the same league. Help."

"I got you, girl."

Transferring the steak cubes to the marinade, I peeked at her over my shoulder. "How was your first week?"

"It was weird not sitting with Lucia, Jane, and Meghan."

My hands were too steaky for a hug. I settled for a sympathetic smile.

"It's not that bad though," she continued. "Kimberly has had my back through the whole thing. Last year, she cursed Lucia out. They almost got into a fight. This week, she sat with me at lunch and said she wasn't dealing with the girls until they got their heads out of their asses."

"I'm glad you have one good friend."

She playfully kicked my backside. "I have more than one good friend. How was your week?"

"Bizarre."

The two of us talked while I cooked up and served dinner. After, we went upstairs and Jordan descended on my closet.

"Tell me this," she said, "is sex on the table?"

"It's been on the table since I laid eyes on him after break. The trouble is Derek Grayson, King of the Breakfast Bunnies, is playing the slow card."

"Breakfast Bunnies?"

"You don't want to know." I flopped onto my bed and watched her tear my closet apart. "The point is he's not shy about sex, and yet, he's been turning me down. I don't know if we'll do anything more than fool around tomorrow night."

"You'll want to wear the underwear I got you either way."

Heat flooded my cheeks. "I think he'll like them."

"If he's got a pulse, he'll love them." She pulled out a light green dress I bought in Italy. "This is cute. Do you know where you guys are going?"

"Hold on. I'll ask him."

I fished out my phone and sent him a quick text.

Me: Can I get a hint of your date plans? Should I wear something fancy?

His reply came back almost instantly.

Derek: My parents won't be home tomorrow night and I want us to be able to talk about everything in private.

Me: Should I be going to your house? I promised my mom I wouldn't. What if your parents come home early? Also, the guards will tell them I was there.

Derek: The guards won't say anything. They're there to keep me safe, not report my movements. And my parents won't catch us. They are handling some stuff that isn't likely to wrap up early.

Me: So our big date is canceled?

Derek: No, we're going to do everything I had planned, ending with me counting the freckles on your back.

I burrowed into my pillow, fighting a smile.

Me: I don't have freckles on my back.

Derek: How would you know? I should check to be sure.

Me: Good idea.

The bed dipped. "What are you grinning about over here? Is he giving it up or what?" Jordan stuck her face next to mine. "Count the freckles on your back? Does that mean you're getting it from behind?"

"Jordan!" I shoved her. She collapsed on the bed howling. "Why are you like this?"

"Who knows?" she teased. "It's definitely the green dress though. You'll look so hot in it, he'll be bending you over the table before dessert."

"Thanks. I don't know what I'd do without you."

"As repayment, you can help me think of something to give Adam for our anniversary."

"Has it been a year already? Wow."

"Yeah." Jordan's smile was infectious. It filled me with happiness seeing my cousin in love. "But what do you get the guy who has everything?"

"We'll come up with something. Between us, we know everything about Adam Moon."

We stayed up so late brainstorming gift ideas that Jordan ended up staying the night. I checked my phone all through breakfast the next day.

My first date with Derek Grayson. When is he picking me up? What does he have planned? What exactly does playing with me while he counts my freckles mean? Are we making love tonight? Can we risk it when his parents could come in at any time?

I glanced at my screen for the twentieth time in ten minutes.

"Stop freaking out," Jordan said. "You've had many first dates by now."

"But this is Derek and there's a lot going on with us. My nerves are justified."

Jordan speared a piece of watermelon and put it on my plate, knowing it was my favorite. One of the many ways she was the best cousin ever. "You're going to have a good time."

A smile tugged at my lips. "I know I will. I didn't think it was possible to feel this way and I have this with four amazing guys. I want Derek and me to be as close as people can be. He doesn't let others in, and I'm fine with that, as long as he makes an exception for me."

"What about Michael, Cole, and Landon? If you guys are going to do this whole thing, they should be close too, right?"

"They are united in making sure no other guy touches me, so that's a start, but yes, I'd love it if they were all friends. Michael, Cole, and Landon seem cool, but Derek has always been a bit of a lone cat."

"Well, I guess you guys don't have to be like Adam's family, all living together under one roof and raising each other's kids. Four guys. Four separate relationships."

"I never really asked them how they pictured the future," I said. "We haven't talked about the future at all. In my head, I did see us like Adam's family but... what if that's not what they want?"

I pressed my lips together. My stomach was churning—twisting and writhing as pressure built in my throat.

We're young and in high school. Sharing a girlfriend might seem perfect now, but what about college? What about marriage, kids, buying a home, and meeting the parents. None of their families know that I'm dating all four of them. Why did I never think to ask why they haven't told them?

"Uh-oh. I said the wrong thing, didn't I?"

"No," I rasped. "You said the right thing. I've been so loved up, I haven't been thinking. It's our senior year. College acceptances will be rolling in. What if we end up in different places? Or what if they stay to be with me? They've worked too hard to compromise their futures over me. I should have thought about this. We should have *talked* about this."

"Yep, I definitely said the wrong thing." Jordan walked around the island and hugged me. "Don't spin out. Just have the conversation now. You might not all live in a big mansion on the hill with twenty kids, but that doesn't mean you can't carve out your own happily ever after."

Melting into her hug, I replied, "Of course, you're right. Thank you."

I said that, but I spent the rest of the morning and most of the afternoon going back and forth on what we talked about. I must have picked up my phone a dozen times to start messages to the guys. Every time, I shook my head and tossed the phone back. If we were going to have a serious conversation about our future. We should do it in person.

I forced myself to sit at my desk and watch a movie. Derek called me partway through.

"I'm leaving Evergreen," he said. "Chances of your mom calling the cops if I drive off with you again?"

"Slim. I told her we're dating. She's cool with it." I made a face. "Well, not *cool*, but she won't try to stop me."

"Glad we don't have to go through her too. My mom and dad are crazy about privacy, but otherwise, they've been the relaxed, hands-off types my whole life. Now I'm hit with *groundings* and *family meetings*. What the fuck is that about?"

I chuckled. "You're living a completely different life, my friend. Us normal kids get grounded for forgetting to take out the trash and not making the bed. Two things I'm sure you've never done."

"And you'd be correct." He sounded amused. "I tried the 'I'm eighteen' card, and Mom blew up. She gave me the speech about living in her home and abiding by her rules. I think she got that from one of her scripts."

"So we're definitely in for it if we get caught."

"I love my mom, but she's not keeping me from you. Don't worry about that for a second."

Love spread through me like blazing heat. "You say the sweetest things to me, Derek Grayson. Careful, or I'm going to think your soul is a teddy bear instead of a wet cat."

"Wet cat?"

I laughed. "I have to get ready. I'll see you in a bit. I love you."

"Love you too."

Taking out Jordan's pick, I spread it on the bed and then hunted for the perfect accessories to match. I began the day nervous about the date and the conversation to come, but one talk with Derek and it melted away. I loved him and he loved me. Everything else would work itself out.

The doorbell rang almost exactly one hour after we spoke.

"I'm leaving, Mom," I shouted as I raced down the stairs. "We'll be back before eleven. Don't wait up."

"Zela, hold on. I want to speak to him."

I froze with my hand on the knob. "Speak to him? About what?"

"Just wait here." Mom opened the door herself and stepped outside. I caught a glimpse of Derek's smile morphing in surprise before the door slammed in my face.

I pressed my ear to the wood, listening. Only the soft murmur of voices floated through.

What is she saying to him? Is she warning him off? She promised she wouldn't try to stop me dating him. Or are they talking about his father? How monumentally uncomfortable would that be for Derek. I should rescue him.

The knob turned just as I reached for it.

"—we understand each other. I expect her home at eleven and not a minute later."

"Yes, ma'am."

Never in the last four years had I ever heard Derek so contrite.

Mom kissed my forehead. "Have a nice time, my only one. I *will* be waiting up."

"Yes, Mom."

I waited until her footsteps retreated to turn to Derek. The boy standing on my porch was gorgeous, but then, how could he not be? This son of a movie star had all the beauty people paid surgeons millions of dollars to achieve. His blond hair curled at the temples, still damp from his shower. A simple sweater and jeans concealed his body from me, but I could already picture taking them off beneath his soft sheets.

I can't believe he's all mine.

Derek hooked his arm around my waist and pulled me forward. I crashed against his mouth with a moan on my lips.

"You look incredible," he whispered. "Ready to go?"

"Yes."

We walked hand in hand to his car.

"What did my mom say to you?" I asked.

"You know, the usual mom stuff."

He held open my door for me to climb inside. I considered pushing it as he walked around to his side.

Leave it alone. It's your first date. Just enjoy it.

"What are we going to do tonight? Watch movies in your home theater? Mess around in the game room? Order in?"

Derek laced our fingers together and brought my hand to his lips. A ripple passed beneath my skin as he kissed my knuckles.

"I'm making you dinner. From scratch. All by myself."

"Really? That's so sweet. I didn't know you knew how to cook."

"I don't," he said without a lick of shame. "It's most likely going to be a disaster but it's the thought that counts."

I laughed. "I can help you with dinner. You don't have to poison us."

"Have some faith in me, Manning."

"You just said it's going to be a disaster."

"Shit. Fair enough."

We laughed. I let go, forgetting about everything else and just enjoying being with Derek.

The ride to his place we spent talking, joking, and listening to music. The guard let us in at the sight of Derek's car. He gave me a curious look as we rumbled through the gates but didn't attempt to stop us.

"Are you sure he won't tell your parents?"

"Not unless they ask and they have no reason to. I told them I was going out tonight."

"I promised my mom I wouldn't come here and I broke it in less than a day."

Derek put his mouth to my ear. "I love our morning meetups, but we shouldn't do the things I'm going to do to you outside."

I released a shuddering breath. My core pulsed with need. "You don't get to say things like that and then turn me down for sex. Just giving you a heads-up."

His chuckles ghosted over my ear. "We'll do it when the time is right. It may be tonight. Who can say for sure?"

"We can."

He leaned away, grinning. Derek was enjoying this way more than I wanted him to.

He parked and then came around to open my door.

"Such a gentleman… all of a sudden."

"Hey, I've always been a gentleman." He tucked my hand under his arm. "I treat women right. I wasn't raised to do anything else."

"So, it's going to be all holding doors, flowers, breakfast in bed, and foot massages from now on?" I teased.

"I didn't say that."

The world spun. Derek whirled me around and pressed me against a column. The air whooshed out of me as he draped himself on my body.

"If you wanted a guy like that," he said, "you wouldn't be with us. You want someone who'll bend you over in the dirt, smack your ass, and then treat you like an equal and remember you're smarter than we'll ever be. I am more than happy to be that guy for you."

My chest heaved. Pressure was building in my lower belly to the point I feared I would explode. "We're having sex tonight," I growled. "Don't fucking think you're going to tease me, Derek Grayson."

He laughed low in his throat. "I like you giving me orders."

I rose up to kiss him when something flickered out of the corner of my eye. The guard walked out of the shadows, doing his rounds. He glanced at us pressed against the column—my dress up around my waist and Derek's thigh between my legs—and kept going like he didn't see anything.

"Let's take this inside," Derek said.

"Let's take it upstairs."

"We have to eat first," he said with a grin. "I'm starving."

Derek threaded our fingers together and led me inside to his kitchen. My fervor cooled as we passed through their saloon doors into the sparkling, marbled space. Bright red and orange peppers, leafy broccoli, asparagus, chicken, and a bunch of spices were spread across the island waiting for Derek to turn them into something delicious. Beneath the bay window, the breakfast nook had been transformed by flickering candles and a tiny speaker playing soft music.

"Derek, this is beautiful," I breathed.

"I thought you'd like it. I was going to take you to the best restaurant in the Promenade, but after this week, I figured it was my turn for a big romantic gesture."

"Your turn?"

"Yep." He moved over to the stove and flicked it on. "You were so obsessed with me, you became Zeke. You showed me how much you love me. Dinner is the least I can do."

"Obsessed is a strong word," I muttered. "And I did it because I thought you were my brother. Don't rewrite the Zeke years."

"I will rewrite them."

Derek puttered around the kitchen, pulling out knives, cutting boards, pots and pans. For someone who claimed he didn't know how to cook, he sure looked like he knew what he was doing.

"If anyone asks," he said, "you were a lovesick fan trying to get close to the son of Naomi Grayson. I fell in love with your brand of crazy and the rest is history. We are *not* telling our future children you thought I was your brother. Especially, not the part where you seduced me anyway."

"I didn't— We never— There was no—"

There was so much to unpack in those freaking statements I didn't know where to begin.

"I didn't seduce you!"

"All that time you spent in my bed?" He winked. "Brothers and sisters don't normally sleep together."

"Maybe not in the States, but that's not weird in other places. I just wanted to have you to myself."

His grin grew more knowing. "Repeat that to yourself and hear how it sounds."

I huffed. "It's not weird. And it's not obsessive."

"It's both of those things and you can add possessive to the list. It's alright, Zee, I said I'm into your brand of crazy."

"You're not telling people your version of history. Our future children or otherwise. And speaking of which, are you serious about that or is it one of the many ways you like to mess with me?"

"Am I serious about children?" Derek chopped the peppers as he spoke. It made it hard to study his expression. "Yeah. I've always wanted them. Mom's been going on about her grandchildren since potty training."

"But... with me?"

"Did you think there is any version of the future where you're not knocked up with my kid? I want kids, and I'm having them with you."

I lowered my head. Now it was me who didn't want him to see my expression. "Thanks for informing me," I replied, fighting to keep my voice even. "Anything else I should know about our future?"

"We're going to travel together. See all the places you haven't gotten to yet. We can live wherever you want. I'm not bothered. I can act anywhere."

"What about Cole, Michael, and Landon?" I ventured. "Are they there too?"

"Yeah. They can come. We'll be one Moon-type family."

"That's what you want?"

Derek looked at me steadily. "I want whatever you want, Zela."

I didn't push it further. If I did, I might have burst and spread Zela confetti all over the kitchen. Derek wanted a life with all four of us. This was more than I could have dreamed.

"You want to be an actor?" I asked instead.

"I've learned from the best. Plus, I think I'd enjoy it. You meet cool people, film in amazing locations, and bring stories to life."

I loved this. Planning my future with Derek made me the happiest I'd ever been.

"What about college?" I asked.

"You're going to Somerset, right?"

"I haven't gotten my acceptance yet. I feel good about my application though. I have all As, lots of extra-curriculars thanks to Cole, and glowing recommendations from my teachers since freshman year."

"I told Mom I was going there since I found out it was your top choice. The dean is a huge fan of hers and they have a good drama program."

"You'd be a great actor," I said. "I could tell you were gifted from how well you pretend to not be a nice guy."

"Maybe I'm not pretending. From what everyone else says, I'm only nice to you."

"Hmm. No. You're definitely one of the best men I know."

"I love that you feel that way."

Something in his voice made me look up.

"But you don't know everything about me," he said. "Not yet."

"You want to have this conversation now?"

"Don't you think we should before"—he glanced up toward the ceiling—"we go any further."

He has a point. If this night is going to end the way I want it to, we should get everything out in the open. I just don't want this perfect date to sour.

"Yes, we should," I said. "What's going on with the Network, Derek? Why did you take over for Cameron and what does that even mean?"

He sighed. "We're not dancing around this thing."

"This is what you wanted."

"Okay. You're right. I just..." Derek put down the knife. "Can you take over for me?"

I hesitated.

"Please. If we're going to eat sometime tonight, you should finish this while I talk."

Moving around the island, I accepted the knife. For a spell, the only sound in the kitchen was the soft *thwack, thwack, thwack* of my chopping.

"This will make more sense if I start at the beginning," Derek began. "With the expansion and why the Network wanted it."

"To make millions."

"Yes, but it was more than that. That night in the woods when Cameron recruited you guys, he wasn't making anything up. The Network has grown in the last sixteen years. Meeting the right person at the right party, whispering in their ear, promising them they'll get to mentor the next Steve Jobs before the world discovers his talent.

"That's how my father and his buddies were able to amass the largest secret club of professional athletes, billionaires, musicians, businessmen, and moguls. They don't do this for free of course. They do it for the favors, connections, and perks. The house we stayed at that my father keeps close to the studio, he's got plenty more of them all over the world. He puts up Network members for free and they do the same for him when he asks."

"How?" I asked. "How did he build this?"

"He's a director, Zee. The number of rich, famous people he meets on a daily basis would blow your mind. Not to mention the number of people who fall over themselves just to be in the same room as Mom. They came to him... and he brought them on board."

My hand stilled as the truth hit me. "Your dad founded the Network."

He nodded. "Like Cameron said, Dad saw what went down at Evergreen Academy and he had an idea."

"But where does the expansion fit into all of this?" I threw out my hand. "He's already a billionaire with a gorgeous wife and the perfect son. Why did he get it into his head to spread the messed-up battle system to the rest of the schools and make more millions he doesn't need?"

Derek came closer, pressing his body against me. His presence soothed me even though I didn't want it to. I was so clueless for so long.

"A rich man never has enough money, Zela. That drive that pushes you to reach limits no one else can dream of doesn't disappear when you run past the finish line. It just tells you to search for another race. The Network is made up of those people, and inevitably, they realized they could be doing more.

"I said before the members don't mentor for free. They get perks, and in exchange, getting face time with them is the lure that brings new members like Michael, Cole, and Landon in. One of the members came to Dad a few years ago and pitched him an idea. He said he'd offer more of his time for a price."

"A price?"

Derek took my hand and continued chopping. His touch was gentle as the broccoli stalk became a handful of tiny green trees beneath our knife.

"Think about it, Zee. How much would a new author pay to be mentored by J.K. Rowling herself? How much would Cole pay for tips from Michael Phelps? The answer: a shit ton."

I nodded slowly. "That's what he meant by monetizing the Network," I whispered. "But then, where does the expansion fit in?"

"Breakbattle Academy is just one school and the Elite Class is no more than ten students. Plus, not all of them agree to join the Network. For what they wanted to do, there aren't enough boys to pay."

"Of course. It makes sense," I said grudgingly. "And you're right, people would pay through the nose to get one-on-one attention from the best. So that's the plan, make the boys pay to join."

"No."

"No?"

He shook his head. "That wasn't Dad's plan. You know his story. He grew up middle class. His parents put him in Breakbattle because he was bullied at Chesterfield for being smart. One week of orientation, he's put in the Elite Class and his whole life takes a different path.

"Breakbattle is majority Chesterfield kids and most of them couldn't afford to be in the Network at the prices the members wanted to charge." Derek trailed his finger along my cheek. "He knew excellence could come from anywhere."

"I don't get it, then. What did they decide to do?"

"Dad came up with tiers. The first 'level' is free and it's what they've been doing from the beginning. Recruit the freshmen and be available to all the members in exchange for favors. The next level is email contact. You'll be put in touch with the high-ranking member of your choice for a one-time fee. You can talk to them, get advice, and they'll interact when they want and put a stop to it when they feel like it.

"As the tiers go up, you spend more, but get more one-on-one time. The highest and most expensive tier is basically an internship. For example, a budding director could pay to work on set with Dad."

"No wonder Michael, Cole, and Landon wanted to be a part of this."

"It's why we're all a part of this. The Network isn't evil. No one is trying to hurt people. The members' time is valuable, and they're willing to offer more of it, they only ask to be compensated. Not all of us have parents like mine able to hand them their dreams on a silver platter. If you have the money and ambition, why wouldn't you take advantage of what the Network has to offer?"

Despite myself, understanding wormed its way in. What Jonathan Grayson did made sense. Keep the Network free, but charge for those looking for more. Everyone got what they wanted and the potential was there to make millions.

"Where does Dominick Dupre fit in? I overheard him. He said he was only brought in because of the expansion. Why did your father need a man like that?"

Derek blew out a breath. "Dominick Dupre is a bastard, plain and simple. Everyone knows it. He doesn't bother to hide it. The thing is, the man can squeeze five dollars out of a penny and he's no idiot. He may be involved in some shady stuff, but the SEC has never been able to find something on Dupre Financial Holdings because he keeps his business completely above board. He manages the accounts of almost everyone in Evergreen and he does it well.

"The kind of money the Network wants to play with can't be kept under Dad's mattress, and the members didn't like it being put in an account only he had access to, so—"

"They brought in Dominick to manage their funds," I finished. "Oh my gosh. Oh my gosh."

I pushed the food away. My stomach heaved. I doubled over, head falling onto the marble countertop. "I'm so stupid. I thought— I thought— You don't want to know what

I thought," I cried. "I torpedoed the expansion and I had the Network all wrong."

Derek rubbed small circles on my back. "It wasn't your fault."

"Yes, it was! I told the board not to approve it. I riled up the classes and bred resentment so no one in their right mind would want the battle system in their school."

"Zee, if you knew all of this before, would you have done things differently? Do you honestly think the battle system is good for students?"

"Of course not," I replied without hesitation. "The only people who benefit are those at the top, and in no society has that situation been the best for everyone."

"There you go. You fought for what you believed in. No one, including me, Landon, Michael, or Cole, blames you."

Derek lifted me up by my hair. I looked in his eyes, battling guilt like I had never felt.

"We love you."

"But what's going to happen now?" I croaked. "Cole won't get to swim with Phelps and Michael wants to go to the Olympics. I ruined everything."

"Oh, baby." Derek kissed me gently. "It's not as bad as all of that. We're ridiculously rich and Michael runs faster than comic book heroes. They can still get as far as they want to go, whether the members lend more of their help or not."

He kissed me again, and again, and again until I relaxed into him. I wrapped my arm around his waist, holding him tight.

"As for what happens now," he continued, "we've been scrambling since the announcement to figure it out. Mrs.

Jeong promised to give advanced notice of their decision, but that obviously didn't happen. Dad is out right now working to convince the high-ranking members to stay in the Network. They were looking forward to the money coming their way. Dad basically assured them the expansion was a done deal. Without more recruits, they'll hardly get millions.

"And without the members they joined to meet in the first place, the Elite students are threatening to leave too. It's been a fucking mess keeping things together. Even Hunter wants to leave and the kid worships me."

"Hunter is in the Network too?" I tossed my head. That was hardly the most interesting thing he said. "Hold on, the entire Network is falling apart over this? But why? They don't have to recruit from battle system schools. Why don't they approach college freshmen or award winners or—"

"That's a lot of work, Zee, and they're all busy with their own lives. It's why me, Cameron, and the guys before us handle the recruits. What else do we have to do? And you know how easy Breakbattle makes it. They literally take their smartest, most athletic kids and slap labels on them. We don't have to search for the kids with the most potential. The battle system tells us who they are. And getting them when they're fifteen is the whole point. Teenagers need mentors. Wealthy adults who've already gotten there on their own don't."

"Oh."

He had a point. Michael was headed for greatness. Everyone could see it. Waiting until he got there on his own didn't make sense. No wonder they snatched us out of our beds as freshmen.

"Do you think your dad will convince them to stay?"

He kissed the top of my head. "Yes. They still get a lot out of the Network from favors alone. They're pissed because the dollars spinning over their heads were snatched away, but when they calm down, they'll realize there's no reason to leave."

I relaxed. "Okay, good. The expansion had to be stopped. If I'm honest, I think Whittaker should give into For All's demands and end the battle system completely. But I don't want to get in your way, or Michael's, Landon's, or Cole's. I never had a problem with the Network, just the people you put in charge."

"Cameron went too far. Dad took away his position, but Dominick wouldn't stand for him to be kicked out of the Network. Everything got way out of hand since they tried to change things up. I'm on board with Dad getting things back to the way they were."

"Me too."

Derek cupped my cheek and gifted me another sweet kiss. "Are we good? That's everything, Zee. I swear."

"We're good. Thank you for telling me."

"Of course." He bent to kiss me and paused. "Actually, there is one more thing."

"What?"

"Mom told me who my biological father is," Derek said casually. "I meant to tell you sooner but you kept distracting me."

I gaped at him. "I distracted you? You're the one who rips my clothes off before I say hello."

"The result is the same."

Laughing, I rose up and claimed my kiss anyway. "Do you want to tell me about him?"

"*Mom* didn't want to tell me about him. She and dad fought about it for like a week. Big mansion like this and I still heard them. In the end, you convinced them."

"Me?"

He nodded. "Everything you did to find Jonathan Grayson. Dad didn't want me to go through my life thinking I had to find something missing. He wore Mom down."

"So, who is it?"

"You actually know him. He was her costar from her movie *Monsoon Canyon*."

My mouth fell open. "No way. You mean your biological father is Trevor Philips?"

"Yep."

"But he—he's like in every single one of my favorite movies. He's Will Smith famous."

Derek shrugged. "They filmed the movie while Mom and Dad were basically separated. The two of them got close, kept it secret of course, and Mom got what she wanted out of the relationship—me. Trevor never saw kids in his future, so he was cool with signing away his rights."

Derek released me and reached for the food. He went back to chopping like we were talking about last night's football game instead of the man who brought him into existence.

"I met him once when I was seven. He got a part in another one of Mom's movies and I was running around on set. The manager said I couldn't have any more cookies, so he snuck me one while she wasn't looking."

"Did he say anything to you?"

"Nah. Mom popped out of nowhere and hustled me off. I never saw or spoke to him again after that."

I wasn't sure what to say. Derek truly sounded unruffled, but then, he wasn't like me. He grew up with a father who loved him. He didn't question his life until I bulldozed into it.

"Do you want to see him?" I asked.

"No. He was a nice guy who respected my mom's wishes and gave her the one thing she always wanted. I'll respect his wishes and leave him in peace. Besides, Mom is having puppies over this whole thing. I don't think she could take it if I tried to make contact with him."

I leaned against him. "She loves you. She wants you to be proud of her, and more than that, she doesn't want you to think for a second that you weren't wanted."

"I know. It's just convincing her that I'm okay is important to me. We're a family. We always have been."

"I love this," I murmured. "Us talking, being honest with each other. We should have done this a long time ago."

"It's what we'll do from now on."

Derek finished chopping the ingredients and finally threw them into the pan. My stomach growled in direct response to the sizzling food.

"What about you? How is everything with your mom?"

"It was rough," I admitted. "There was another man and she refuses to tell me who he is. I haven't fully forgiven her for that."

He looked at me over his shoulder. Sympathy shone in his eyes along with traces of unsureness. "She must have her reasons."

"I want to know who he is, Derek. I'm tired of being protected. All the things that have happened to me prove not knowing him has kept me far from safe."

"I meant it when I said I'd help you find him."

I smiled. "I know you did and I truly appreciate it. I just wish I knew where to start. I don't have a name. I don't have anything. Every veiled comment my mom made about 'Jeremy Holt' growing up was about your father. There's nothing to go on except that they were together one time."

"Any chance you could get your mom to break?"

"No. Andronika Manning does nothing she doesn't want to do. I'd have a better chance of convincing the senate and house of representatives to dismantle the government and name me queen of America."

Derek chuckled. "Specific."

"I'm not even kidding. She will never tell me." I pushed myself off the counter. "Ugh. Let's change the subject. This is ruining my mood."

I came up from behind and pressed my cheek on his back. "Go back to talking about our future. How many kids are we having?"

"So many. We're talking an irresponsible amount."

I giggled. "Got any names for these kids?"

"Derek Junior for sure."

"I would not be sure about that one."

"What's wrong with DJ?"

We argued, talked, and laughed back and forth as he cooked dinner. Then we sat down to a meal that proved there was nothing Derek Grayson couldn't do. I swallowed one bite of the chicken stir-fry and moaned pornographically.

"This is incredible. I can't wait to eat what you make for dessert."

Derek caught my hand under the table. "Dessert will be served upstairs and it won't be in the form of food."

I knew my smile was goofy. I didn't care. "Even better."

"We don't have a lot of time though. It's almost nine thirty and we have to leave at ten to get you back before curfew."

"It's okay. If there was anything I would have given up sex for, it's spending the night talking with you. We'll do it next time when we don't have to rush."

"Agreed, but I'm still going to scarf this down so I can get you upstairs and out of those clothes."

"I'm way ahead of you."

Although delicious, I did not savor my meal. We cleaned our plates in eight minutes flat and then grabbed our drinks to go. We stifled our giggles as we climbed the stairs, passing two guards on the way. They watched our ascent with stony faces. Just another night in the Grayson mansion.

Derek's room was the usual mess of books. He shoved a whole stack to the floor and tossed me in their place. We shed our clothes with frenzied hands.

"Now, I believe I said something about those freckles."

An exhilarating mix of desire and excitement thrummed in my veins. Derek flipped me onto my stomach and my heart beat so loud I was sure he could hear it.

The mattress dipped. Derek reached over me and grabbed one of his pillows. "Get comfortable, Zee."

I put it under my chin and sunk into the sweet, downy smell of flower detergent and a scent that could only be Derek's.

"There's one," he said softly. He kissed the small of my back—a kiss so feather-light it felt like a tickle. "And another one. One here too."

I sighed. *Could this be more perfect? What I wouldn't give to not have a curfew?*

"Oh." His husky voice floated up to meet me. "There's one here too, and you said you didn't have freckles on your back."

Derek kissed me again and my eyes popped open.

"That's definitely not my back," I teased.

"I'm just going where the freckles take me." He pressed another kiss on my cheek. "Fucking hell, Zela, you're so beautiful."

"He says to my backside." I lazily kicked my feet in the air. I was completely comfortable with Derek. Comfortable with teasing him and comfortable letting him explore my body as he wished.

"Your front side is pretty amazing too."

Another kiss, much lower this time. I knew what was coming before he slipped his hand between my thighs and nudged them apart. My breath caught.

"I'm pretty sure there aren't any freckles down there."

"You were wrong before," he replied. "I'd better check myself."

I laughed breathlessly. It was cut off by a swipe of Derek's tongue.

"Oh yeah. Lots of freckles down there. It's going to take a while to count them all."

Holy hell. If I wasn't in love with this guy before, I would be now. Why was he so freaking sexy?

"Take your time," I rasped.

"Wanna help me out?"

I got my knees under me and lifted my ass in the air. A moan ripped from my lips as Derek tasted me. Up and down, his tongue unwound my sanity like a loose thread. I whimpered with every teasing of my clit.

A noise made me peek down. He stroked his length furiously—at odds with the slow, lingering way he was eating me out. The sight caused my lower belly to tighten. He must have felt me clench. Derek stuck his tongue through my lower lips. Picking up the pace, he bobbed in and out. That was the final straw.

I buried my face in the pillow, crying out as my orgasm shuddered my body. I collapsed on the bed with no chance to catch my breath before Derek groaned. I gasped as my ass was covered in sticky wetness.

"Shit." Derek collapsed on top of me and kissed my damp temple. "If it's that good, imagine what it will be like when we have sex."

"I don't want to imagine. I want you, Derek."

"I know you do, but not in the woods or ten minutes before curfew. Next time I get you alone here, Zela Rae, you're mine."

"Sounds good to me."

Derek's weight pressed me into the warm, silk arms of his bed. Safety and security existed beneath him. I never wanted to leave. The future Derek saw of us traveling the world with our obscene amount of children was what I wanted. I wanted it with all of my boys. I just prayed Landon, Michael, and Cole wanted it too.

We spent what little time we had making out and whispering sweet nothings to each other. Curfew came all too soon. Derek drove me back home and said goodbye to me on the doorstep with Mom watching openly through the living room window.

I went to bed that night feeling great about my relationship with him. Now I had to speak to Michael, Landon, and Cole.

Chapter Five

Monday morning, I strolled through the halls for the cafeteria. My body hummed from my rendezvous with Derek. We changed it up that morning with roleplay. Derek was enjoying dangling sex over my head, so I would make him as crazy as he made me. Since I was finally in the right uniform, I went full schoolgirl. I put my hair in ponytails and donned knee-high socks that I snuck out of Melody's drawer. I would never ask why she had them. I knew way more than I needed to about Adam's sex life thanks to Jordan.

Derek's jaw dropped at the sight of me. His reaction was almost as delicious as his response. I'm pretty sure teachers weren't allowed to spank naughty students, but we weren't going for accuracy.

Walking inside the dining room, I spotted Landon seated at our table with three apples in front of him. There was no one else there, so I had no clue who he stole them from.

"Landon."

He saw me and his face lit up. "Hey, baby. How—"

I swooped in and gave him a searing kiss. The boys the next table over wolf-whistled.

"Damn. What was that for?"

"I spoke to Derek." I sat in my own seat, heeding the lunch monitor's watchful eye. "He told me the truth about the Network and the expansion. I feel like such an idiot for thinking you could be involved in something questionable. Why didn't you say something?"

Smiling, he took hold of my chin and pulled me in for another kiss. "Because I agreed with you, Zee. I want all the tier stuff Jonathan Grayson is trying to pull off, but I don't want more battle schools. Because of you and Moon, I know what life is like for an F. They can work harder to find recruits instead of forcing more kids into this situation."

"I love you so much right now, Landon Foster. I want to take you into the nearest broom closet and have my way with you."

He jumped up. "What are we still doing here?"

Laughing, I dragged him back down and snuggled into him. "Can I ask you something?"

"Anything?"

"What kind of future do you see for us?"

"Our future?"

"Yeah."

I held my breath, body tensing. The passing seconds were murder on my nerves.

"Well, I see us at Somerset University. Me pre-law and you a math major. I see you helping me with late-night study sessions by stripping off a piece of clothing when I get an answer right. I'm very much looking forward to that."

I rolled my eyes. Of course, there is lots of sex in this future.

"I see us making our own way. Building our own life. A couple of kids for sure. They'll be the best-dressed preschoolers you've ever seen." He draped his arm around me. "What do you see?"

I leaned back to smile at him. "I see the same thing, baby."

Our lips met.

"Guys!" Michael skidded to a stop next to us. He hadn't changed out of his running clothes. His shorts molded to his muscled frame and drew more appreciative stares than I liked. "You're not going to believe this. Come with me."

"What's wrong?"

Michael's handsome face was pinched. "For All. He struck again and... it's worse this time."

"Oh no," I breathed. "Is someone hurt?"

"Come."

We needed no more prompting to trail Michael outside. In front of the basketball gym, a group of kids gathered peering through the doors. For some reason they didn't go in.

Michael pushed through them, his grip firm on my wrist. "Excuse us, guys. Zee, look."

I looked around him. My eyes flared.

The gym was destroyed.

Popped basketballs covered the floor, mixed in among trash and rotting food. Covering my nose, I took the horrid scene in. The basketball nets were shredded and a hammer stuck in the middle of the scoreboard told of its destruction.

"I checked the other gyms," Michael said gravely. "The wrestling mats were torn apart. Dye was put in the swimming pool. The soccer balls were popped and the goals ripped up. The only thing that wasn't hit was the track. For All has officially taken it too far. If they find him now, the administration will have him arrested."

I couldn't deny it. I was looking at thousands of dollars' worth of damage. For All would not come back from this.

I didn't ask why he did this. The why was spray-painted beneath the ruined hoops.

END THE BATTLE SYSTEM

"HOW DO YOU THINK HE did it?"

I picked at my food. My appetite was gone and with it went my desire to talk about For All. The whole situation made me sick.

My new lunchmates didn't feel the same. Everly didn't approve of me sitting with my mixed group of friends at breakfast and dinner, but she could only do something about it during lunch. My class sat with me every lunch period, even if I changed tables.

"Annie stayed late in the wrestling gym last night until right before the doors locked," Lauren said. "Everything was fine, no one came in, and she didn't notice anyone outside."

"Something like that took all night," Isla put in. "I bet he hid in one of the locker rooms, waited for everyone to go to bed, then trashed the gyms."

Murmurs of agreement went around the table.

"This is too much," May said. "They've shut down everything but the track. Why won't For All give it a rest? Doesn't this guy see no one is on board with his lunatic crusade?"

"He's clearly not going to stop until he gets what he wants."

Everyone stared at me. It was a minute before I realized I said that out loud.

"It's true," I finished. "If he was willing to let this go, he wouldn't have escalated this far. I'm afraid of what he'll do next if he doesn't get what he wants."

Everly shook her head. "Whittaker isn't going to end the system."

"I know," I replied. "That's why I'm afraid."

The girls fell quiet. We ate the rest of our meal in silence.

It was a subdued group that entered Mrs. Munoz's class.

"Come in, everyone. Take a seat. We need to have a discussion before we begin class."

"It's about For All," Adeline stated. "What are Whittaker and Argyle going to do to stop him?"

"This is of course about this morning's incident. Despite our hopes, it's become clear the security measures we've put in place aren't enough to stop these attacks against the school. It may have seemed like the principal was ignoring For All, but in reality, he was exploring every other option but the ones we have to adopt now."

"What does that mean?" May spoke up.

"It means that as we speak, security is conducting a search of your rooms."

"What?"

The first cry set it off. The room erupted into shouts, arguments, and calls of invasion of privacy. Mrs. Munoz let it go on without comment.

"Are you finished?" she asked when the girls quieted down. "Good. As you know, the rules state that we can search your rooms if the need arises and that time has come. The guards concluded the damage to the equipment was done by a blade. The student could still have this weapon on them. I'm sure you'll agree our first priority is locating and confiscating it. Yes?"

A shiver skittered up my spine. The grave faces of the girls spoke to the same feeling. No one else shouted about their rights.

"We hired assistant coaches last year to watch over your practices," she continued, "but we still offered leeway by leaving the gyms open throughout the day and lending select Elite students' keys. All of those keys will be reclaimed, and from this point forward, no one is allowed into the gym without supervision.

"Finally, the destruction of school property was extensive. We'll spend thousands of dollars to replace the scoreboards and equipment. Money that will come from this year's senior trip fund."

"No," Lauren moaned. "You mean our trip to New York is canceled?"

"I'm afraid so."

"Fuck," Everly cried, uncaring of our teacher. "It's not fair. We didn't do anything wrong."

"I'm sorry, ladies. Our athletic program is just as important as our academic one. This has to be our first priority and the money must come from somewhere. We can't hold battles until everything is fixed and replaced."

"Which is what he wanted."

Munoz inclined her head. "I'm certain it is. And he got his wish. The last thing I want to make clear to you before we begin is that what happened today is a criminal matter. If the search of your rooms doesn't turn up the culprit, we're handing the matter over to the police and they will interview you."

"Well, none of us did it," Everly replied. "We already know it's one of the boys. Mrs. Munoz, we have to save the trip. Can we do something? What if we get our parents to donate money? We could do a bake sale? Or a fundraiser?"

"Good idea, Miss Mackenzie. Why don't we brainstorm at the end of the day?"

The girls perked up. The biggest thing on their minds was spending their last year together cruising around New York and why wouldn't it be? According to them, For All was just a bitter F boy that had nothing to do with them.

Melody sought me over their heads. The look on her face matched mine. We didn't know how this would end or how far he would go, but a knife-wielding kid with something to prove was all of our problems.

"THEY TORE MY ROOM APART," Cole said. "Whittaker had them upend the couch, remove my mattress, look in the toilet and behind the television. He's not playing around."

I cuddled in tighter. A frigid wind whipped through the clearing that night, teasing the trees and slapping our heated cheeks. It didn't help that we were naked. Soon, it would get too cold for us to meet out here.

"He can't afford to play around. For All has a knife. One student has been killed on campus. He won't let anyone else get hurt."

Cole kissed my temple. "Are you okay on the girls' side? I don't like you so far away with all of this going down. At least as Zeke, I could keep you in my bed where you belong."

"It's you I have to worry about. You and the other guys." I lay on his chest and listened to the steady thump of his heart. There was no better music. "For All has to be a guy, and he's not shy about attacking the Elite Class."

"New For All hasn't tried to hurt us. Stink bombs, bloody messages, and computer viruses are nothing compared to sabotaged bleachers, poisoned contact solution, and drugged water bottles. If he was truly willing to do anything to get Whittaker to give him what he wants, he would have switched to personal attacks a long time ago."

Fear choked me, edging out all the high from having sex. Cole's point was terrifying for its truth. We once had a For All that was willing to do whatever it took to achieve his endgame, and my boys were hurt in the process. What if new For All decided that was his only option?

"Cole, don't say that."

"Think about it, Zee. New For All took over in our sophomore year. That means he's either a senior or a junior by now. He's running out of time to have his demands met and Whittaker is no closer to giving in. What happens when he gets desperate?"

"Cole, please. I can't go there. The thought of him hurting you…"

I trailed off, biting my lip hard.

"Hey." Cole held me tighter. "I'm sorry. I didn't mean to scare you. You shouldn't be scared, Zee. No one is going to mess with us. Whittaker upgraded the locks. Sondheim roams the halls. And Michael, Landon, and I learned our lesson about leaving our stuff around. We're safe, Zee. I promise."

"I just want this to stop," I croaked. "I want the battle system to end, too, but this isn't the way."

"It will stop. They'll find him and it will all be over."

I took a deep breath, held it, and then let it go. I repeated it until my heart slowed. Cole wanted me on the boys' side to protect me. I wanted to be over there to protect *them*. My boys would not be caught in the crossfire of For All's crusade.

"Want to talk about something else?"

"Yes," I said. "We can talk about where we'll meet up. It's getting too cold to be outside."

He blew out a breath. "I was thinking about that too. I was one of the lucky ones with keys to the pool. That's gone, so there goes my plan to chase you around the locker room."

I laughed. "I'm not too fond of locker rooms since freshman year. Your chances of getting lucky in there were slim from the start."

"Shit." His smile was tinged with regret as we shared the memory. "Then I better get creative. Michael swears he has a way to sneak you in the dorms but he won't spill. He says he won't let you get caught with one of us before he has a chance to be with you."

"Can't blame the guy."

"Yes, I can."

My unease leaked away. My loving, cranky asshole had that effect on me.

"I'm coming to your place this weekend. We'll have to get in enough to hold us for the week."

Cole leaned back to hit me with wide eyes. "Challenge accepted."

"That wasn't meant to be a challenge," I replied, grinning.

"Too late."

We talked and made love one more time under the cloudy night. When we were spent and warm beneath the blankets, I chanced the conversation I had been waiting for.

"Cole?"

"Yes, Zee?"

"Where do you... want to go to university?"

"Didn't I tell you?" He shifted onto his side, facing me. "I'm going to Somerset."

"Really?"

"They've got a great swimming program. They took Chris from crazy good to insanely good, and I'm basically a legacy. Coach has had his eye on me since Chris told him my parents produced two of us."

"That's what you want? It's your top choice?"

He nodded like it was no big deal. The joy bursting inside of me said otherwise.

"I'd miss Mom, Dad, and Toby if I went out of state."

I flicked his nose. "And Christina."

"Maybe some days." Cole pressed his forehead to mine, smiling into my eyes. "I'd definitely miss you though. You didn't think I'd leave you, did you? Play the long-distance game while Michael, Landon, and Derek have you all to themselves? Not a chance."

"I would have happily done long distance with you, Cole Reed. If there is somewhere else you need to be to pursue your dreams, then that's where I want you to go."

"Somerset is exactly where I need to be. Everything I want is right here."

We kissed gentle and unhurried.

"Can I ask you something else?" I whispered.

"Is it if I want to go again? Because the answer is yes."

"This isn't a good angle to kick you up the backside, but it's coming."

"I'm already turned on, Zee. You don't have to tempt me."

I laughed. "Seriously. I want to know where you see us in the future. After college and all of that."

"Where I see us?"

"Yes, and not just me and you. Michael, Landon, and Derek too."

His smile dimmed. "I don't know. I haven't really thought about it."

"You haven't? But you're Cole. You plan out every minute of your life."

He flipped onto his back, staring up at the sky. "Yeah, but you were never part of it."

I froze. "What does that mean?"

"Not what you think, so don't freak out. I love you, Zela. I love you so much it doesn't make sense. It's like that cartoon love where hearts pop out of my eyes when I see you. Cupids dance around my head and I float off the ground."

I brushed my lips against his shoulder. "I'm not hearing a problem."

"Because you're not a problem. My plan was to get through high school avoiding serious relationships. Didn't think it'd be a problem since everyone in my class was a guy. I wasn't counting on your fake wig-wearing ass."

Chuckling, I cuddled closer. "I messed up the great Cole Reed's plans."

"Completely. I didn't think I'd fall in love with you. I didn't think my best friend would fall in love with you too. None of this was what I expected, and it's so much better than my plan. Since I've been with you, I've accepted I don't need to have every step mapped out. So no, I haven't thought about five years from now. I just think about now. And how lucky I am to be with you."

"Damn," I whispered. "He's far gone."

"Fuck you," he shot back, laughing.

"So you really haven't pictured little blond babies or a big mansion with all of us living together?"

"You mean have I pictured living like Moon?" His voice grew serious. "Honestly, no. One or two blond babies would be nice, and a house for just me and you. It wouldn't bother me if you were still with Michael, Landon, and Derek, but Adam's dads are like brother-husbands. They love each other as much as they love his mom. The only one I'll ever be close to like that is Michael."

I was quiet as I absorbed his speech.

"Are you upset?"

"No." I was surprised to find I meant it. "I'm in four relationships, not one. You want us to have a life and family that is just ours. I understand and I want it too. I just hope we can find a better way than me jumping from house to house, family to family."

"We will, but we don't have to figure it out right now." He rubbed my thigh. "We have to go soon. Want to sneak in one more time?"

My smile returned. "Do you have to ask?"

Cole kept me out until the very last minute. We snuck a quick kiss on the quad and then ran for our campus. I burst inside and nearly ran into a wall of flesh.

"Whoa." Welsh reached out to steady me. "Easy there, Miss Manning. I came to check the door locked properly. What were you doing outside this late?"

"It's not late. Lights out isn't for an hour."

"That may be, but not many students have a reason to walk around an empty campus at nine o'clock at night. Why were you out there instead of in your room studying?"

"For the reason you said." My tone was even. "I was out for a walk."

She lifted a brow. "Alone?"

"No. My boyfriend was with me."

"I see."

"We didn't break any rules. We're allowed outside until the doors lock and we didn't go into the gyms. How else are we supposed to spend time together?"

"I didn't say anything." Welsh stepped to the side. "Go on, Miss Manning. Straight to your room."

"Yes, Ms. Welsh."

Melody was sitting up in bed reading when I came in.

"There you are." She set her book down and patted the spot next to her. She treated me to a surprisingly tight hug.

"Is everything okay?" I asked.

"I know you don't have to tell me where you go, but can I admit I'm a little freaked out? There's a guy with a knife running around campus."

I hugged her back. "I'm sorry. I should have checked in. Of course you're freaked out. We all are—or most of us are. All the other girls seem to care about is their spring break trip."

"Ugh. It's senior year and they refuse to let anyone ruin it. I'll pay for the stupid trip myself if it gets everyone to talk about what's important again."

"I'm with you there."

She let me go. "I was so excited about my last year with Adam and now I can't wait to get out of here. Let's just double-lock the doors and get some sleep."

I pushed our desk chairs in front of the door to make her feel better.

The next morning, I woke before my alarm. My internal clock rang with Derek time. I showered quickly and donned my uniform.

"Bye, Mel," I whispered at the lump stirring beneath the sheets.

I grabbed my phone and it vibrated.

Derek: I can't meet you this morning. I'm sorry. I love you. See you tonight.

My heart sank. *Tonight? Does that mean he's not coming to breakfast?*

I typed out the question. Derek didn't reply. My phone was a silent brick in my pocket on the way down to the cafeteria. I searched for him immediately, but Derek was nowhere to be seen. A second sweep revealed Michael, Cole, and Landon were missing too.

I got my breakfast and then rolled up next to Hunter. He bent over the table, ignoring his food, and scribbled in his sketchpad.

"Hey, mentee. Have you seen the guys?"

He beamed at me. "Morning, Zee. Your timing is great. I just finished this."

"Finished what?"

"I didn't let you have the first one. This will make up for it."

Hunter tore out the page and handed it to me.

"Goodness, Hunter." Pleasing, awed surprise tugged a smile to my lips. "This is amazing."

The sketch was of Derek and me the way we used to be. Propped against his pillows, we were in mid-conversation—or argument—from my exasperated expression. A book dangled from Derek's fingertips and a smirk on his mouth. The drawing was even more special because it was me next to Derek. Zela, not Zeke.

"You're incredibly talented, Hunter," I said. "All the little details you drew from the part in my hair to the stripe on my socks. Do you think you'll pursue art?"

He shook his head. "It's just a hobby. I used to draw pictures for my mom to make her smile. I got better so she wouldn't have to fake it over my stick figures."

I laughed. "Well, you made me smile too, and I needed it. I'm making this my background." I snapped a pic with my phone to prove it. "So have you seen Derek or the guys? I'm worried something is up."

Hunter's ever-present smile twitched at the corners. "Something is up, Zee." He leaned in, lowering his voice. "With the Network. Derek's been saying everything is fine, but I got this weird text this morning."

Hunter pulled out his phone and handed it over.

TM: Member meeting. Strongly advised that all attend. If unable, your leader will relay details. Location, date, and dress code to come.

"Why is this weird?" I asked.

"We don't have member meetings. Ever. Having one in the middle of this shit storm doesn't fill me with confidence."

"Who is TM?"

"Top member."

"As in the highest member of the Network?"

He nodded.

Jonathan Grayson.

"The leader of the Network suddenly calls a mandatory meeting," I mused aloud. "I agree. Something is up. What do you think—"

Hunter's gaze flicked over my head. "Hold on. Whittaker is here."

No sooner had the words left his mouth than the principal's voice rang out.

"Attention, students. Quiet down. I have an update in regards to the latest attack against the school."

A hush fell over the room as though a switch had been flipped. Whittaker took his place at the front of the head table. Behind him, a solemn troop of teachers, two guidance counselors, and a vice principal formed a line.

"First, I'd like to assure you all that there is no reason to panic. We are committed to keeping you safe, and measures have and will be taken in the aftermath of the destruction. With that said, the search did not turn up the culprit."

Whispers broke out.

"At this point," Whittaker continued, "we're turning the matter over to the police. They will maintain a presence on campus from this point forward."

Principal Whittaker swept out his hand. We collectively swiveled around and I laid eyes on none other than Detective Langman.

Playing high school security guard can't be detective work whether For All has a knife or not.

"Do your best to cooperate with them," said Whittaker. "The self-named For All's terrorizing against this school ends now."

Chatter filled the room as Whittaker took his seat. I read "For All" and "police" on everyone's lips.

"It's horrible what's going on," Hunter said. "Cameron murdered and every day we wake up to a new surprise from For All. I'm shocked parents haven't pulled their kids out of here."

"Trust me, my mom is ready and willing to send me to Chesterfield High. If this keeps up, I won't be able to stop her." I nudged him. "Are your folks threatening to pull you out?"

"My place isn't close by. I don't want to leave my friends either but, like you said, I may not have a choice."

"Hey, guys."

Justin, Owen, Tanner, and Nico strolled up with their trays.

"Why is the head table filled up?" asked Tanner. "What did we miss?"

I sat back, letting Hunter explain. My mind was busy with the implications of Whittaker's announcement. The hunt for For All was heating up. Detective Langman was here.

But is he looking for our mysterious attacker or is he looking for Cameron's killer? Or third possibility, is he looking at me?

I hadn't heard from him since Mom shut him down at the station. She made him direct all further questions to our lawyer who dances on a pedestal of alibis, lack of evidence, and no witnesses. It's possible I was still his number one suspect.

In all of this time, he must have found something that pointed him to the real killer. His suspect pool was limited to the people on campus that weekend. It couldn't be that hard to narrow it down to the people who had a grudge against him.

"—give him what he wants. Would it be the fucking end of the world if Breakbattle was like every other high school in the world?"

Tanner pierced through my thoughts.

"The battle system sucks," he hissed. "We all know it and we'd say it if Whittaker didn't come down on students who do. For All has to do this cloak-and-dagger shit because he'd be ignored like the rest of us if he said it to their faces."

"We don't have to be quiet," Melody replied. I hadn't noticed her arrive. "Zela and I have come up with a bunch of protest ideas. We can get the media involved, organize sit-ins, pass around petitions. People were too scared to get active in Stand Up before, but we're seniors now. We've got our college acceptances and we can't be punished for exercising our rights."

"We can be punished," Tanner argued. "Whittaker basically shut us down after the basketball game."

"So, we don't let him this time. If you feel this strongly, Tanner, do something about it. Something that will get our cause the right kind of attention."

Electricity charged the air as their gaze locked across the table.

The bell rang.

I left them to it. Crossing the cafeteria, I considered how much trouble I'd get in if I stormed the boys' campus looking for the guys.

"Watch it!"

A hard shove almost propelled me into the doorframe.

"How did you become Elite when you can't manage walking?" Zach spat.

I straightened and leveled them with a glare I wish would pop their heads. I was sick of their petty bullshit. Serious problems were plaguing the school. When was Zach going to grow up?

"Easy," I said through gritted teeth. "I beat your cheating ass."

Shannon couldn't help a parting shot. "Stupid bitch."

"That wasn't nice."

The dry voice killed any thought of a reply. I held still as Langman stepped in front of me.

"Sweet couple."

I scoffed. "Lord willing, they never spawn. I hope you noticed I was well within my rights to stomp them into the floor, but I didn't because I'm a pacifist."

A ghost of a grin crossed his face. "I think you need to be advised of your rights again. Stomping people into the floor is not on the list."

"Neither is being late to class. See you around, Detective."

I made to go around him.

"Sooner than you think." Langman smoothly blocked my way. "We've come to interview the students. Congratulations, you're the first one."

"I don't know who For All is."

He swept out his hand. "Please, follow me."

"My mom says I'm not allowed to speak to you without our lawyer."

"We can wait for your lawyer to arrive. It's entirely up to you, Miss Manning."

I reached for my phone.

Wait. Maybe I shouldn't. He just wants to speak to me about For All and that will be a short conversation. I can get this over with and get on with my day.

"Fine."

"Wonderful. Your principal granted us your library for the interviews."

The two of us walked lockstep through the main building. Out of the corner of my eye, I picked up on the side glances Langman threw me.

He's wondering how this thin young woman killed the great Cameron Dupre. Answer: I didn't.

Ever the gentleman, Langman held open the door for me to go inside. I went over to the tables in the back and sat without prompting.

"Thank you for speaking with me, Miss Manning." Langman sat on the opposite end and smiled at me. His smile was charming enough to be disarming. I bet he teased a few confessions out on his affable nature alone. "Why don't we jump right in?"

"I'd like that."

Langman pulled out the notebook I knew well. "Where were you between nine p.m. and six a.m. Sunday night?"

"I was in my dorm room. One good thing about being the odd girl is my roommate can vouch for me."

"I'm sure she will." Langman wrote something down. "Do you have any idea who For All is or why they're carrying out these attacks?"

"I'm pretty sure For All is a guy and my boyfriend pointed out that he must be a junior or senior by now. Other than that, I don't know. As for the why," I continued, "he's been extremely clear. He wants the battle system done away with."

"Why do you believe they're a junior or senior boy?"

I walked him through my reasoning.

"How can he be a junior if this began in your freshman year?"

"Hmm. You know more about this than I thought."

"You didn't think I'd do my homework?"

"He could be a junior because the new For All started up when we were sophomores."

"New For All," Langman said without skipping a beat. "And the old one you accused of being Cameron Dupre."

I stiffened. I walked right into that. "Yes."

"How did you know Mr. Dupre was behind the sabotage against the Elite boys?"

"He admitted it to my face."

"And what made you so sure he wasn't behind the incidents in your second year?"

"He had nothing to gain from driving us out of our rooms with a stink bomb or giving us our tablets. Someone else took over, and like you saw in the video, Cameron didn't know who they were."

The faint scratchings of his pen seemed louder in the empty library.

"Around the time of the incidents, did you see anything or anyone that seemed out of place?"

I shook my head. "And I wouldn't have if he's in another class or grade. They keep us separated."

"Alright, Miss Manning." He flipped the notepad over. "Anything else you want to tell me?"

"Only that I don't believe he'll stop until he gets what he wants. The battle system should end. Breakbattle can have advanced classes like normal schools do, but they don't have to take it this far. For All is right to hate it. It's already taken the life of one girl."

Langman's brows snapped together. "Taken the life of a girl? Who are you referring to?"

"Rebecca Taylor. Don't you remember? The girl who committed suicide years ago because the boys drove her to the edge with nonstop battles."

He looked at me blankly.

"She's the reason the campuses were split."

"I'm afraid I don't know the school's history very well," he admitted. "I moved to Chesterfield recently. I am sorry to hear that though."

"They should have scrapped the system as a disastrous experiment then."

"The argument could be made, yes, but it doesn't excuse what For All has done. The school intends to press charges for the damage to property."

"It's not the way I would have done it." I leaned back, folding my arms. "Better to exploit the weaknesses of the system and let it fall apart on its own. You never get your hands dirty."

Langman gave me a long look.

"What?" A smirk twitched at the corner of my lips. "Pacifist, remember? I don't get physical with people, places, or things. I agree with his goal, but how he's going about it doesn't make sense. I don't like that he's not smart enough to see that. It worries me what he'll do next."

"He won't do anything next. The CPD is taking over and two officers will be posted here. We'll find For All."

Like you found Cameron's killer, went unsaid.

Langman's expression changed. "Miss Manning, about Cameron Dupre..."

Unease tickled my spine. Did the guy read minds?

I rose to leave. "I can't talk to you about Cameron."

"Then don't talk. Just listen."

I paused hovered over the chair.

"I will be honest with you, the investigation has hit a wall," he started. "We know he fought with someone in that room and died from a blow to the head. The blood on him was most likely from the assailant. The issue is we can't compel a blood test. And before their rich parents made them lawyer up, Cameron's friends swore up and down that he didn't have a problem with them or anyone else."

Slowly, I returned to my seat.

"We don't have a string of threatening texts. He didn't call any strange numbers. We haven't discovered so much as a spam email on his computer. The only one we can see with a clear motive is you. The private investigators Dominick Dupre hired are combing through every statement and scrap of evidence and they came to the same conclusion."

"I didn't—"

"I know."

The denial lodged in my throat. What did he say?

Langman leaned in, holding my gaze unflinchingly. "There's a reason I came here today. I spoke to Jonathan Grayson and he finally told me the truth behind your midnight escape to the cabin. If you became Zeke to get closer to him, finding out he wasn't your father made Cameron's blackmail video useless. There was no reason to kill him over a secret that was out."

I surged forward. "You believe I'm innocent?"

"I do and I want to prove that definitively by running your blood, Miss Manning." His pepperminty breath passed over my face. "When it comes back as not a match, I can clear you as a suspect and we can move on to other viable leads. The alternative is I put on the record what Mr. Grayson told me—which he asked that I not do if I can help it."

Of course he did. The scandal would be massive. I can see the headlines now. "Film legend Jonathan Grayson Sterile." "Who is Derek Grayson's True Father? Vote Below."

I found a birth certificate and blew up their happy façade. Still, Jonathan told the truth to keep me out of trouble. The least I can do is take a test I'll fail.

"Okay. I'll give you my blood."

"Thank you, Miss Manning. I'll have techs here within the hour."

Langman was good for his word. Forty-five minutes later, he and his techs carted off a vial of my blood. I considered telling Mom about this, then threw the thought away. It wasn't a big deal. Langman believed me. The results would eliminate me from suspicion and once and for all we'd put this horrible chapter behind us. No need for Mom to pay lawyer fees when I was innocent.

Class was underway when I got onto the Elite floor. Melody shot me huge eyes as I passed her, trying to communicate something. I smiled to let her know I was okay and took my seat.

"Okay, Zela. We're on page forty-six. Begin analyzing the text and answer the response questions. You can have an extra ten minutes to finish."

"Yes, Mrs. Munoz."

I kept my head down and did my work. After the bell rang for lunch, Melody came over to my desk.

"Do you want to skip the cafeteria and eat in our room?" she asked. "All anyone is going to talk about is For All and the police. I want to pretend for a second everything is normal."

"You read my mind."

We grabbed some food from the dining room and took it upstairs. I propped my tray on one knee and my tablet on the other. Some peace and quiet to hang with Melody and watch a movie was exactly what I needed.

She climbed up next to me. "I'm in the mood for something funny. There's not much to laugh about these days."

"Agreed. Wanna try something new or an old favorite?"

"Old favorite."

A notification appeared on my screen. I swiped it away and pulled up Netflix.

Melody's tablet dinged.

"One second." She heaved herself up.

Hmm. Old favorites. We've got Bridesmaids, The Other Guys, Mean Girls.

"Zela."

It's been a while since I've seen Mean Girls.

"Zela, you need to look at this."

"Look at what?"

Suddenly the tablet was out of my hands and Melody's was in its place. I screwed up my face at the upside-down A spinning on the screen.

"Ugh. He hacked your tablet? Why?"

"It's not a hack. It's a video. You got it too." She showed me the notification I ignored.

Email. ForAllForYou@gmail.com

"He's got his own email address? He's getting bold."

"Zela, look at this." Melody tapped the screen, hitting play.

The two of us leaned over the screen as the symbol flashed out and was replaced by a single chair and white backdrop. A figure stepped in front of the camera.

"Shit," Melody breathed. "Is that him?"

I shook my head, not able to conjure the words to reply. The lens aimed at a backside in uniform pants. His hands hung by his side, concealed in gloves.

"Hello, Breakbattle." A deep, electronically altered voice filled the room. "It's time we talked."

The figure abruptly fell out of frame. I lurched up, but just as quickly, he reappeared. For All sat down and gave us a perfect view of the black cloth sack over his head.

Squinting, I studied every inch of him.

"I can't make anything out. Skin color. Build. Nothing," I said. "The camera is too close."

"No, I think I saw—"

"There has been a lot of talk about me, what I've done, and why," For All stated.

All inclination to talk fled. For All had our complete attention.

"I want to make it clear that I mean no one harm. The weapon you're worried about is a Swiss Army knife I borrowed from confiscated property. It's been returned with everyone none the wiser. Most importantly, I don't have it or any other weapon."

This would be a relief... if he's telling the truth.

"With that distraction out of the way, we can get into what's really important," he said, and I was sure he was a he more than ever. "Ending the battle system.

"I want to be clear, I will not stop until this is done. And you should applaud me for it—no, you should join me. I'm not talking about the self-satisfied Elites who've fooled themselves into thinking able bodies and growing up with an army of mommy-funded tutors make them better than everyone else. I'm talking to the Cs, the Ds, and the Fs.

"This system is bullshit and you know it. The administration has fooled you into thinking you have access to more resources and opportunities than you'll get elsewhere. All you have to do is win a battle. But it's a lie."

Melody and I were rapt. We hardly blinked. I barely breathed.

"At literally any other school in the country, you'll go to the library when you want. You'd show off at school dances with the other kids. You'd go on the same field trips, experience growing up together, share the same memories. You wouldn't live in the shadow of a legacy that drove a young girl to her breaking point.

"At any other school—at the school just twenty fucking minutes from here, you'd be treated as equals despite your test scores or how fast you run."

Passion laced his voice as it rose. Despite this, For All didn't gesture, wave his hands around, or get agitated. He remained perfectly still. So still, a mannequin could have been sitting in that seat.

"The battle system is wrong. It discriminates against you all the while convincing you you're only getting what you deserve."

He leaned forward. I couldn't see his eyes, and yet I felt them pierce me.

"I'm not saying you deserve more," he continued. "I'm saying you deserve what every other public-school student has. Access to an equal and fair education. Lowerclassmen, I ask you, take back what is yours."

"He's got a way with words, doesn't he?" Melody rasped.

I could only nod.

"*Demand* what is yours. And if they won't give it to you: refuse. Refuse to obey their class timeslots. Refuse to stay out of their dances and movie nights. Refuse to let them hold your property hostage. Refuse to battle."

"Refuse to battle?" I repeated.

"That's right," he said as though he heard me. "Refuse to battle. They force you to participate in this backward system by dangling privileges over your head and threatening your grade, but if you all stand together, you can take that power back."

He leaned back, adopting a pose of stillness once again. "This isn't about me. I'm not doing it for myself. I'm speaking up for you. If you don't want this and you'd rather continue along as the Cunts, Dumbshits, and Failures, then do nothing. Keep your head down, trudge to graduation, and I'll do it with you.

"I swear here and now that I will stop if you choose not to take up the fight. For All will go dark and everyone can return to their regularly scheduled lives. But I hope you stand up. Lowerclassmen, I pray you refuse."

The screen went dark. I jerked like I had been slapped. Yanked from the trap of his words, I blinked at the tablet as I tried to make sense of what happened.

Melody recovered much quicker. "Did you see it, Zee?" She tore the tablet out of my hand and furiously swiped the screen.

"Did I see what?"

"Right here." She tapped the hooded figure. "His patch. Look at his patch."

My eyes bugged. "Oh my gosh, Melody."

It was blurry. A moment caught just as he sat down, but there was no denying that was a big, bold B on For All's patch.

OUR RELAXING, MOVIE-time lunch was scrapped. We used the little time we had left to obsess over every line, inflection, movement, and shadow of For All's video. Walking into Munoz's class, we heard the girls having the same conversation. They huddled around Everly's desk, bent over her computer.

Isla ran up to Melody. "Mel, did you get the video?"

"We watched it five times."

"But did you see the patch," Lauren piped up. "He's a B."

"Why would a B do this?" May asked. "They don't have it that bad."

"They don't have it as good as us," Everly replied. "I said whoever was doing this was bitter that they couldn't hack it."

A whoosh of air blew my skirt.

"Ladies, please," Munoz cried. "Sit down."

Munoz tossed her things on her desk, looking frazzled. Her blouse was untucked and a dab of mustard decorated the corner of her mouth. It seemed For All interrupted her lunch too.

Everly stood. "Mrs. Munoz, did you—"

She put up her hands. "I've seen the video. We all have. Principal Whittaker is handling it as we speak."

"But did he notice the patch?"

"Yes. We saw the B." Munoz clutched her chest and released a long breath. "The officers have been informed. They will conduct another dorm search and pull the B students out for questioning. Girls and boys to be safe. When For All is found, he will be expelled. It doesn't matter that he claims he will cease his attacks. I'm just relieved this is over."

"Best part," said May, "is that they can make him pay for the damages and the senior trip will be back on."

The girls clapped. Their spirits were lifted. All was right in their world once again. My world, not so much.

After class, I texted the boys. I hadn't heard from either of them since Derek bailed on me that morning. By then I knew Hunter was right that there was something wrong. At least one or all of them would have sent me an explicit text before the final bell rang if it was a normal day.

Me: Is everything okay? Is there another issue in the Network?

My cell vibrated a couple minutes later.

Derek: Meet me tonight in our place.

Me: I'll be there.

THAT NIGHT, I STRODE through the woods to a chorus of snapped twigs and chirping insects. Nighttime didn't make the menagerie of trees and moss spooky. On the contrary, I enjoyed the peace of this place where I could be with the men I loved. If only it didn't come with the harsh memories attached.

I broke through the trees. Derek was waiting for me. He wasn't alone.

Michael, Landon, Cole, and Derek ended their talk at my arrival. Michael held out his arms for me and I ran to him without a thought. His piney body spray filled my nose. I breathed deeper, exhaling worry as I inhaled him.

"Guys, what's going on?"

"I'm sorry we didn't tell you sooner." A hand grasped my arm and tugged me free of Michael. Derek turned me to face him. "The recruits were on me all day."

"Why? Is it your dad? Was he not able to convince the members to stay?"

"Oh no," Landon said. "The members are going to stay."

I glanced between them. "That's good, isn't it?"

"The members are going to stay because they finally got what they wanted," Derek replied. "My dad is out, Zee. They voted unanimously to have him removed as head of the Network. And they chose Dominick Dupre to take his place."

Chapter Six

"What are you going to do?"

"I don't know, Zee."

Michael's throat rumbled against the back of my neck. It was tranquilizing—as tranquilizing as his slow, deliberate massage of my thighs—but I refused to be calmed.

The boys didn't have any more to tell me the night before in the clearing. It followed that Michael wouldn't suddenly have information nine hours later in time for our run, but I put off meeting Derek to get this time alone with him anyway. We needed to talk and I needed to be with him.

"Why won't you meet me in the clearing? You like playing hard to get, Michael Young?"

The two of us sat on the grassy pitch in the middle of the track. I leaned against his chest while he ran his hands over my body. Maybe we didn't need to go as far as the clearing. Here would do.

He chuckled. "Not playing. I don't want our first time to be in the place I committed the second worst thing I've ever done. And if I get you alone out there, I *will* end up inside of you."

His growl enticed a shiver. He was much better at this waiting game than me, or so it seemed. Hearing him talk like that reminded me he wanted us to be together as badly as I did.

Michael kneaded harder and a sigh left my lips unbidden.

Careful with this guy, Zela. He's doing a great job of distraction and you're due a serious conversation.

I pushed through the Michael haze. "Second-worst thing you've done?"

"I manipulated a drunk kid into telling me he caught his mom cheating and then told everyone to get into the Network. He actually thanked me for listening to him because he had no one else to talk to. I felt lower than shit."

He kissed the spot just below my ear. "But still the worst thing... was the locker room."

"We don't have to go there, Michael," I whispered. "I forgive you. You can forgive yourself."

"I'll never forgive myself."

"Everything is perfect now." I twisted around to look into his eyes. "Because I'm with you."

Michael gave me one of those sweet kisses that sped my pulse. His hands didn't pause in their massaging as his tongue swirled with mine. He moved further up my thigh and my core responded.

I broke away, gasping. "Oh, Michael. I'm doing it so much these days my panties get wet if one of you even blows on me. You can't tease me like this."

He put up his hands in surrender. "Whatever you say. But how about this? Next week Thursday. Me and you. My room."

Squealing, I spun and threw my arms around him. "Yes, yes, and yes."

"Damn," he said, grinning at me. "You don't have questions?"

"None. Just tell me what to do."

"I'll give you a full rundown of the mission later."

I kissed him again. "I feel ten times better now. It's a shame to spoil it by talking about Dominick but we should. What's going to happen with him in charge of the Network? Will you drop out?"

He sighed. "I only know what people have said about him," Michael admitted. "None of it is good. I want the connections the Network promises. Adisa Ele called me personally and said he can't wait to meet me the next time he's in the country."

"That's... great?"

Cracking a smile, Michael bumped our heads together. "It's amazing. He's a famous runner in Africa. He was born and went to school here. He joined in college and moved. The guy wouldn't know I existed if not for the Network. I don't want to leave because of Dominick, but there are changes coming, Zee. Chances aren't good we'll like them."

I nodded. "I can't imagine how Derek feels. His father built this up and the guy he brings in to help snatches it away."

"He had help. It was the members who voted him out."

Michael gripped my thighs and kneaded tight muscles. "As soon as I know what to do, I'll tell you. Right now, I want to talk about us. Derek sees you in the mornings and Landon and Cole are with you at night. I need more of you all to myself. I have serious Zela withdrawal."

"Ugh. I know. We have to go back to running together. I miss watching your ass in these shorts."

"Hmm. I knew there was a reason you run slower than you have to."

I nipped the tip of his nose. "To be fair, I'd be trailing you even if I ran flat out. I might as well enjoy the view."

"You can enjoy this too."

Michael flipped me onto the grass. My yelp was cut off by his lips crashing on mine.

All that stuff about talking and we spent the final hour until the breakfast bell making out.

Michael carried me piggyback over to the girls' side.

"Tomorrow morning, let's sneak away for breakfast," I said. "We can eat on the bleachers. Just the two of us."

"And the morning after that. And the morning after that. And the morning after that."

I pecked his cheek. "Yes, yes, and yes."

Michael dropped me off in front of my door and I nearly skipped upstairs. Life was pushing in on all sides, but being here with my boys made it all worth it.

I walked into our room in time to catch Melody going out.

"Do you mind waiting? I'll take a quick shower."

"Sure."

Twenty minutes later, the two of us headed over to the main building. Someone waited for us just outside the doors.

"Adam," I cried. I full-speed tackled him in a hug.

Adam picked me up and twirled me. "I miss you, Zee. It sucks over there without you."

"I swear you love my boyfriend more than me," Melody teased.

"It's true. I do." I squeezed him tighter to be extra obnoxious. "It's why I get to steal him away to Europe this summer."

"Don't pack me in your suitcase just yet," Adam said. "Dads haven't said yes."

"I have complete faith in your mom. You're going and we're going to have an amazing last summer together."

His brow shot up his forehead. "Last summer? What are you talking about? I'm going to Somerset with you."

"You are?"

"I got my acceptance letter yesterday." His face split into a grin. "Mom broke laws opening it for me, but we're all excited, so I forgive her."

"Congratulations. That's amazing." I celebrated with a kiss on both cheeks. "I wonder if I got my letter. I have to call Mom."

"While you do that, I'll take over hugging and kissing Adam."

"Good deal."

The sound of their smooching was my soundtrack as I dialed Mom. She picked up on the first ring.

"Zela, what's wrong? Did something happen?"

"Nothing's wrong, Mom. I called to ask if a letter came for me from Somerset."

"Oh. Well, as a matter of fact, I'm looking at it right now."

I tensed. "Is it... a big envelope?"

"I'd say so."

"Thick? Like it's stuffed with papers and catalogs and the keys to the next four years of my life?"

"It's pretty thick."

I screamed.

"Heaven's sake, Zela. I was holding the phone to my ear," she scolded without any heat. "Congratulations, my daughter. I'm so proud of you."

"Thanks, Mom. Open it. Open it, open it, open it. Read the letter to me."

She laughed. "You can read it this weekend. I want to see the look on your face when you open your first acceptance. Now we wait for your Ivy League acceptances."

My enthusiasm didn't lessen. "Mom, I applied to Princeton, Columbia, and Brown because they were equally as tough as Somerset and it was stupid to hang my hopes on one school, but if that envelope truly says what I think, I'm not going anywhere else."

"Why not? You want to teach math at the collegiate level. That requires an impressive resume."

"Somerset is impressive. Plus, it's close to home. I don't want to be far from you, Jordan, and Aunt Bev."

"Only one, you have been my life and my companion for the last eighteen years. The thought of you far away is hard for me to accept. But no one will stand in the way of your greatness, Zela Rae. Least of all me."

I swallowed hard, pressing my lips together. My mother so rarely said things like this to me. It made it all the more special when she did.

"You could never be in my way, Mom."

Mom roughly cleared her throat. "Well, um, just come home and we'll celebrate. All four of us."

"Can't wait."

I hung up and dropped my phone in my bag. Adam draped his arm around me.

"Sounded like good news."

"Big envelope."

It was his turn to hug and kiss me.

The three of us walked into the cafeteria laughing and crowing about life in college. If Adam and Melody felt the sting of their impending breakup, they didn't show it. Their faces shone talking about how they'd set up their dorms and what they'd do the first time they were out from under their parents' noses.

"I'm looking forward to having my own bed permanent-ly," Adam put in. "When I'm at home, one or all of my sib-lings wander into my room at night."

"Ahh," I crooned.

"It'd be cute if they weren't in their bed-wetting phase."

I cringed. "Fair point. Okay. You get that one. As for me, the first thing I'm going to do is order a large, greasy pepper-oni pizza and eat it on my bed."

Melody laughed. "You've thought a lot about this."

I picked up the food trays and handed it to them. "Yep. I love my mom and she's an amazing cook. But she's deathly serious about health food only. She's even more serious about not eating anywhere other than the kitchen. I'm going crazy. I may even drip on the sheets."

"You're both thinking too small," said Melody. "I found a freshman bucket list online the other day. I'm working my way through the whole thing. Pull an all-nighter. Take a spontaneous round trip. Or I could—"

"Mel."

Tanner, Nico, and Owen pushed through the food line.

"Mel," Tanner repeated. "We need to talk to you and Zee."

"Morning, guys. What's up?"

"We're in."

"In what?" I asked.

He jerked his head at Melody. "She said you guys thought up ways for us to protest and get noticed. We're in. We want to do it."

Owen and Nico nodded behind him.

"We got For All's message," Tanner continued, "and he's right. This shit goes on because we let it. He's one person and he messed with the system many times. If we all fight back, we could end it for good."

"Or you could get suspended in your final year," Adam said seriously. "Are you sure about this? With the video out there, anyone who protests will look like they're supporting him."

"We do support him," Nico piped up. "We weren't behind that psycho stuff in freshman year, but that wasn't new For All. He's not dangerous and he'd never hurt anyone."

Nico's talking like the guy is his lifelong friend instead of a faceless figure on a screen. His video had more of an impact than I knew.

"We're sure, Adam. It is our final year. We deserve to spend it like normal seniors with dances, spring break trips, skip day, and all the other shit they'll tell me I can't do because I failed a test years ago." He focused on Melody. "So how about it?"

Melody was already reaching for her bag. "Zee and I made a great list. It'll be tough, but we'll have the most impact if boys and girls get on board." She led the three of them away, food forgotten. "I loved what Zee did last year training the lowerclassmen."

"That was cool, but we want to do what For All said and refuse..."

"So much for thinking it was over," I said softly.

Adam moved to my side. I let him enfold me into his side. "I can't say for sure what is going to happen, but I do know one thing, this is far from over."

"I'M SO PROUD OF YOU, cousin."

"I can't wait to say the same when your acceptances come in."

The seeking rays sought us through the blinds. It was well after when we usually got up, but we stayed up so late the night before talking that sleep had trouble letting us go.

Jordan and Aunt Bev were waiting for us at home with my unopened letter, balloons, and cake. They kicked up a fuss shouting and clapping before I pulled the letter out. It was official. I was going to Somerset University.

The mattress squeaked under Jordan's shifting. Crystal clear memories of my night with Cole floated through my head.

"Soon we won't be able to do this," Jordan said. "Go to each other's houses whenever we feel like it and stay up all night talking. I thought our first fifteen years apart prepared me for this, but I was wrong. I'm going to miss you, Zee."

Emotion welled in my throat. "Don't say that. It's not going to be like before. We'll see each other more than once a year for one. Also, I looked up the flights from New York and it's less than two hours away. If you get into Columbia, we can alternate weekends we'll visit each other."

"Are you serious? 'Cause I would love it."

I reached for her under the blankets. "Of course I'm serious. You're basically my sister and you know how I get about my siblings."

We cracked up, easing the tense moment.

"I'm so glad we can laugh about this now," said Jordan. "You were straight obsessed with that guy."

"I'm obsessed with all of those guys. Cole and I are going to the park today. I can't wait to have more than a stolen hour with him."

"Need help picking out an outfit?"

"Always."

I finally pushed myself up and went to my closet.

"So did Adam give you the news?" I asked.

"He did and we're going to celebrate tonight."

"Are you also going to talk about the long-distance thing?"

"I haven't gotten into Columbia yet, Zee."

"You will. Unless the admissions board is made up of idiots, and Ivy League schools tend not to hire dummies."

"*If* I get in, we're both willing to do long distance. I love him and I don't want to be with anyone else. We'll make it work."

Footfalls sounded behind me. Jordan reached over my shoulder and took down a light, floral shirtdress.

"This one with your strappy, yellow sandals. Cute and comfortable."

"What are you doing tonight with Adam?" I asked while I changed. "Can I return the favor?"

"We're doing a double date with Kim and her boyfriend, then we're parking somewhere quiet. I've got something special planned. He won't care what I'm wearing after that."

I finished getting ready just in time to reply to Cole's on-his-way text.

"I'm going down for breakfast."

"Be down in a sec," I called after her.

I pulled up Derek's number.

"Morning, Zela."

"Hey. How are you?" I sat on the edge of my bed. "I wanted to talk after the clearing, but you've been so busy."

"I'm sorry. Everyone is looking at me to tell them what's happening, but I'm the last person Dominick Dupre would share his plans with."

"I wish I could understand why the members chose him over Jonathan."

"They were looking for a regime change. Dad wouldn't monetize the Network the way they wanted, and then he went incognito over the summer. He focused all his attention on me and our family stuff. Dupre seized his chance to sway them to his side."

"I'm sorry."

"Stop it, Zela."

I blinked. "Stop what?"

"You know what. You're apologizing because you believe you're to blame. You're not."

"If I hadn't—"

"If you weren't the push that made him confess, who knows how long you would have gone on thinking I was your brother. You would have chased a lie forever, and I would still be living in one. Dad said himself he'd lose the Network a million times before he lost me. The soft old man isn't angry over this."

A smile found its way through my guilt. "You're soft too, Grayson. I bet you love that he stayed home and showered you with attention. You can't fool me. You're both a mommy *and* a daddy's boy."

"Watch it, Manning. That ass isn't so fine I wouldn't spank it again."

Pure naked lust erupted in me like a sprung tap.

I spread out on the bed, playing our romp in the woods on a loop. "Well... if you think that's what I deserve."

"Dammit, Zela," Derek hissed. "My mom's waiting for me in the car and now I'm hard as fuck."

His voice was thick with the same lust and my smirk widened. "Hmm. I should be punished for that too."

"Yeah, okay. I've got to hang up. I love you. Wear that outfit again on Monday."

The call ended on my giggling. Derek and I had amazing chemistry in bed, but we also needed to laugh, joke, and stay up all night talking about everything and anything. With every day that passed, my certainty grew stronger that what we were building would last.

My phone went off.

Cole: We're here.

The doorbell rang as I reached the period. Downstairs, I heard Mom open the door and then the murmur of voices. Cole and Toby greeted me when I came out. Cole with a wave of his hand and Toby with a wag of the tail. The loveable pup bounded up, planted himself in front of me, and waited expectantly for his love.

"Hi, Toby. Hi, handsome boy." I rubbed him all up and scratched behind his ears. My reward was a long, wet tongue licking my arm.

"Where are you three going?"

"To the park," I said. "We'll have a picnic and tire Toby out."

"The Chesterfield Park?"

"No, the one by Cole's house."

She shook her head. "Do you need to drive an hour when there's a park around the corner?"

"I take Toby to the Evergreen dog park," Cole cut in. "They're used to the big guy there. He wants to play with everyone, but people sometimes freak out seeing a dog this big running at them."

The Great Dane barked like he was agreeing.

Mom made a face at him. She was many things but a pet person wasn't one of them. "I see your point. Alright. Just be home before curfew."

"Bye, Mom. Love you."

In the car, Cole leaned over and whispered in my ear, "Everything I said was true, but let's be honest, all I'm worried about is getting you home. We have a challenge to complete."

"We're doomed to fail that challenge, aren't we? We'll never have enough."

He groaned. "This is why you're the one for me."

I poked him playfully. "Let's go to the park, have a nice date, and then we'll go back to your place and go at it until curfew."

"If you insist, I have no choice but to say yes."

The drive to Evergreen must have been an hour, but it never felt long with Cole. Toby stuck his head through our seats every now and then to get the attention back on him. I was happy to oblige.

"Toby, sit. Sit, boy." The dog ducked out of the way, letting me see Cole. "Would you make fun of me if I said I could do this for the rest of my life? Me, you, a dog, and nothing to do but be with each other."

"Yes, I would make fun of you."

"Cole!" I swatted his arm.

Laughing, he tried to get away. "Kidding. I love this, Zee. I'd whisk you away every weekend if I could."

I said nothing. Just laced our fingers together and relaxed.

Cole turned onto a narrow path and we were greeted by a sign that read Evergreen Dog Park. The parking lot was nearly full. In the distance, dogs ran around free of their leashes. Some of them chasing each other and some chasing their tails.

Toby barked, signaling his readiness to join the fun.

"Zee, would you mind getting the basket out of the trunk while I get him on his leash?"

"Does he need one?"

He nodded. "There's a private spot toward the back of the park. It's right next to a stream. He'll try to take off the second we get in the park, so the leash will keep him with us."

"Okay. We can eat first and then run around with him. Did you bring his toys?"

"I brought one Frisbee and a bone. Any more and you'd get ideas that we were staying here longer."

I shook my head. Cole had me torn between my romantic side and the one that wanted to take his clothes off every time he walked into a room.

"What did you make for lunch?"

"My chef made sandwiches, pasta salad, homemade chips, and guacamole."

"Ooh. That I will rescue from the trunk."

I climbed out and went around to the trunk.

"Thank you."

A few feet away, a woman with a service dog crossed the path in front of an idling car. She waved at the driver and thanked them for letting her pass.

Cole popped the trunk. I lifted the top.

I'll be making fun of him too.

Nestled on the fabric was a soft, blue blanket and basket with a matching bow. I peeked inside the basket.

Champagne glasses, silverware, and those look like roses to me. He does have a romantic—

A harsh glare reflected out of the corner of my eye. I looked up just as the car accelerated. The shrill squeal of rubber on pavement reverberated in my soul, and I rooted to the spot, eyes growing wide.

"Zela!"

Hands grasped and yanked me away. The car rammed through the spot I had been in. We collapsed as the scream of metal on metal ripped through the parking lot.

No.

It was me screaming.

Cole's car smashed into the wheel stops and it startled Toby into a furious barking fit. The car reversed, whipped around, and peeled out of the parking lot. A chaos of noise, terror, and shock overwhelmed my senses.

"Zela?! Zela! Are you okay?!"

"Stop!"

"Zela?"

"Don't worry. I'll help you."

"You're okay, Zee." Cole's voice tried to reach me. "You're safe."

He held me tight as the panic attack ravaged my bruised body. My breaths came in rapid pants. I couldn't breathe—couldn't remember how.

"It's okay, baby. I've got you. No one is going to hurt you."

Cole crooned in my ear softly and soothingly as the last vestiges of my demons fled to the deepest corners of my mind. I buried my face in his neck, crying.

"Toby, stop," Cole ordered. "It's okay, buddy."

"Are you sure you're okay?" someone said. "That was awful."

"We're fine," said Cole. "But could you call the police?"

"Already did. We got the license plate number too."

"Thank you."

The next half an hour was a haze. Cole wrapped me in our picnic blanket and had me sit on the grass next to Toby. The loveable giant wasn't a guard dog, but he gave a good impression of one sitting erect by my side and huffing at anyone who got close.

Cole fielded most of the questions. He appeared cool and calm as he told and retold the story to the police. Only I noticed the slight tremor in his hands.

He's being strong for me. Protecting me.

I'm certain I never loved him more than I did right then.

"The driver was probably drunk," the officer told him. "We see it all the time. Kids come out here with a trunk full of booze and find secluded spots in the woods. He lost control, panicked, and hightailed it out of here."

"Can you find them?"

"We have the license plate. We'll track them down. Now get in. We're taking you to the hospital just to be sure you're alright. Your parents can meet you there."

"What about my dog?"

"My partner can run him up to your house."

"Okay. Thank you."

The officer went off to talk to his partner. Cole came over and gathered me in his arms. I didn't stop him carrying me to the police car. I couldn't walk, even if I wanted to.

"There goes our romantic picnic and all-day sex challenge," I croaked.

He paused buckling my seat belt. I thought that was what he was doing anyway. He blurred through my tears.

"Thank you. Y-you saved my life."

"I owed you one. You saved me and I saved you." He kissed me—a light, gentle kiss that mixed with the salty wetness on my lips. "I'll always save you, Zela."

"KNOCK KNOCK. CAN I come in?"

"Adam?"

I struggled out of the cocoon of blankets.

"No, relax. I'll come to you."

The sheets lifted and Adam slipped inside. "Hey, best friend. I heard you had quite a date yesterday."

"You could say that."

Adam opened his arms. "Come here."

I needed no more urging to fall into his warmth.

"Are you okay?"

"Yeah," I replied. "The doctors checked me over to be sure. A few scratches, but nothing serious."

I rested my head on his chest and pulled the covers to my chin. I'd been in my bed since Mom brought me home from the hospital. I was content to stay for the rest of the weekend.

"I'm so happy you're alright. Ms. Manning made it clear there wouldn't be any trips to Evergreen for a while, so I drove down first thing. Mom is here too."

"My mom said I couldn't go to Evergreen?" I sighed. "I can't say I'm surprised."

"So a drunk driver almost hit you in the middle of the day?"

I nodded. "Cole pulled me away just in time."

"Did you see their face?"

"It happened too fast. Someone else caught their license plate."

"Good. They better find that piece of shit. Almost hitting you and then racing off? They better pray I don't find them myself."

"Don't go chasing after drunk drivers. I need you right here."

Adam cuddled with me for most of the morning up to the announcement of a second visitor. Jordan came in, saw us, and joined the pile.

They distracted me with talk of our trip and Adam's progress getting his dad to agree.

"It's Mom against Ryder," he said. "Every time she turns my other dads' nos into yeses, Ryder comes in, reminds them it could be dangerous, gets their worry back up, and then they say no again."

I laughed. "So you're just sitting on the sidelines watching them ping-pong back and forth?"

"Pretty much."

"My mom keeps dropping hints that she's coming with us," Jordan put in. "I'm starting to think she's not kidding."

"Why would I be kidding?"

Aunt Bev materialized in the doorway. She gave me a tender look. "How are you doing, favorite niece?"

"Much better now."

"You have more visitors. They say they're your boyfriends."

Adam untangled himself from me. "That's our cue to give you privacy."

Cole, Landon, Michael, and Derek came in. They drove in one car and showered me in their love and attention all at once. Chocolates, flowers, kisses, and promises they'd find the person who almost hit me themselves.

I don't believe they felt better about what happened at the end of the day, but having all of them with me chased away the thick sludge of fear that pinned me to the spot, and replaced it with love and contentment.

The next day, Mom got me to school minutes before the automatic gates closed for the school week. Melody hugged me tight when I got to our dorm.

"Adam told me what happened," she said into my hair. "I hope the police find that idiot."

"Me too." I peered over her shoulder. "What's all of this?"

"I was going to surprise you."

Melody's bed was covered with little brown packages. She ripped one open and showed me the contents.

"I had these made for us, Tanner, and the lowerclassmen," she explained. "What do you think?"

I pulled out one of the button pins. The face boasted a simple design. The school colors covered the face in diagonal stripes. Smack in the middle was one bold, golden letter: R.

"It stands for refuse. We're all going to wear them and make it clear to the administration that we're not playing along anymore." Melody's voice rose with excitement. After years of trying to get people to care, students were finally taking action. "I've checked and rechecked the student handbook. Button pins aren't against the school rules unless they depict something obscene, offensive, or gang-related. Whittaker couldn't argue these fit the description no matter how he twists the definition. We can't get in trouble for wearing them."

"Doesn't mean we won't be punished anyway." I said that, but I took a pin and stuck it through my lapel. "Teachers are going to have a lot to say about it. Whittaker and Argyle will have a lot to say about it. And Everly Mackenzie will have the *most* to say about it."

She scoffed. "Leave Everly to me."

"These are great, Melody."

"Thanks. Want to help me give them out at breakfast?"

"Hand me a box."

We went down with our boxes and skipped past the food line. Melody veered toward the girls' tables while I headed for the boys.

I started with the senior Fs since they knew me. I explained what the pins stood for and pretty much exactly what For All outlined—refusing to challenge others in battles or accept challenges. Ignoring time slots, passes, and tickets and using every campus resource despite the letters on our patch.

One of the boys, Lucas Neil, shook his head. "Seriously? It's all good for you because you're Elite. You don't have anything to *refuse*. We're the ones who'll get in trouble."

"Yes, you will."

He blinked at me. He wasn't accepting that response.

"It's true," I went on. "I can go where I want. Do what I want. And I don't have to battle if I don't want to. I have everything *you should have* and I'm guessing you don't think that's fair."

The boys shared a look.

"Of course it's not fair," said Neil.

I held up the pin. "Then do something about it. I'll support you. I'll back you up. But there's only so much I can do. I truly believe we can change the system. We just have to do it together."

Neil studied me for a long time. He seemed to be looking for a trace of insincerity, and the other guys were waiting for him to find it.

"Fuck it." Neil plucked the button out of my hand. "Our dorms are shit. Our classrooms are shit. And Coach wouldn't let me try out for the track team because I'm not Elite. This system is bullshit and I didn't want to be a part of it anyway. I'm cool with not playing along."

He put his pin on and then reached for the box. "Give me those. No offense, you gave a good speech, but it's hard to hear over the E on your chest. The guys will listen if it comes from me."

"I get it." I handed them over without a fight. "Go to Melody if you need more."

I returned to our table to find Melody had already blown through her box. Everyone sported a button on their chest.

Michael stood when he saw me.

"I got our breakfast, Zee. You ready?"

I kissed him. "I'm ready."

"Can I lodge a complaint?"

Breaking away from Michael, I glanced down at Landon. "A complaint?"

"Yes. Why does Michael get to have you all to himself for breakfast? This is when you and I make out and cause everyone to get uncomfortable. It's our thing."

I bent and gave him a peck. "We can make people uncomfortable at dinner."

"Count on it."

Michael and I strolled out to the track bleachers to have our breakfast.

He spread his long, slender body the length of the seat and relaxed with his head on my lap.

Michael parted his lips for a grape. "I feel like I should be feeding you. You had a rough weekend."

"This is perfect. You're doing everything you need to do to take care of me, Michael."

He caught me as I reached for another grape. "Not everything."

My heart picked up speed. Michael's gaze held me spellbound as he kissed my wrist. My vein pulsed beneath his lips.

"Why are we waiting until Thursday?" I gently traced his mouth. "If we can sneak into your room, let's go now."

"Sondheim has a weekly staff meeting on Thursdays. It overlaps with both of our lunch periods. I was going to sneak you a boys' uniform. If anyone passed us in the hall, they wouldn't look twice if we kept our heads down. This is the only way I could see to get you to myself. I'm willing to risk it if you are."

"I'm willing"—I bent and kissed him—"to risk it right now."

"Thursday," he whispered.

I nodded. "Thursday."

MELODY AND I MET AT the base of the stairs. Not by chance. She texted me as I was finishing up my breakfast/ make out session with Michael and asked me to walk in with her as a united front.

"Why does this feel like we're walking onto a battle-field?"

She cracked a smile. "Because the Elite girls put down coups with extreme prejudice."

"You're the most popular girl on campus. You can get people to listen this time."

Her gaze drifted up the stairs. "We'll see."

We walked into Mrs. Munoz's class and the girls were up to their usual—chatting about the weekend, taking out their homework, or setting up their desks. Shannon was the first one to notice us.

She took one look at our buttons and rolled her eyes.

"Of course you're a part of this shit." Shannon waved her phone at us. "Zach told me all about it. Your little protest isn't going to work."

Everly poked her head out from behind her computer. "Protest? What protest?"

"Yes, ladies." Munoz's tone held a distinct note of warning. "What protest?"

"The lowerclassmen aren't participating in the system anymore," Melody said. "Neither are we."

"Is that so?"

"Yes." She tapped her pin. "For All was right about that at least. It's not fair the way they're treated."

"This is a discussion for after class and you can trust we'll have it then. Sit down."

I went to my desk without argument. Everly glared daggers at me as I passed by. I believe this fell under not staying in my lane.

THURSDAY COULDN'T COME fast enough. Life at Breakbattle was heating up. Lowerclassmen strode through the halls proudly displaying the pins on their lapels. Every day the number of students wearing them multiplied. From freshmen to seniors, Cs, Ds, and Fs announced their right to refuse.

Whittaker and Argyle had yet to address the situation although Mrs. Munoz made it clear she'd be speaking to them. So far, the upperclassmen limited themselves to glares and hissed comments, but I sensed the tension brewing.

Maybe it was my recent brush with death but their attitude stoked my ire. Why were these assholes so intent on maintaining the status quo? The lowerclassmen didn't want to take anything from them, they just wanted to enjoy the same privileges they do. The privileges they would get if they went to a regular school.

Their attitude was really pissing me off, and an afternoon with Michael was the perfect way to unwind and remember what was important.

My eyes flicked to the clock all morning, waiting for the bell to free me. At 11:59, I threw my books in my backpack and hopped out of my seat.

"Enjoy your lunch, ladies."

I intend to.

I hurried out of the Elite Wing and into the dorm building. Michael slipped me the boys' uniform that morning. He had no choice but to sneak it out of the laundry. Whittaker confiscated my Zeke uniforms last year. I guess he was worried I'd pull my boy act again.

He was right.

I put the uniform in my backpack and then left for lunch. The boys ate first and then girls. The guys would file out and head to class where Michael would be expected if he hadn't feigned sick this morning. The nurse told him to return to class when he felt better.

I scarfed down my chicken burrito and fruit cup in record time. Melody gave me a knowing look.

"Good luck," she whispered. "Hope you guys pull it off."

"Thanks. See you in class."

Casually, I stood and made for the exit. Welsh glanced at me for a second, then her eyes slid away and she went back to patrolling the lunchroom. Students could leave the dining room as they pleased. She had no reason to look at me twice.

Ducking into a bathroom, I changed quickly and then leaned against the door to wait. Michael would come for me when the coast was clear. We didn't have to stay in the lunchroom, but most people did. The hallways would empty out and we'd be together.

My heart rattled around in my ribcage, reminding me of a caged bird. Waiting for Michael to be ready was beautiful torture. It was excruciating not being able to show him how I felt physically, but the anticipation tingled beneath my skin.

"Zela?" Michael knocked twice. "Are you there?"

I came out and threw myself in his arms. "Let's hurry. I want us to have plenty of time for all the things you're going to do to me."

Peals of laughter filled the hall. Michael pulled me close and rubbed my nose with his. "Wow. It's insane how much I love you."

"I love you too."

People would have thought we were up to something if they saw us speed walking to the dorm. Thankfully, no one did.

We didn't slow down until we reached the Elite floor. I closed my hand on the knob and Michael moved in front of me.

"So, uh... I did some stuff." He ducked his head. "I wanted it to be special."

I pressed against his chest. "It will be." Reaching around him, I gently pushed it open.

Michael held my hand as we walked inside. I clapped my hand over my mouth, holding in a gasp.

"Did some stuff" hardly did justice to Michael's efforts. Pink rose petals covered the floor, leading a trail to his bed where he scattered them on the sheets. My gaze drifted up to the ceiling and the fairy lights overhead.

"I thought it'd remind you of our first date," said Michael. "The fireflies."

"It's perfect," I whispered.

"Not yet."

Michael grasped my waist. Walking backward, he guided me over to the bed. I held my breath, knowing what was coming next. Michael undressed with slow, sure movements.

Now that we were here, he didn't seem nervous. The same couldn't be said for me.

I rubbed my suddenly slick palms against my pants. It felt like the first time just like it did with Cole and it would with Derek.

He pushed down black silk boxers and kicked them away. I let out a shuddering breath.

I'd watch him run and think this brown Adonis couldn't possibly be sexier. My eyes raked his bodily greedily. *I was wrong.*

Michael reached for me. My borrowed blazer slipped off my shoulders and pooled around my ankles. My pants followed. Michael sat on the bed, drawing me with him. He brushed his fingers along my thigh and slipped beneath the hem of my shirt. The clock was ticking on our time together, but I didn't rush him. He pressed his lips to my stomach and dropped little kisses around my belly button as he removed my top.

"You're so incredibly beautiful, Zela." His breath ghosted over my heated flesh. "How did I get this lucky?"

"You—"

He drew my panties down in one smooth move. My tongue glued to the roof of my mouth and stayed there. I didn't want to speak and break the spell. Instead, I reached behind me and undid my bra.

"Beautiful," he breathed.

I bit my lip to hold in my smile. I certainly felt beautiful when he looked at me like that.

Michael guided me down onto his lap. He cupped the back of my head and kissed me. Not the sweet, gentle

Michael kisses I treasured, but a fierce, almost hungry kiss that revealed just how hard waiting had been for him too. His tongue swirled in my mouth and I moaned as I melted into him.

I gripped his shoulders and pushed him back. I climbed over him and crawled to the head of the bed, feeling his eyes on me as I went. I slipped under the sheets and then patted his side for him to join me. He did just that.

We roamed each other's bodies beneath the covers. Michael was everywhere. His lips on my chest. His legs tangled with mine. His fingers teased my nipples to hardened points.

Michael moved on his back and drew me on top of him. Our lips didn't break contact as he continued his exploration of my body. One hand tweaked my nipple, drawing breathy moans, and the other began a slow descent down my stomach.

It wasn't fair him putting me on top. My body trembled under his attention. I could barely stay upright.

I propped myself up on a hand that shook and reached between us. I grasped his length at the same time he slid inside of me. Breaking our kiss, I nuzzled his stubbly cheek and pressed my mouth to his ear. I wanted him hearing my cries—experiencing what he did to me.

His length was warm and smooth in my palm. I matched his pace, starting slow and tugging pleasured groans free from his lips. Our hands moved faster and faster and the room filled with our cries.

I collapsed against his chest. My arm gave out as my orgasm crested. Michael propped up my waist with his free hand, keeping me where he wanted me.

"Yes, Michael," I breathed. "Just like t-that. I love you so much."

I pumped him harder and heard his sharp intake of breath. His nails dug into my side and then next I knew I was on my back. I blinked blearily at him as he slipped out of me and moved his hands to the back of my thighs.

"Baby, please," I whispered. "Don't stop."

"I'll make it up to you." Michael gave me one sweet kiss. "The first time you come for me," he spoke against my lips, "I want to taste it."

I almost came right there. His head disappeared under the covers and he took my legs and draped them over his shoulders. His mouth found me in the perfect world we created for ourselves. The lights shimmered above me. Through my haze, they truly looked like flitting fireflies.

Michael stole between my lips. My orgasm came roaring back, building as his tongue darted in and out. I came so violently my back arched off the bed and I almost knocked him off. He held me fast, his mouth on me as I rode the crashing wave down.

"Fucking hell," I gasped. "I can't believe we waited this long to do that."

His chuckles reached me from under the sheets. Michael stretched out next to me and pulled me on top. "No more waiting. Never again."

He folded his hands behind his head and smiled. It suddenly hit me what he wanted me to do.

My cheeks warmed. "Wait. You want me to…"

He gripped my ass and guided me back. "If you want to."

I'd never been on top before. Derek and I were still working our way to sex while Cole and Landon liked me on my back, on my knees, a few times against the wall, and once upside down. But never had I been on top.

"This is a first for me," I admitted. "I love that I have one saved for you."

"There are many firsts in our future, Zela."

My heart fluttered with so much love for him. That was the sexiest thing he'd said to me all day. Our future.

Michael reached between us and positioned himself at my entrance. I took him inside and hissed. Michael was far from small.

He gripped my waist, murmuring sweet nothings to me as I adjusted. I began to move, rising all the way up and then rocking down. The brief flash of pain disappeared beneath pure, euphoric pleasure. The pressure in my lower belly built fast. I wouldn't last long and I knew my Michael was close.

I moved faster. The mattress squeaked to the tune of my bouncing and joined the music of our moans. Moving his hands to my breasts, I lowered myself just a little so I hit at just the right angle. My cries were near screams.

We were in perfect rhythm—moving as one.

"Yes, Zela. Fuck, I'm almost there."

"S-same time," I rasped.

Closer and closer I got to the edge, moving faster than before, and then Michael reared up, driving deeper inside of me, and sunbursts exploded in my mind. He held me upright as my orgasm wracked and ravaged me.

"Wow," I breathed. I collapsed on top of him, snuggling into him. "Why haven't I tried that position before? I'm a big fan. We're doing that again."

I felt his laugh against my cheek. "We can do anything you want as many times as you want." He kissed my damp temple.

My sigh was one of deep contentment. "Can I ask you something?"

"Oh. Is it finally my turn?"

"Your turn?"

"For the big question about the future. The guys told me you've had the talk with them."

"They did? Since when do you all talk?"

He chuckled. "You know, we're actually becoming friends for real. Cole and I apologized to Landon for the shitty way we acted when he came out. Derek apologized for being a shit."

"He wasn't so bad," I said with a giggle.

"Derek had a soft spot for you since freshmen year. You were lucky to miss Derek Grayson at his best."

"Sounds like it. But what about you? Where do you see us in the future?"

Michael cupped my ass and drew me closer. "Thankfully, I had plenty of time to prepare an answer, and the truth is I don't see my life much different than it is now. I want to live with Mom, see Dad in Europe every summer, run, study to become a doctor, and... be with you."

"What about Derek, Cole, and Landon?"

"I could see us living like Moon and his family. We can squeeze out a couple of kids and raise them together."

Happiness filled me to bursting. I could have lifted off the bed and floated away. "I can see it too." I kissed his chest once, twice, and then again. "I can also see us going for round two."

He hummed low in his chest "I can too but not today. We have twenty minutes left."

Disappointment battled with my happiness. "What about next time? Can we be together every Thursday?"

"I can't pretend to be sick every week, baby."

"No. Of course, you can't."

My dismay must have come through loud and clear because Michael hugged me tighter. "We still have the weekends. I've never been happier that Breakbattle allows us out."

"Mom isn't letting me go to Evergreen for the time being. Not after the almost hit and run."

"Hey." Michael grasped my chin and tilted me back to look in his eyes. "I promised we were done waiting. I'm yours to take advantage of now. Whenever you want me, I'll find a way to make it work."

"Really?" A grin stole over my face. "Because I want you right now."

"And watch me make it happen."

I shrieked as he flipped me over again.

WE DRESSED CLUMSILY. It was hard to do it properly when we couldn't stop kissing each other long enough to do up our buttons.

"I have to stay," Michael said in between kisses. "I don't want anyone to see me out when I'm supposed to be laid up in bed. Will you be alright getting back?"

I drew back, coming up for air. "I should be fine. There are a few more minutes until lunch lets out. I'll run back before anyone sees me."

"Okay. I love you."

"Love you too."

We kissed at the door and then I snuck out. I practically floated down the hall. All the trouble I would get in if I got caught was completely worth that stolen hour with Michael.

I reached for the door handle the moment it turned. There was no time to react as it flew open and I came face to face with Zachary Fields.

We stared at each other—panic on my face and surprise on his. It winked out in a breath and his shock was replaced with irritation.

"What are you doing here?" we said at the same time.

Zach's reply was quick. "None of your business. Get out of here before I tell Whittaker."

He shoved past me. I didn't bother to watch him go. I had already been caught by the worst possible person. I needed to get out of here before anyone else saw me.

My race to the girls' campus was even more frenzied than the one to Michael's room. I set foot on our side seconds before the lunch bell rang. I had fifteen minutes until class.

I'll have to take the quickest shower on record. I straight up smell like sex.

I burst onto my floor and came to a jerking halt. Standing in front of my dorm was Langman and a female officer.

"Detective?"

"Ah. There you are, Miss Manning."

I approached them slowly. "What's going on?"

"Can we speak inside?"

"About what?"

"About the results of the blood test."

"Okay." I unlocked my door and let them inside.

"Is there something wrong with the blood?" I asked as I toed off my shoes. "Do you need another sample?

"The sample you gave us was perfect." Langman looked me up and down. I realized how I was dressed and quickly shed my stolen blazer. His expression didn't change. Neither did the intensity of his stare.

Great. I smell like sex. I bet I look like it too.

"We were able to prove conclusively your blood is not a match to the blood on Cameron Dupre," Langman said.

"Wonderful. Then it's all over."

"Not quite."

"What do you mean?"

"We found something else in your blood."

The running clock and the little time I had to get ready for class nagged at me. "What? Just tell me what you came here to say."

"I came here to say I found DNA in your blood. The same DNA as Cameron Dupre."

My brows snapped together. "What are you talking about?"

"I'm talking about a familial match between you and our victim."

A roaring buzzed in my ear.

What is he saying?

"Zela, he was your half brother, and with that said, we have more questions for you."

The world stopped. I stopped. Stopped moving. Stopped breathing.

"He was your half brother."

"Your half brother.

"Your brother."

Langman's expression flickered. "Miss Manning, are you alright?"

He said something—shouted it—but I heard nothing as darkness claimed me.

Chapter Seven

Needless to say, I didn't make it to class that day.

I sat at the kitchen table, staring into the depths of my mug. By some miracle, I made it through Friday's classes and came home. Mom buzzed around the kitchen preparing miso salmon and homemade spring rolls. I stared at her whenever her back was turned.

Cameron Dupre was my brother which meant only one thing. My father was Dominick Dupre.

Derek said a lot of local businessmen taught guest lectures that year. I should ask if Dominick was on the list.

Why? a harsh voice cut in. *You already know the truth. At some point Dominick and Mom met. Blood tests don't lie.*

I dropped my head in my hands. My body felt tight and uncomfortable—like I had been zipped up in someone else's skin. I didn't know myself anymore. I didn't know anything anymore.

Cameron Dupre was my brother. The boy who bullied me, framed me, blackmailed me, attacked my boyfriends, and made my life a misery, was my brother. How could I reconcile that? It was a truth too big for me to deal with, and I hadn't begun to process the fact that the man I'd been warned about since the first week of orientation is my father.

Landon's words roared through my mind.

"It sounded like Jonathan Grayson was a total shit to her. What if this other guy was even worse?"

I would say he was worse. Why did Landon have to be right?

I glanced at Mom again. *This was the man she was trying to protect me from. I understand why. If it was me, I might have done the same in her place. But is it better that I know? Is it better that I found my true brother months after he was murdered? Is it better that my father is a person openly despised?*

Tears stung my eyes. I dropped my head so Mom wouldn't see. Part of me felt like I should grieve. Cameron was gone and I'd never know another side of him—if one existed. There could have been a day when we reconciled. Out of high school and reminded of what truly mattered, Cameron and I could have stayed up late reading and talking. Someone took all hope of that away from us.

"Zela? Zela?"

I jerked. Mom appeared in front of me.

"Yes, Mom?"

"I asked if you wanted three spring rolls or four."

"Four, please."

She made no move to get them. "What's wrong? Are you crying?"

"Yes," I said honestly. "It's been a rough week."

Her face softened. "Of course it has, my Zela. A drunk fool almost killed you." She walked around the island and enfolded me in her arms. I hugged her tight. "I knew I should have kept you home this week." Mom kissed my forehead. "Take some time, relax, connect to your energy, and if you're not ready by Sunday, you can miss the first day."

"Okay. Thanks, Mom."

She kissed me again and my rush of love for her tinged with guilt.

What do I have to feel guilty about? I didn't go looking for Dominick Dupre. The truth came to me.

The doorbell rang.

"I'll get it," Mom said. "You eat and then get some rest. You look very pale, my only one."

Mom left the kitchen and answered the door. I didn't move from my spot.

What do I do? I should tell her I know. We—

"Please, Ms. Manning."

I snapped my head up.

"I won't stay long," Derek said. "I just want to make sure she's okay."

"Alright. Twenty minutes. Zela needs to eat and get some rest."

Derek stepped into the entrance of the kitchen. I saw him only hours ago. He tried to kiss me goodbye on the steps of the school. I was so out of it I walked off. When I realized what happened I was halfway across the lawn and Mom was waving at me from the car.

He took a step but I shook my head. I gestured upstairs. Without a word, we headed to my room.

"Zela, what's up?" he asked. "Did something happen?"

I walked to the other side of the bed and sat, keeping my back to him.

"You've been acting weird all day. You didn't come to me this morning. You sat at the Elite table instead of with us. You didn't... kiss me goodbye."

I pressed my lips together. They trembled with all the things I wanted to say.

"Did I do something?" Derek's voice took on a tone I'd never heard from him before. "Tell me what and I'll fix it."

"You can't fix this." I blinked and teardrops splashed onto my clenched hands.

Heavy footfalls thudded behind me. Derek ran around the bed and knelt at my feet. "I'm sorry, Zela. Whatever I did, I'm sorry. Just tell me what to do."

I cupped his face and pulled him in for the kiss we'd both been missing.

"Stop apologizing, dummy," I whispered. "You didn't do anything wrong."

"Then what is it?"

"I got some news on Thursday."

Derek brushed away a tear. "The kind of news you cry over. Tell me what happened."

I opened my mouth to tell him I needed time to process. My head was wrecked. I didn't know how to feel about the situation, let alone how to talk about it.

I opened my mouth... and it all came out.

I told Derek everything about the blood tests, the results, and the man who fathered me. He paled with every word.

"Dominick Dupre? Is he sure?"

"Langman said they ran the test twice. They're sure. We're a familial match."

"Holy shit." Derek fell back on the floor. He stared unseeingly somewhere to his right. I heard his thoughts churning away.

I hesitated. *I need to know. One day I'll ask the question. Let it be now.*

"Derek," I began. "All the stuff I've heard about Dominick Dupre. Tell me why. Why do people say he's a bastard?"

"Zee, we don't have to—"

"I need to know."

His eyes traced my face. He must have seen something because he nodded. "Okay. First, you should know that nothing's been proven. It's whispers about other people's whispers that built his reputation."

"What do the whispers say?"

Derek took my hands and pulled me down to him. "They say that he advises dangerous people. Mafia, cartels, CEOs who get crafty with the pension fund. He's smart enough not to handle their money, but that doesn't stop him telling *them* how to handle it."

I sucked in a breath. "How could he get away with that?"

"Like I said, whispers. Nothing has ever been proven. No money in his business that shouldn't be there. No surveillance shots of under the table payouts. But Dominick takes a lot of lunches with people you wouldn't let know your address."

"Is that it?"

"No. There's one more thing that I know about..."

"What is it? Please, I need to know."

Derek grabbed my waist and pulled me closer. He wrapped me securely in his embrace as though he thought what he'd say would break me if he didn't hold me together.

"There was a nanny."

"A nanny?"

"Years ago, when we were kids obviously. Cameron's nanny disappeared. I remember my parents talking about it one night when I wandered into their bedroom. They thought I was sleeping."

"What happened?"

"She was young and lived here on a visa. One morning they found her room empty and her gone. Dominick said she must have been homesick and wanted to leave without a fuss. The problem was Cameron's birthday was a few days away and she got them both tickets to go to Evergreen Playland."

I filled in the blank. "Why would she do that if she never planned to take him?"

"Exactly. There were other things too. The police got on to her parents and they confirmed she didn't go home. Plus, she told her friends more than once that Dominick wasn't a nice man, and she only stayed because she loved Cameron."

I nodded slowly. "So, you're saying my biological father is a suspected murderer who is tangled up with the mob?"

"What I'm saying is a lot of stuff that has never been proven."

I tried to swallow around the lump forming in my throat.

"What about Cameron?" I asked. "You've known him longer than me. What was my brother really like?"

"You know what he was like," Derek said softly. "You've known him for years."

"There had to be more to him."

"I'm sure there was but I never saw that side. Cameron and I weren't friends. I didn't have friends before you."

"You wouldn't have had me." I didn't want to say it. The certain truth that tormented me since I discovered Langman at my door. "You were the wrong brother. If I had known the truth, it would have been Cameron. I would have come for him. I would have devoted all my time to winning him over. The day in the woods that set us on this path. I only freaked out because I thought he killed my brother."

"You would have freaked and refused to go along either way. That's who you are."

"With how desperate I was to earn your trust?" I cried. "Who knows what I would have done for Cameron's?"

"Not that."

"He died never knowing the truth. Everything would have been different if he knew I was his sister."

"You can't know that."

Derek's touch was gentle as he caressed my thighs with small, calming circles. "You can't torture yourself with what might have been."

I choked back a sob. Derek's love and warmth couldn't reach me in the place I was in.

"What might have been is all I have. He's dead, Derek. My chance to have a relationship with my brother disappeared one horrible night and I didn't know to care until now." Hot, furious tears ran down my face. "Do you know how awful that makes me feel? The only brother I'll most likely have and I skipped the memorial they held at school because I didn't want people to stare at me."

Derek took hold of me and gave me a little shake. "You didn't know, Zee. I love you, and I love that your possessive streak brought us together, but don't use it as a reason to torture yourself with guilt. If you had known, nothing would have stopped you from being there. Hold on to that."

I tossed my head. "No."

"Zee—"

"No," I cried. "It's not enough, Derek. I have to find him."

"Find who?"

"The killer. I have to find the person who killed Cameron." As I said it, I never felt more certain of a single thing.

He gaped at me. "Find the killer? Zee, that's what the cops are doing."

"And they're getting nowhere." I wiped my face using the hem of my sleeve. "Langman told me himself. Months later and their only suspect was me. Private investigators were brought in and they clearly don't have a clue because they haven't arrested anyone yet."

"And you think you're going to find something the CPD and a team of investigators can't?"

"I'm going to try."

"You can't—"

"Zela?" Mom sounded from the other side of the door. "It's time for Derek to leave."

"Okay," I called. "He's going now."

He grasped my forearms when I tried to get up. "No, Zee. I'm not leaving until you agree you won't go after the killer. Promise me."

"I won't. You know me too well by now, Grayson. I could give you a promise, but we both know I won't keep it."

"Zela," Mom said again.

"You have to go."

Derek didn't move.

"I'm not letting you go after a killer," he said through gritted teeth.

"You're not stopping me either. He was my brother. I have to do this."

"What is with—!" Derek stifled his shout. He took a deep breath and tried again. "I want his murderer to be brought to justice as much as anyone, by the *police*. He doesn't deserve your eternal love and loyalty because you share the same DNA."

"Yes, he does," I replied, feeling it with every fiber of my being. "That's what family is."

Derek shoved away from me. "Ugh!"

I went after him, pulled his hands away from his face, and tugged him toward the door. "If we push Mom, she won't let you visit at all. I love you," I said under my breath. "I know you want me to be safe, but I need you to understand that I'm not changing my mind."

He stopped dead, pulling me up short. "Then you're not doing it without me. I'll help you."

I turned on him. Determination etched into every line of his face. "You don't have to be a part of this," I said.

"Like I would let you do this alone. Besides, you need me anyway. If you're going to find out what was going on with Cameron in his last year, we have to talk to his friends and you have charges pending against all of them. They can't, and won't, talk to you. I can get them to talk to me."

"Zela," called Mom. "Open the door."

I peered over my shoulder. "But you—"

"I love you."

Derek pulled me in for a searing kiss that made me stumble back onto the bed. Then he blew out of the door shooting a goodbye over his shoulder.

Mom came inside. "Are you sure everything is okay?"

You should tell her. Now is your chance to before it goes any farther.

"Everything is fine. Let's eat, Mom. I'm starving."

"ZELA, THAT CAN'T BE true."

Landon looked like he had been sucker punched. Still his reaction to the news was a lot better than mine.

"It is true."

"Holy shit," he breathed.

The two of us sat on the grassy pitch in the middle of the track. It was early Monday morning. Michael looped around us, giving us space to talk. I already told Michael what I learned about my parentage. I asked Landon to join us so we could have that talk. Later tonight, I would talk to Cole.

I saw Derek that morning in the clearing. He wouldn't stand for me to miss another morning meetup. This time we talked and he tried again to change my mind. When it didn't work, he recommitted himself to helping me.

"Dominick Dupre is your father," Landon repeated.

"Yes."

"Cameron is your brother."

"Yes."

"And you want to find his killer."

I nodded.

"Holy shit," he said again. Landon scrubbed his face, suddenly looking like he felt every minute of his six a.m. wake up. "This is insane, Zee."

"I know, but I had to tell you. All of you. I don't want there to be secrets between us." I leaned in and pecked his nose. "That said, you guys won't change my mind about this. He was my brother. If the police can't find his killer, I will."

Landon snapped up. "Not without my help and *not* alone." He peered at me hard. "I'm serious, Zela. If I found out you arranged some back-alley chat with a suspected killer and went there by yourself, I'd lose it. Whoever this guy is, he beat Cameron to death and he was twice your size. Do not fight me on this."

Despite everything I was going through, a smile tugged at my lips. "I wasn't going to. I need to do this, but I don't need to do it alone. We can keep each other safe."

He opened his arms and I fell into them. I breathed in his sweet, citrusy scent. "This went much better than my talk with Derek or Michael."

"Just wait until you get to Cole."

My smile evaporated. "Oh, yeah. That won't go well."

WON'T GO WELL WAS THE understatement of the century.

"Fuck no."

"Cole—"

"Come on, Zela!"

Cole stalked up and down the rim of the pool. Coach was back in his office. He had to be here, but he trusted us not to dump dye in the pool. It left Cole free to yell at me.

He was fresh from a swim, dripping wet and wearing the school swim trunks that I always thought were skimpier than they needed to be. Of course on Cole, I liked them.

Desire stirred in my lower belly, responding to his anger like an aphrodisiac. On a normal day, this fight would end in sex. I didn't expect it today.

"What do you think you're going to do that the police haven't done already?"

"Something was going on with Cameron last year," I replied. "He went through the trouble of kidnapping and dragging me to the woods to prevent me from ruining the Network's plans, and then he pretends I don't exist. He wasn't himself. You must have noticed."

Throwing up his hands, Cole said, "Yeah, he was off, but what does that prove?"

"I don't know, Cole. I don't know anything yet. I just know where I'm going to start. The fundraiser."

He stopped pacing. His expression smoothed out. "The fundraiser."

I nodded. "It was months before his death and walking into the room covered in Cameron's blood implicated me more than it did anyone else, but that overheard argument is proof someone was pissed at Cameron. They attacked him."

"But you didn't see who it was."

"No, but we were at a high-society gala at the Evergreen Country Club. I doubt some random wandered in off the street. The only conclusion is—"

"The person who attacked him was at the party." Cole's anger fled. He gave up pacing and sat next to me. "The place was stuffed with the board, the Network, and their families."

"A long list but a lot smaller than everyone in Breakbattle."

"If the fight is connected to his death," he reminded. "Cameron wasn't the nicest guy. The killer might be someone else who hated him."

"It's all I have to go on right now." I placed my hand on his knee. "Do you understand why I have to do this?"

"No."

"Will you not fight with me about it at least?"

"No."

I cracked a smile. "I won't ask you to help me, but—"

He scoffed. "Of course, I'm helping you. I already know where to start. Christina's coach wants me to tour the campus and check out the swim team. Santiago got into Somerset. I can track him down and talk to him while I'm there."

I opened my mouth to say I'd go with him.

No, I can't. Even if Mom let me out of the house, Santiago wouldn't talk to me to tell me I was on fire.

"Good idea. Thank you for doing this."

"I think this is crazy and I won't give up on convincing you to stop," Cole said. "He may have been your brother, but he's not worth you getting hurt over."

I let the comment pass through without consideration. I loved my guys, but they didn't need to understand this. I was doing what I had to do.

I tapped my lips. "Kiss, please."

Cole pulled that face that scared others off but that I found cute. "You don't deserve one."

"I always deserve a kiss."

"No."

"Right now." I hooked my finger through his trunks, drew it back, and let it snap.

Growling, he grabbed my head. "Fuck you," he said before giving me a hot, spine-melting kiss. We went at it like we were fighting—our tongues clashing together and triggering heated moans.

He tore away, breathing hard. "It's not too cold tonight. Let's go to the clearing."

"Let's go."

In the end, my conversation with Cole went a lot better than expected.

THE NEXT MORNING, MELODY and I woke to a new message on our tablets.

"Zela, did you read this?"

I looked at her reflection in the vanity. "Read what?"

"Morning assembly directly after breakfast. The whole school is supposed to report to the auditorium."

"We don't have to ask what this is about."

I read in her eyes that she was thinking the same thing.

"We have a right to protest," she said.

"And Whittaker has a right to detention."

"Detention won't hurt us. This system does."

I sighed. "I wonder why he can't see that. This school is ranked the best in the country, and they turn out a high number of graduates who go on to become a success. The Elite Class and their resources are great, they really are, but we shouldn't go through battles and tournaments to get through them."

"That's just it though, isn't it," Melody said. "In Whittaker's head, we all have the same chance to prove ourselves and those famous alumni reinforce that he's doing everything right."

"I'd like to sit down and talk to him like I did with the board. Explain to him what it's really like."

"Do you think he wants to hear from you after the whole Zeke thing?"

I cringed. "Not even a little bit."

Melody climbed out of bed and hugged me from behind. "We're at the point where we have to make him listen and we will. He can make us go to all the assemblies he wants. I won't quit."

"Me either."

We finished getting ready and went down to breakfast. There was a different energy in the room. Too quiet. Too tense. My friends and I didn't talk much. I think we were all feeling the weight of the pins on our chests.

Most of us were up and heading toward the auditorium before the bell rang. Seeing all the teachers and staff lined up on stage, I sharply recalled my first day at Breakbattle Academy.

Cameron was the first person I met. He was the first person I spoke to. I thought he was angel-crafted perfection, then he opened his mouth. My first rival. My brother.

"Fill in the front rows and then move back," Argyle instructed. "Quickly, please."

The boys and I parted at the second row. They went one way and Melody and I went the other. We grabbed two seats on the aisle.

"Good morning, everyone," Argyle began. "I have a few updates and then your principal will address you. First, I want you to know the police have concluded their interviews and the secondary search of the B dorms and classrooms. At this time, they are not certain of who For All is, but they will not give up and neither will we.

"Despite the claim that he will stop now, For All committed crimes against this school and he will be held accountable for them. He is not a hero. He is not a martyr. For All is a vandal. At this point, I'd like to urge anyone who has information about For All to come forward. You will not be punished. Our only desire is for the attacks to end and you all to feel safe in your school"

I looked down the row of Elite girls. They were all nodding their heads. If one of them knew who For All was, they'd give him up so fast For All wouldn't have time to blink.

"An officer has been officially assigned to the school and they will work with the security team to ensure there are no more incidents," she said. "This brings me to my next announcement. All of the gyms will be open by Friday. We replaced the pool water last week, and this week the new mats will be brought in and the scoreboard replaced."

Half the room erupted into cheers. The half that wasn't wearing pins.

"Any questions before I give the floor to Principal Whittaker?"

Everly raised her hand.

"Yes, Miss Mackenzie?"

"What about the knife? You said the police's search didn't find anything."

"Forgive me, I should have said the knife was found where For All said it would be in confiscated property. And while we're relieved he doesn't have a weapon, confiscated property is locked in a drawer in the administration office. We're highly disturbed that he broke in not once, but twice for a knife he shouldn't have known about." Her hard gaze passed over us, lingering on those with pins. "This is why I'll say again, he is not someone to look up to."

Whittaker got to his feet. "Thank you, Mrs. Argyle. On that note, I should speak."

She stepped aside for him to claim the podium. Whittaker walked up and adjusted the mic. He took his time taking out a set of note cards, placing them in front of him, and then smoothing his jacket. You could hear a rat breathing in the walls it was so quiet.

"Students," he began, "I'm disappointed. Why am I disappointed? I'll tell you."

Melody and I shared a look. I could tell neither one of us knew what to make of his calm, even tone.

"I'm disappointed because in the midst of attacks, police, and the school board's decision, select students have decided now is the time to pile on more. For All's video was not a call to action. It was an incitement to legitimize his actions and make you all a party to them. And to my disappointment, students fell prey to his propaganda."

Whittaker stepped out from behind the podium.

"I am not a harsh man. I am not unfair."

I could have imagined it, but I thought he glanced at me when he said that.

"I want you all to have the best education and I ensure I hire the best teachers to provide it. Do you disagree? Tell me, students, from the Elite Class to the F Class, do you believe your teachers are giving you a subpar education?"

No.

The answer came unbidden. To admit it now would be foolish. Despite this, I couldn't say Dawson and Dr. O'Quinn were bad teachers. F teachers or not, I learned a lot from them.

"Let me ask you this," Whittaker went on. He began striding up and down the length of the stage. "For All spoke of your rights, but what rights is he referring to? Your right to an education? You are receiving an education and the battle system doesn't hinder it. On the contrary, it is written in our rules and charter that you all must receive what is required to complete assignments and pass your exams. No one here has given you a book report and then told you to battle for the book. We don't ask that you swim a fifty meter and then battle to get into the pool. The education you're entitled to is given freely with no restriction."

He paused at the end of the stage. "But then... For All isn't speaking of that right, is he? He's speaking of the right to tablets, dances, birthday parties, televisions, movie nights, and field trips to Orlando, Florida. But here is the issue, none of those things are rights. They are exactly what we call them: privileges.

"It is a privilege, not a right, to go on non-academic field trips. It is a privilege, *not a right*, to have a dorm with a television and computer. You can devote your entire life to constitutional law and you will never find the grounds to state your public high school owes you a party on your birthday."

He resumed striding. Our heads moved side to side, following him as one.

"But here at Breakbattle, we do grant you these privileges and they are available to *all* students. We do not discriminate against you by class, wealth, or any other metric. If you want that party, battle for it. If you want to change classes, the tournaments are open to all. What you earn and how far you go has always been squarely on your shoulders.

"For All would have you believe otherwise, but make no mistake, this is about him and not you. His deep-seated hatred of the battle system is something we've seen a few times. Hours of training or studying that don't move you forward can wear on you."

He gestured at us. "You're giving your best, so how could the problem be you? No, it's the system. It's rigged. It's unfair. It can't recognize your talent. It must be changed. This is the common progression of thoughts from those embittered by the system. We understand this frustration and we want to help you, For All."

Whittaker's tone shifted as he spoke to the masked activist. "I know you're in here, young man. Trust me when I say I don't want the situation to escalate farther than it has.

Come to my office, turn yourself in, and we can discuss the best way to move forward."

He fell silent. Below him, we looked around as if expecting someone to jump up and say, "It's me."

No one did.

Whittaker released a deep sigh. "Think about it and make the right choice."

"In the meantime, I must make one more thing clear." Whittaker's tone shifted. "Your right to protest is not in question, but the way you have chosen to do so will not be tolerated. For All was mistaken in the notion that we won't carry out the stated penalties if you decide to refuse to participate in the battle system."

Whispers broke out around the room. The spell had been broken.

"You could not walk into the classroom, announce you won't do your assignments, and then expect there to be no consequences," Whittaker said. "Battles are a part of your curriculum and if you refuse to accept them, your grade will reflect it. I suggest you all remove those pins and focus on earning what you want the right way."

Whispers reached a crescendo and erupted into full blown shouting.

"That's not fair!"

"We've never had a fucking choice in this place!"

"Get rid of the ten-point penalty!"

"Silence!" Whittaker's bark cut through the protests. "You've been informed. What happens next is entirely up to you? This assembly is dis—"

"Excuse me. If I could say something."

Miss Val went to Whittaker's side and put a hand on his shoulder. We couldn't overhear their conversation but the shaking of his head said no loud and clear. Miss Val didn't move. After a minute of back and forth, Miss Val walked up to the podium.

"Before you all leave, I think it's important to circle back to one thing the principal said. If anyone is feeling frustrated, trapped, or helpless for any reason, I want you to know you can come to me at any time. You don't have to wait for our scheduled appointments. Talk to me," she implored, "and I'll do everything I can to help."

"What does that mean?"

I snapped around. Tanner was on his feet.

"Everything you can to help," he shouted. "What if the reason we're feeling frustrated, trapped, and helpless is because of the battle system? How will you help us then, Miss Val?"

"Sit down, Mr. Grady," Whittaker ordered. "How dare—"

Miss Val put up her hand, halting the principal in his tracks.

"If the battle system is effecting you to the point of damaging your health or wellbeing," she said clearly, "then owing to my responsibility as your therapist, I will grant you the right to refuse. You will no longer have to participate in the system."

"Miss Moon!"

Whittaker's cry kicked off chaos like I had never seen. The teachers swarmed her. The students screamed across rows. And through it all, Melody and I gaped at each other, reflecting in our eyes that we were laughably wrong about how this assembly would go.

THE WEEKS THAT FOLLOWED were the strangest I'd ever experienced at Breakbattle and I dressed as a boy for three years.

Whittaker ordered us out of the room after Miss Val's announcement. Luckily for me, my best friend was Adam Moon. He kept me informed of the whole story. The part where Whittaker went off on her and she gave as good as she got. The day after that when all four of his dads stormed the office and they had an hour-long meeting. Not even Adam knew what they talked about.

He told me about Whittaker trying to argue Miss Val didn't have the authority to excuse students from the battle system and her shooting back she had the authority to do what she needed to protect her students, and if he didn't like it, he could fire her.

"I bet he wanted to," Adam said. The two of us stretched out on the bleachers watching Landon practice. "But Mom is the best therapist the school has ever had. Parents call specifically to praise her and the work she's done to help their kids."

"She's helped me," I agreed.

"He won't get rid of her. So now he's got to decide what to do because Mom is serious."

Miss Val was serious and hence the battle between the upper and lowerclassmen reached a fever pitch. The assembly had the opposite effect Whittaker wanted. The number of students wearing pins the next day basically covered all the lowerclassmen in every grade.

Unfortunately, the Bs, As, and Elites couldn't leave it alone. They said to take them off and the lowerclassmen refused. Then they took it a step further and challenged them to battles. All of them were bullshit since the lowerclassmen didn't have privileges for them to take. They refused and went to Miss Val. She backed them up and Whittaker held out on the ten-point penalty for one week. Dozens of parents called him shouting about targeting and bullying. The punishment for refusing a challenge was quickly reduced to a week of detention.

This didn't stop the upperclassmen or sit better with the Cs, Ds, and Fs. Battle lines had been drawn in the sand and the only place where the upper and lower classes mixed were at my table in the middle of the cafeteria.

I hated seeing the school like this. Even though I once worked behind the scenes to whip them up into this kind of frenzy, I'd hoped by this time we would have learned something.

"I honestly don't know what's going to happen," I said aloud. "Breakbattle can't go on like this. It's been weeks and every day more people join For All's fight, and the upperclassmen get more vindictive about it."

"They like their privilege system and they don't want to lose it," Adam said. "The school funnels most of the budget toward them. They can't afford to give us all televisions, smartboards, and special field trips. If Breakbattle becomes a regular high school, equal education means we all live like Cs."

"Not all of us." I bumped his shoulder. "We're getting out of this asylum and going to Somerset. But this is all about the school we'll leave behind. No one should go through the stuff I went through, and they definitely shouldn't be treated like Rebecca Taylor once was."

He bumped me back. "It's a good fight and your friends are all happy to fight it for you. I know you have other things to worry about."

His statement killed any lingering good mood. Adam was correct. I cared about the lowerclassmen and their fight to change the school, but I had my own fight. Cameron's killer would be found and brought to justice if it was the last thing I did.

Adam rested his hand over mine. "How is it going so far?"

"I've hit a wall. The boys are great. None have gone back on their promise to help me. Derek unearthed the guest list to the fundraiser. Cole cornered Santiago at Somerset. Michael is helping me narrow down who couldn't have been on campus the night Cameron was murdered. And Landon was incredible. He convinced Henrietta and Declan to gift Cameron's mom a free beauty consultation to ask her questions about what was going on around the time of his death."

"Wow. What did you guys find out?"

I rattled it off. "Every Network recruit from school was there along with their parents. Plus, the Network members that live in the area. There were also the school board and their families. From there, Cole asked Santiago if Cameron had a problem with any of them."

"What did he say?"

"No."

"No?" he repeated. "None of them?"

"Santi told him their senior year wasn't very different from the rest. He admitted there was tension between Cameron and Derek because he wanted his position back, but since Derek was in the cabin with me, he's off the suspect list."

"And you're at square one."

"Pretty much. Michael and I shortened the list by asking who couldn't have been on campus, but there are still about twenty people left. One thing we know for sure is that something was going on. Cameron's mom said as much to Henrietta. When he was home on the weekends, he'd stay out late and be secretive about where he was."

"Did Santiago at least know what that was about?"

"Cole went back and asked him and he assumed at the time that Cameron was out hooking up. But he didn't ask about it and Cameron didn't say."

"Real close friends those two," Adam muttered.

I squeezed his hand. "They can't all be like us."

Adam gave me a smile. "So what are you going to do now?"

"The same thing I've been doing. Continue digging into his life until I find someone who can tell me the truth. This might not go well, but I'm going to talk to Beth."

"Beth? Should I know who that is?"

I shook my head. "She's a freshman and a friend of Cameron's. Langman made it clear that I was eliminated as a suspect so she shouldn't hate me anymore."

"And if she does?"

"It'll be a short conversation."

He chuckled. "Good luck, Zee. I really hope you find something that the police can use. It's terrifying to think we could be going to school with a killer."

"It is terrifying. Especially because no matter how I look at it, I don't see how a grown man or woman could sashay onto campus, stroll into the dorm, kill a student, and then walk out without anyone noting they were there."

"A parent could," he replied. "All they'd have to do is say they're there to see their kid."

"Whose parent would want to kill Cameron? Why? What could push them to take that risk?"

"The alternative is that it's a student."

"A Network student if this is connected to what happened the night of the fundraiser. We were the only kids there."

"Could this be about the Network?"

"I— I just don't know." I pressed my fingers to my temples. I had a perpetual headache these days. "I'd done everything possible to stay out Cameron's life. If only I'd gone around the corner and looked for the person who attacked him at the fundraiser."

"Don't torture yourself with if onlys. Worry about what you can do now. If this Beth is a friend, maybe she was a closer one than Santiago. She might know what he was dealing with back then."

"I hope so. I'm going to talk to her tonight after dinner."

"Good." He kissed my cheek. "Let me know if you need my help."

"I will—"

"Stop kissing my girlfriend, Moon."

Landon had his opponent pinned face first in the mat. It didn't stop him clocking us.

Adam got up, hands raised. "I'm backing away from the Zela. My hands are where you can see them."

I laughed. "Will you two quit it? Adam sees me as a sister."

Landon released the boy and backed away, preparing to circle him. "I don't see him kissing Esme this much."

"You don't see me with Esme at all," Adam replied.

"The point stands."

Rolling his eyes, Adam said bye and loped off the bleachers.

Landon soon finished practice. He came out of the locker room damp and smelling sweet. I wished not for the first time we could find somewhere to be alone.

"Why don't we go out this weekend?" Landon asked. "I looked it up and there's a drive-in movie right outside of Chesterfield. Do you think your mom would go for it?"

"I think so. She's even starting to thaw on not letting me go to Evergreen. It just freaked her out that I was almost killed and she had to speed from an hour away scared out of her mind. I understand that she wants to keep me close."

"Seems like you understand your mother a lot more in general."

I nodded. "We're in a good place now. She doesn't know why, but I've finally forgiven her for all of it. Jeremy Holt, Jonathan Grayson, and Dominick Dupre. The many fathers of Zela Rae Manning. Wouldn't that make a good movie title?"

"Are you kidding? Girl dresses up as a guy and infiltrates a boys' campus all to find her family. Through the years, she uncovers secrets that turn lives upside down. That movie would make millions."

I laughed. Why in the hell was I laughing? I had no idea. My life was just so ridiculous laughing about it was the only reasonable thing to do.

"They'd ask Asher Monroe to play you," I said. "Ooh! Or Jake T. Austin."

"Damn. You think I look like those guys?"

"Oh yeah."

"Well, you for sure would be played by Indiana Evans."

"I could live with that."

We looked at each other and cracked up.

I love this. The last few weeks have been so intense. Nice to just goof off with my boyfriend.

"So are you going to talk to Beth now?"

I lost my smile. It was nice while it lasted.

"Yes, I am. I'll drop by her room after dinner and see if she'll talk to me."

We stopped in front of the side entrance. Landon spun me around and pressed me to his chest. "I don't like that I can't go with you. Maybe you should bring Melody."

"I haven't told Melody that Cameron's my brother or that I'm looking into his death. Besides, I'm just asking her questions about his life. She's not the killer. She wasn't here when he died and she didn't go to the fundraiser."

"No, but she's gotten in your face before."

I raised a brow. "She's like twelve. If she tries it again, I can handle myself." Rising on tiptoe, I kissed him. "Stop stressing, baby. I'll call you guys after if I find anything out."

"Okay."

I went to my room, showered, and started on my homework. Melody came in to drop off her stuff and then left for dinner. I stayed in to work on my project. The concept of slowing down didn't exist in the Elite Wing. Munoz assigned us a twelve-page report on an influential woman and poster to go with it. I was almost done on the paper and Mom loaded me up with markers, glitter, and cardboard to finish off the poster.

My body cut up paper and spread glitter on auto-pilot while my mind returned to Cameron. I wasn't sure if Beth could help me, but I had nothing—no, less than nothing. I needed someone to point me in the right direction.

Was this about the Network? Cameron was attacked at the Network's crafty fundraiser. But then it comes back to why? He wasn't fighting the expansion. He didn't have a position to steal. Why would anyone hurt him over that?

If it's not his secret club, then it was personal. And I'll need someone like Beth to shed light on his life outside of Breakbattle.

I glanced at the clock. Five minutes until they closed the dining room. Beth would be here any second.

I left my work on the bed and stuck my head outside. Girls filed in one after the other, talking about their homework, weekends, and some of them had For All on their lips. He hadn't struck since his video. Everyone wondered if he took a step back because his work was done, or if he was gearing up for the next hit.

Beth walked in alone. Her head was stuck in a book and she strode to her room without looking up. I seized my chance and stepped out behind her. Silently, I followed her to the door.

"Beth."

She jumped. The book sailed out of her hand and hit the door.

"What the hell? What do you want?"

"I need to talk to you." I gestured behind her. "Can we do this inside?"

Her eyes narrowed. "Do what? What would you need to talk to me about?"

"Like I said," I replied, "let's do this inside."

"You're... not still mad about before, are you? My mom talked to Cameron's mom. I know the evidence cleared you."

"This isn't about that, but it is about Cameron. You said you were friends with him?"

She nodded.

"It's not right that the killer is still out there. It's even worse when you think how much time the police wasted on me when they could have been looking for the actual murderer. Cameron deserves justice and I want to help him get it."

"You do?"

"Yes." I smiled. "So can I come in?"

"Oh, yeah. Come in."

Beth twisted her key in the lock and motioned for me to go in first. My eyes swept over the room. I liked what she'd done with the place. I didn't put any effort into decorating my dorms. What was the point when I already had the perfect room a few miles away at home?

Beth clearly did not feel the same. She had everything from flower wall decals, a plush purple rug, star string lights, and her name spelled out in big bold letters above her bed. Beth even added her own furniture.

"You can sit there." She pointed at the matching purple beanbag at the foot of her bed. "So what did you want to talk about?"

I sat and half disappeared into the smushy purple seat. I ignored it and focused on why I was here.

"I don't know as much about Cameron as I wish I did," I began. "What I do know is he was having problems with someone last year. I stumbled on two separate fights. Do you know who it was?"

She shook her head. "I know what you're talking about though. I remember Cameron was off back then. He'd come over and be on the phone the whole time, glaring at the thing like he wished he could chuck it in the pool. Other times, he'd ignore his texts. I asked what was up a few times, but he said it was nothing."

I eyed her. She seemed like a sweet kid when she wasn't accusing people of murder. The question was how did she become friends with Cameron? She was five years younger than him and again, she was sweet.

I better find a good way to phrase this.

"How did you two become friends?"

Good enough.

"Cameron is—" She stopped. "I mean, Cameron was my next-door neighbor. My mom started doing the stay-at-home-mom thing around the time his nanny left. She offered to watch him for free. Mrs. Dupre couldn't turn that down."

"Oh. That makes sense."

Beth gave me a knowing look. "It's cool. Everyone used to ask us that. Why was this older, hot, rich boy that could convince any girl off the street to give him company wasting his time with me? Cameron told them all to fuck off."

She shrugged. "What can I say? I've known him since I was three. Mom taught us to swim together and we'd pass out head to head on the couch during naptime. Even after he got too old for babysitting, he had my back. I think he liked it."

"Liked what?"

"Having a little sister."

He had a little sister. Me.

"What was he like?" The question was out of my mouth before I could stop it. "We had our issues, but there had to be a different side to Cameron."

"Hold on."

Beth went over to her nightstand and rummaged around in the drawer. She pulled out something I couldn't see from my spot on the floor.

"He liked cars," Beth said. "His dad collects old rare ones and Cameron could tell you everything about them right down to how many stitches were used to put together the seats."

Beth plopped down on the beanbag, scooching me over. She presented her find. It was a tiny photo album. I took it from her quicker than necessary but she didn't notice. I flipped to the first page and there he was.

A young Cameron beamed at me through the shiny plastic cover. He couldn't have been more than eight years old. Holding his hand was little Beth. Behind them, was a multi-million-dollar backdrop.

"Where are you guys?"

"In front of Cameron's house," she replied.

I turned the pages. It was the scene Beth told me about. The two of them were on the couch passed out. Their tiny faces were innocent in sleep.

What if that had been us? Me and Cameron taking naps together?

The picture formed in my mind hazy and undefined. It disappeared the harder I tried to hold onto it. I couldn't see myself in a happy moment with Cameron Dupre—no matter how much I wanted to.

A knot lodged in my throat as I flipped through the photos of a happy Cameron and the little sister he chose to love.

"We loved video games," Beth chattered on. "We would stay up all night playing. And he was obsessed with old rock bands. The Who, Eagles, and Deep Purple were his top three favorites."

"What about his parents?" I cut in. "Were they close?"

Emotion welled up inside of me, threatening to strangle with every word of the guy I never got to know.

The whole time the one I came to Breakbattle for was you and I missed you.

"Not so much with his mom. Mrs. Dupre is nice enough but she's always busy with her charities, fundraiser, nonprofits, and all of that. She was never home and when she was, the phone was glued to her face."

"And his dad?"

"Cam loved his dad. Dominick actually did spend time with him." She laughed. "It was so cute. He had a little desk in his office and when he'd work from home, he put Cameron there with his crayons and juice box so they could be together."

"That is cute." Surprise laced my voice and it felt justified. Was there a nice side to Dominick Dupre?

"He didn't stop as Cameron got older. Dominick took him to work with him all the time. He taught Cameron everything he knows."

She dropped her head on my shoulder. "Dominick is wrecked over this. Losing his only son and the police haven't found who did it. I still can't believe it. Who would want to kill Cameron?"

I was ready as the tears came. I wrapped my arms around Beth and let her cry.

"I want to find them too," she said between sobs. "I wish I knew something that could help."

"You are helping, Beth." I looked at the album. "You've helped me more than anyone."

"I don't know who was getting to him but his girlfriend might."

My hand stilled on her back. "Girlfriend? What girlfriend?"

"I never met her but a few weeks before he died, I caught him in his swimsuit dripping wet by the pool and snapping pics. I asked what the hell he was doing and he said he was just sending Em a few previews so they'd both be wet. He could be gross like that."

I giggled. Oh my goodness. Cameron Dupre had a sense of humor.

"So he had a girlfriend but you never met her? She didn't go to the funeral?"

"Dominick made the funeral family only and us. Plus, I say girlfriend but she could have been his sexting buddy or something. I don't know how serious they were."

"But whatever they were doing, they were doing around the time he was killed. He may have confided in her." I was warming up to this quickly. "I have to talk to her."

"I hope you find her and that she knows more than I do." Beth snuggled in further. "Thanks for this, Zela. I've missed him so much. It was nice to talk about him." She pulled back and looked me in the eyes. "And thank you for trying to do something. I'm sorry I ever thought you could hurt him. You're good person."

"You're going to be okay, Beth. Just..." I wrapped her hands around the album. "Hold on to the good memories. Remember your funny, happy, protective big brother."

Her smile trembled at the corners, but it held. "I will."

I didn't leave right away. I stayed with Beth until I was sure she was okay. Then I returned to our room and found Melody on her bed working on the same project I needed to finish.

"Hey. Your phone's been going off nonstop."

"Of course it has," I said, "because I chose to date the most overprotective guys on the planet."

"You love it and you know it."

"Shh." I winked at her. "Don't let them know."

I turned on my phone to three calls and seven texts.

Me: Chill, my loves. The one hundred pound fifteen-year-old girl didn't hurt me.

Their replies came back almost instantly.

Landon: Did she know anything?

Cole: What did she tell you?

Michael: How close was she to Cameron?

Derek: You promised we'd do this together.

Me: This I had to do on my own and not just because you can't come on the girls' side.

Derek: Did she know something about Cameron?

Me: She knew he was hooking up with someone before he was killed. Maybe Cameron complained to her about the guy who cut his face and shoved him against the door.

Michael: If we could just get a name. He might not be the killer but at least we'd know we need to look somewhere else.

Derek sent me a text outside of the group chat.

Derek: Zee, meet me tomorrow.

Me: I meet you every day. I'm not about to forget.

Derek: Tomorrow especially. I have to talk to you about something.

Me: Okay. I love you.

Derek: Love you too.

I sent private I love yous to Cole, Michael, and Landon and promised to tell them the rest of my conversation with Beth the next day.

I tossed my phone on the nightstand and reached for my project.

"Melody, quick question."

"Yeah?"

"Do you know an Em? She might have been a year ahead of us, or she lives in Evergreen."

"Em as in Emma or Emily?" she asked. "I know an Emma who is six and lives a few houses down. Then there's Emily. She's twenty-something and works in my favorite store in the Promenade. Is it Emily you're talking about?"

Is it? Could Cameron have been hooking up with a twenty-something-year-old shop clerk?

"Maybe," I said. "How well do you know her?"

"She is super sweet. Whenever they get something in stock that she knows I'll like, she sets it aside for me. I've gone out to lunch with her and her girlfriend a few times." She shook her head. "Or I should say fiancée. She told me she proposed a few weeks ago."

"Fiancée? Is there any chance Emily would have hooked up with an eighteen-year-old high school boy?"

Melody laughed. "What are you talking about? She's not into guys and definitely wouldn't go for high school ones. Why do you ask?"

I considered how much I should tell her. "I'm trying to track someone down for a friend, but all I've got is a nickname."

"Why doesn't your friend tell you the full name?"

"She doesn't know," I said simply. "Sexting buddy."

Melody formed an "o" with her lips. "Gotcha. If you want to pass on my advice, keep those things anonymous. It can get a lot less sexy outside of cyberspace."

My brows shot up my head. "Are you speaking from experience?"

It was her turn to wink at me.

THE NEXT MORNING, I met Derek in our usual place. We kissed hello like people who hadn't seen each other in months.

"What's going on?" I asked. "What did you want to talk about?"

"It's about the Network."

"I thought everything was quiet?"

"It was quiet. The Network went dark and Dad started to believe Dupre took over just to shut it down. That is until"—he took an envelope out of his pocket—"we got this." He handed it to me. "We all got one. It's an invitation to Dupre's house over winter break. I told the guys I would tell you about it."

I didn't take out the invitation. "What does this mean?"

"Whatever his plans are, he's going to announce them at this party. The entire Network is invited all the way down to the recruits. And you have to be there."

The envelope shook in my hand. "Me? Derek, I don't want to see him. I'm not ready."

"This isn't about him." He stroked my cold cheek. "It's about Cameron. His old friends will be there. Heath, Santiago, and the rest. They might know more about his death. They could tell us who Em is."

"They won't talk to me."

"Most likely not, but you'll be close by." He kissed the tip of my nose. I did it to my boys all the time. I loved the rare moments they did it too. "I won't push if you really don't want to go."

My first instinct was to refuse. I had too much to sort out. Watching Dominick Dupre take apart the Network while my heart worked to reconcile that my father wasn't a good man seemed like a terrible idea.

"I'll think about it," I said. "Let me see what I can find out about Em. We might not need to question his friends if we find her."

"True." Derek used his hold on my chin to pull me in for a kiss. "While I have you here..."

"It's too cold for you to strip me down and tease me."

"I'm saving that for this weekend. What I really want to do is sit here and talk books with you."

"What a coincidence. I want that too."

Almost an hour later, we headed back to the main building. Derek kissed me goodbye in front of the door to the girls' campus.

I reached for my phone instead of the handle. I waited for a reasonable time to call. That time had come.

Langman answered on the third ring.

"Hello, this is Detective Langman. What can I do for you?"

"Langman, this is Zela Manning.

"Miss Manning? Is there a problem?"

"I wanted to ask you about Cameron Dupre. Did you ever speak to a girl named Em? Or Emma or Emily?"

"No, I can't say that I have."

"But you have his phone. Did you find the half-naked swimsuit pictures he sent to Em?"

"I didn't find— Hold on. What exactly is going on here?"

"I spoke to one of Cameron's childhood friends. They told me he was hooking up with a girl named Em around the time of his death. She might know who he was having a problem with."

"We've interviewed Beth and she mentioned that she believed he was dating," said Langman. "He and this Em could have been involved, but by the time of his murder, her contact information was deleted from his phone and those pictures erased. None of the texts we read were of a romantic nature."

I deflated. "Did you find anything else on his phone?"

"I can't discuss this with you, Miss Manning. Thank you for making sure I was aware of all the information, but I'll handle things from here."

Miss Val's door flew open.

"—later. I hope you have a great day of classes."

Zach walked out. "I'm in the F Class, Miss V. That's impossible. Bye."

"Bye, Zach."

Miss Val landed on me. "Zela. How lucky is this? Come in."

"Miss Manning? Miss Manning?" Langman brought me back to the conversation.

"I have to go, Detective. I'll call you if I have any more questions."

"No, you w—"

I hung up.

"Morning, Val." I hugged her tight. Adam's mom was the best. Mine took top spot and then there was Aunt Bev, but she placed third for my favorite moms of all time. "How is everything going? Any luck getting the rules changed officially?"

She blew out a breath. "Working on it. How about you?" Val shifted the conversation. "Do you want to come in?"

"I have to get to class."

She waved that away. "I can give you a note. Come inside. I'll make us some tea."

I surrendered my feeble fight and followed her in. I sank into the seat that was always mine during our sessions and wondered if this was fate. I'd never needed to talk to a therapist more.

"You must be on the hook for updates," Miss Val said. "I'm making progress convincing Adam's dads to let him go backpacking with you. Ryder is starting to thaw."

"I really want him to come. He says you guys haven't explored Europe much."

"We usually visit family or take trips to the Caribbean." Val set my mug on the coffee table. "With all the kids, we're not up to longer trips yet. I want him to have this experience with you."

Miss Val claimed her armchair and beamed at me. "Alright. Now tell me what's on your mind."

I chuckled. "How do you know something is on my mind?"

"You have four boyfriends. You've been outed and forced onto the girls' campus. The student body is locked in turmoil, high school is ending, and university is ahead. Of course you have a lot on your mind."

A smile tugged at my lips. "That's why they call you the best."

She laughed. "Do they?"

I sobered quickly. "Actually, there is something I want to ask you."

"I'm listening."

"Val, what if you...?" I trailed off. Picking up my cup, I took a few sips to delay finishing my question.

"What if I what, Zela?" she asked calmly.

"What if you had the chance to see your father? Talk to him. Visit his home. Find out more about him. Would you go?"

"No." Her response was immediate.

"No? Honestly?"

"Honestly. I once had that chance, Zela, and I made the decision not to take it. Have you found yourself having to make the same decision?"

I nodded.

"What do you want to do?"

"I want to know him. I want to know my father. I want it so bad that I've made decisions I can never take back to get close to him. This time, I don't want to make the wrong one."

"What are your fears?"

"I'm afraid I'll hurt Mom. I'm afraid that the rumors about him are true. Dominick Dupre made a terrible first impression. What if that's exactly who he is?"

"Dominick Dupre?"

"He's my father."

Miss Val was a professional. Of all the things I'd told her in this room, she never visibly reacted—until now.

Her eyes flared. "Your father? But that means Cameron..."

"Yes," I whispered.

"Oh, Zela. I'm so sorry."

"I am too. I find my real brother months after he's murdered. I discover my father has mafia ties and probably killed his nanny."

"That was never proven."

"Imagine only having that to hold on to? 'At least the cops can't prove it.'" I gulped down some more tea. "I have an invitation to a party he's throwing. Do you think I should go?"

"I don't know."

I heaved a sigh. "Val, come on."

"Zela, this isn't me playing the you-must-discover-the-answers-on-your-own game. I really don't know. I come from this from so many angles. As a mother. As someone who grew up not knowing my father. As a person who cares about you, and as your therapist. Each one as a different answer."

"Then, can I admit I'm happy there is someone else as confused as me?"

"Yes."

I smiled despite myself. She might not have had an an-swer for me, but this was helping.

"Okay. Let me ask you this," Val said. "When you got the invitation, what was your first thought?"

"I want to go."

She nodded like she knew it would be. "Maybe there's your answer."

IT SEEMED SO SIMPLE that day in her office, but as we neared finals, I flip-flopped on my decision so many times Derek said he'd have sex with me if I made a choice and stuck with it. I chased him through the halls for that one, but when I caught him, he pushed me into a bathroom and we got each other off, so I don't think he learned his lesson.

Having everyone close to Cameron in one room was a chance I couldn't pass up. I could speak to his mother or lis-ten in on the boys talking to his friends. My desire to go was rivaled by my need to avoid Dominick Dupre. I didn't know how to feel about him yet. If I witnessed him act like the man everyone said he was, the decision would be made for me.

"You won't go near him," Cole said under his breath. "You won't have to talk to him. We don't even have to stay long. We can get in, talk to Heath and the guys, and then get out."

The two of us were in the library studying and sneaking kisses. Finals began and our teachers gave not one iota that we were seniors with college acceptances in the bag. The first day and I felt like I pulled out my brain and squeezed every drop of knowledge I accumulated over the years on my exams. I was wrung out.

Spending time with Cole perked me up considerably. Our exams weren't scheduled for the same days or on the same topics, but we studied together anyway. Mostly for the kissing.

"That's true," I said. "I'm overthinking this, aren't I? I just need to focus on why I'm doing this. Someone killed my brother. This is bigger than me."

Cole held my hand under the table. "You're allowed to be freaked. I would be too if Mom up and told me I'd been fathered by Dominick Dupre."

"I hope that never happens. I can't fall in love with any more brothers." I cringed. "That was weird. Way too soon for that joke."

He laughed softly. "It's going to be okay, Zee. Come with me to the Promenade this weekend. We'll get you a dress for the party, grab some lunch, and then drive up one of the secluded dirt roads and have sex in the back seat."

"Ooh. Yes to all of the above."

We leaned in at the same time. Cole's kisses were fierce, demanding, and passionate, just like him. He kissed me like he wanted me with every fiber of his being and he did it every time. No quick pecks for him.

Proving that miracles are real, we all survived finals. Friday afternoon, I hugged my friends goodbye one by one and wished them a happy holiday. Our relief at being away from Breakbattle was carved into our faces. For just a little while, a ceasefire had been called on the battle between the classes.

Saturday morning, Cole showed up at my door and whisked me away to Evergreen. The party was being held three days before Christmas. It gave me two days to find a dress.

"You'd think it would be Christmas themed," I called to Cole.

"He chose the date so everyone could be there from members to recruits. That's it. It's not a celebration."

I plucked a dress off the rack and held it up to my frame. "Alright. I have mixed feelings about Christmas, so a black dress works for me."

"I like it." Cole appeared at my side holding my purse and a bag with the shoes I bought earlier. He was surprisingly cool about holding my things. According to him, Christina wished for a little brother solely for the purpose of him holding her shopping. He was used to it. "Get that one."

My find was a halter dress with no back and a deep slit up the leg. Of course he liked it.

And I'll like the way he'll look at me in it, so this one it is.

I purchased the dress and then we spent the rest of the day exactly like we planned—back road car sex included.

I made it through the next couple of days secure in my decision. It wasn't until I was hours away from the start of the party that I realized it was a monumentally stupid idea.

"What was I thinking?"

Jordan tracked me as I paced a hole in the carpet.

"This isn't even about Dominick. If Cameron's friends knew something, they would have told the police a long time ago. It's been almost a year since he was killed. What am I going to find now?"

"They might have held back something they didn't know was important at the time," Jordan said. "It's worth a try, Zela."

Jordan knew the truth about Dominick. Of course she did. I told her everything.

"The longer this goes on, the more I give up hope. He was killed in a school full of people. Why doesn't someone know something?" I cried.

"Someone does," she said, "and one day, either you or the police will find them. Trust me. Now take a breath, let it out, and finish getting ready. Remember why you're doing this."

I breathed deep till my heart slowed. It helped me get through dressing, putting on my makeup, opening the door for Derek, and the biggest hurdle of getting into his car.

"Are you okay?" Derek kissed the back of my knuckles. "It's not too late to back out."

"I'm okay."

"The offer still stands to leave early. We planned on having our first time over break. We can find a spot and..."

"We'll see what happens."

On a regular night, I'd jump on the suggestion in his voice. Tonight was not a regular night. Jordan warned me once about using sex to feel better. I didn't want my first time with Derek to be a distraction from my daddy issues.

We changed to lighter topics for the rest of the drive. All of my boys got into Somerset University, although it wasn't a surprise.

"Are you going to live in the dorm?" I asked.

"Are you?"

"Yep. I want the full college experience."

"As long as you get a single room, I'm cool with that."

I shoved his shoulder. "What about you?"

"I thought I was, but Mom practically burst into tears when she saw the dorm catalog. She's been going on about her 'baby' leaving for the past two weeks."

"You do live closer to Somerset than I do. There's no reason for you to move out."

"There are a lot of reasons."

Amusement beat back the confusing swarm of emotions ripping into me. "It would be fun for all of us to be in the same dorm again. Having you, Cole, Michael, Landon, and Adam right down the hall is my dream."

"Why is Moon on the list?"

I shot him a grin. "Maybe I love him as much as you guys."

"Don't ever say that again. The smug bastard lords it over us enough."

I full-blown howled. My heavy mood lifted as we turned onto a street lined with cars.

"Thank you." I kissed his cheek. "You always make me feel better."

"It's what I do."

Derek pulled up to a house I'd seen before. Ten years later, the Dupre mansion looked the same down to the vintage cars in the driveway. Derek put his hand on the small of my back and kept me close. He presented his invitation to a man in a three-piece suit.

"Derek Grayson and Zela Manning."

The guy looked me up and down. "This is a private party, sir."

"She knows about the Network."

He said no more. Bowing his head, he gestured for us to go inside.

Stepping over the threshold was like passing through to another world. Mansions were no stranger to me. Wealth and riches had become a norm. But none of the amazing houses I'd seen over the years had prepared me for this. Every single thing I laid eyes on screamed money so loud it deafened me.

Priceless works of art led the way to the front room. They were displayed front and center, demanding to be seen by all who visited. Lights shone down on us from a chandelier that showed its age as well as the other pieces in the house.

I wasn't fooled. Just one of these antiques could pay off her mortgage and set my mother up for life.

"Nice place," I said simply.

"See the floors." He pointed out the black and white glittering tile. "That's diamond inlaid marble."

"I'm sorry. Did you say diamonds? Like *diamond* diamonds? Real ones?"

"They are very real."

"Do owners of financial companies all live like this?"

Derek gave me a look I didn't like. "Let's just say not even my parents could afford one million dollars per square meter."

My stomach twisted. Even if this was paid for legitimately, this bordering on obscene display of wealth added to the picture forming in my head. The cars lined up in the front, the Rembrandt next to the coat rack, and diamonds you walked on. The Dupres wanted everyone to know they had money.

"If you'll come this way, sirs, madams," a voice said. "The party will be held in the great hall."

Music floated out of the room and beckoned us. The great hall boasted few decorations, but the space spoke for itself. Servers weaved through expensively dressed people of all shapes, sizes, colors, and cultures. I'd say it was a diverse group if it wasn't for the fact I counted so few women.

"Does the Network recruit women at all?" I asked. "Are the women here members or spouses?"

"Spouses or moms. We get our new members from the boy campus, so Dad kept it men-only to be their mentors."

"That's stupid."

He barked a laugh. "It is, isn't it? But who knows, that rule may change tonight."

I put my head on his shoulder, sending love his way. "Is your dad coming to the party?"

"The bastard sent him an invitation and he tossed it in the trash. I volunteered in his place."

"Zela. Derek."

Landon waved to us from the other side of the room. Michael and Cole were with him.

"Did you see?" Cole spoke so quietly his lips barely moved. "Dowell is over there and I saw Santiago come in earlier but I don't know where he went."

Landon pointed over our heads. "Do you see that potted plant under the Caravaggio? I'll get Heath over there and ask him about Cameron. You hide behind it. He won't notice you."

"This is all so cloak and dagger," I said.

My heart fluttered in my chest, fed on pure nerves. I pressed my palm over my breast and breathed the way Jordan told me.

"Let's wait until there are more people and noise to cover us," said Landon.

The five of us remained in the corner talking and watching people come in. Everyone was here. Hunter strolled in with an elderly man who sat in the first chair he found and closed his eyes. Boys I recognized as freshmen, sophomores, and juniors joined the party with their chaperones in tow.

"They're here with their parents," I spoke up. "Doesn't this mean the secret is out?"

"Yes," Derek replied. "They have to know why they're here. What we don't know is why Dominick outed us."

"For some reason, secrecy isn't important anymore," I said.

Someone caught my eye.

"Oh my gosh. Zach? What is he doing here?"

The current F student stepped inside the great room looking like he was wholly where he belonged. He stopped a server and lifted two glasses off his tray. One he gave to the pretty older woman by his side who shared his nose.

"What the fuck?" Derek hissed.

"Was he not kicked out?" I asked.

"I made Dad toss him on his ass first thing," Derek said. "He drugged you, cheated during the tournament, and lost anyway. He wasn't staying after that."

"Dominick must have brought him back," said Cole.

"Why would he do that?"

None of us had an answer.

"I can't believe both of them are here," Landon said. "Zach's mom, Crystal, hasn't been in the public eye lately. His dad is divorcing her and it's getting pretty ugly."

"How ugly are we talking?" I asked.

"She took a baseball bat to his Maserati and he called her a plastic whore in the media."

"Holy shit."

"I almost feel bad for the guy," Michael added.

"Don't." Derek's voice was hard. "He hurt Zela and I should have kicked his skull in a long time ago."

I rubbed his arm. "No violence, my love. There has been more than enough of it."

"I don't know about that," Cole said in a voice that prickled my skin. "Look at that smug as shit smirk. He hasn't learned his lesson yet."

"Guys, remember why we're here. The place is packed. Let's find Heath."

Our group split apart with no more talk about Zachary. I couldn't fathom why Dominick Dupre allowed him back or why he risked letting these parents know their kids were snatched out of their beds by a secret underground club running beneath their noses.

These folks don't look pissed though. Smiling faces, tinkling laughter, and charming conversation surrounded me. *Everyone is acting like this is just another party.*

I located the Caravaggio and potted plant. I tucked myself away and continued scanning the crowd. This was the largest collection of famous men I'd ever seen—that any person has ever seen. Not even the Grammys had this kind of guest list. Movie stars, musicians, athletes, CEOs, politicians, and authors mingled on the diamond floors.

"—next for you, man."

"I got into Somerset."

I plastered myself against the wall. Landon and Heath were here.

"You still doing wrestling?" asked Heath.

"I'll do it for fun. I'm going pre-law with the goal of opening nonprofit homes for LGBT kids living on the street. We'll provide services, help them with emancipation, and whatever they need."

"That's cool, Landon." He sounded like he truly meant it. "Cameron said back then that you had other plans. It's good you're thinking bigger than sports. The Network is proud of their professional athletes, but I've always said that's thinking too small. You blow out your knee and where the fuck are you? Sitting alone in your mansion hoping a cereal company puts you on their box. I set my sights higher. I'm at Harvard studying political science and I intend to take my career all the way to the top."

The top? As in... the head of the government?

A vision of President Dowell flashed in my mind.

"Cameron had plans too," Landon said. "To takeover Dupre Financial Holdings and dominate the financial sector. He would have done it too."

"Damn right he would have. Fuck. I miss that guy."

"It's crazy that they haven't arrested the guy who killed him," Landon said. "If you ask me, it must have been that guy Cameron was fighting with at the fundraiser."

The fronds brushed my cheek as I leaned in closer. Landon was good. He should be an actor too.

"Did he tell you about that? I never got him to talk to me about it."

Oh no. Heath doesn't know either.

"Cam didn't give me a name, but I could tell something was up with him," said Landon.

"Seriously. He was acting weird since the year started. Blowing us off and stuff. Santi and I guessed he was hitting some girl outside of school. He just smirked when we asked though."

"You don't know her name?"

"Nah. Like I said, he wouldn't talk to us and barely hung out. He and Santi fought about it all the time."

He and Santi were fighting?

"It must kill him now. All that bitching and arguing over nothing and then Cameron is killed before they could put it right."

"That's got to be tough. Was it just Cameron keeping to himself that bugged Santi?"

"It was lots of stuff. None of it matters now."

"Did he—"

"Hey, let's not talk about this anymore. It's a party. So are you still dating that girl-boy, Zeke?"

I stiffened at the change of conversation.

"Excuse me?"

"Because you should ditch her," Heath went on, clearly not picking up on his tone. "She's caused the Network a lot of trouble. One of the board members let it slip that her interview swayed them to vote against the expansion. A girl like that will bring you down. You don't want her crazy in your life."

"I want her crazy in my life every second of every day. A girl like that pushes you to become a better man just for the sake of deserving her. One day, she is going to be my wife and we'll push out a horde of ridiculously photogenic babies. Until then, you watch your fucking mouth."

I clapped my hand over my mouth. I had to. I was afraid I'd burst out how much I loved him.

Oh, Landon. You've completely blown it... and it's the sweetest thing you've ever done.

"Chill out, Foster." Heath's tone was decidedly cool. "It was friendly advice."

"I don't need your advice."

I heard a muttered curse and the heavy footfalls of someone stomping off. Landon peeked his head around the plant.

"Sorry, baby. My questioning didn't get very far."

Snagging his collar, I kissed him hard.

"I'm going to be your wife, huh?"

"That's correct," he said a tad huskily. "You can only marry one man and since I was your first love, it's going to be me. The other guys will have to suck it up."

This argument we could have way, *way* down the line. Instead, I kissed him again till my lungs cried for air.

"I love you."

"I love you too," he said. "But we should take a break from making out and talk about what I did get from him. Cameron was fighting with someone and that someone was Santiago."

Reality harshly popped our bubble. "You're right. Santiago didn't mention it to Cole. Not just that, he specifically told Cole that their senior year was like every other, while the truth was they were fighting about Cameron blowing him off and being secretive."

"Strange. Michael, Cole, or Derek could try talking to Heath again. I'll go at Santi with what we know."

"Good idea." I flicked his nose. "You're amazing. I have to find a bathroom, but I'll catch up with you later."

"Alright."

I walked out of the great room and one of the staff came up to me immediately.

"Are you looking for the bathroom, madam?"

"Yes."

"It's down that hallway and to your left. There's a sign."

"Thank you."

I walked down the hallway and turned left. I glanced at the door with the sign and looked away, not slowing my stride. I didn't need the bathroom.

Months had passed. Cameron's room might be packed away and bare. Still, I wanted to find it. I wanted to see the space where my brother grew up and discover if it was as cold and meant for show like the rest of this house.

One by one, I visited the dining room, kitchen, library, two guest rooms, and a study. I crept up the back stairs just off the kitchen. His room had to be on the second floor.

The passage was shrouded in darkness. I couldn't chance turning on the lights. As my eyes adjusted, I moved down the hall continuing my exploration. My heels were soundless on the plush carpet. No one would know I was here.

My fingers closed around the third knob on the left. I glanced in and four pairs of eyes look back at me. The Who poster covered most of the wall.

This is it. I threw open the door. *It's Cameron's—*

A tall, large figure emerged from the gloom. "What do you think you're doing?"

I stumbled back, clutching my chest. "I'm s-sorry. I didn't know—"

"Someone was up here. Obviously."

"I shouldn't have done this. I'll go—"

"Get in here."

"Mr. Dupre—"

"Now, girl," he barked.

My sense told me to disobey the command, yet my trembling body took me inside. I reached for the switch. Light cast over the space and the man before me. Dominick's face was expressionless as he took me in. I read nothing that gave away why he'd been alone in the dark in his son's room while a party raged downstairs.

Not for the first time, I wondered how such a severe, rough-looking man produced a boy with the face of an angel. And now I'd have to wonder how he produced me too. We looked nothing alike. I didn't have his thick brows, small eyes, wide-set nose, or thin lips. I didn't have the contempt etched into all of them.

"I know you."

I paused five feet away from him. "Yes. We met at career day."

"The upstart little F."

"I'm an upstart E now."

"I know that too. Zela Rae Manning," he said, surprising me. "The girl who single-handedly destroyed our plans for the expansion."

"I wouldn't say I did it single-handedly." I raised my chin, steadily holding his gaze. "I had some help."

The corner of his mouth twitched in what might have been a grin. It was gone as quickly as it happened.

"It's not an issue now. The Network has moved on."

"So I've heard." I turned away from him and swept the room. It was exactly like I hoped. It appeared as though Cameron just stepped out for a minute. Posters of old rock bands and vintage cars were on every wall. A massive bed took up most of the space. It was covered in green silk sheets to match the green desk chair and green curtains. Green must have been his favorite color.

"Why were you in here alone?" I found myself asking.

"You'll be giving the explanations. What are you doing up here?"

"I wanted to see his room," I admitted. "I never got a chance to know the real Cameron. I regret it now."

Heavy footsteps advanced on me. I whipped around.

"Don't spout your bullshit in here. In my son's room," he barked. "My boy was no fan of yours and the feeling was mutual. I saw the little video you made together."

My heart rocketed against my ribcage. He wasn't going to hurt me but those cold, pitch black eyes looked truly frightening flashing with anger.

"It's in the past, Mr. Dupre." I willed my voice not to shake. "I've forgiven him and moved on. What else could I do? Cameron is gone. Holding a grudge poisons you. There is no point."

"I don't agree. Grudges are not poison. They're fuel. The grudge I hold for the person who killed my only son will see they get the punishment they have coming to them even if I'm not alive to enact it."

I took a step back and he moved with me.

"I am not that person," I said clearly. "I didn't kill Cameron."

"I know that, girl. Your blood wasn't a match for the blood in the room."

My flicker of shock was brief. "Of course you know. You're his father." I looked around his room. A space the complete opposite of the cold, lonely, art museum outside. "And you loved him," I said. "I can't imagine what you're going through."

"No one could understand." He moved away, walking toward the window. "To lose your only son. Your heir. Your legacy. My boy was going to do great things. He would have conquered the world and the weak men within it. I raised him to be everything I was and everything I couldn't be."

Dominick's grief didn't manifest in tears or a choked throat. He seemed a man perfectly in control. But as I gazed at him standing by the window—and the picture of him and young Cameron hanging inches away from the curtains—tears prickled behind my eyes. Dominick Dupre was the saddest man alive.

Swallowing hard, I quickly wiped away a trail of wetness staining my cheek. "I want you to know that no one is giving up. We will find the person who killed Cameron."

"Your reassurance is not necessary. I have the best investigators money can buy searching for the rotted piece of shit. It's only a matter of time."

I stared at my father's back. "And what will you do if they find him?"

"You ask a lot of questions, girl, but you don't have a right to the answers. Get out. Return to the party. There is an announcement coming. Tonight, things are going to change."

I left.

Left the room, left the mansion, left the neighborhood.

The frigid, stinging wind slapped my cheeks as I walked off blindly in any direction. I didn't stop until Derek found me an hour later, almost to the highway.

Chapter Eight

"Are you okay?"

"Yes."

"Are you sure?"

"Yes."

"Are you lying to me?"

I chuckled. I was in my room putting away my Christmas presents. The morning dawned with our first gift, a cold snap that dipped temperatures to almost freezing. Jordan and I took full advantage and busted out hot cocoa, blankets, and a pile of Christmas movies. We watched them back-to-back before her roaring fireplace.

Now I was home and calling all of my boys to hear about their celebrations. My final call only wanted to speak about one thing.

"Derek, I swear I'm fine. I've apologized over fifty times to each of you for wandering off and scaring you. I got overwhelmed. I felt a panic attack coming on and needed the fresh air. I just wasn't thinking straight."

"You can't run away from us." Derek was laced with concern. As guilty as I felt for causing it, it warmed me that the guy who regularly called me clingy was fussing over me. "The next time it happens, come to us so we can take care of you."

"I will."

"Damn it, Zela," he cried.

"What?" I asked with a laugh. "I'm agreeing with you."

"I know something happened when you disappeared. You don't get panic attacks for nothing. Why won't you tell me?"

I sighed. "I did tell you. I went to find Cameron's room and stumbled in on Dominick. We talked for like five minutes and then I left."

"He said something to you. Did something."

"He didn't lay a finger on me or threaten to. All we did was talk about Cameron."

"I don't believe you."

"Of course not, my stubborn love."

He mumbled something I didn't catch. "Did Landon tell you he talked to Santiago? He threw what Heath said in his face and Santi told him to fuck off. Said it wasn't his business."

"Yes, he told me. Heath didn't have a lot more to say either. Then Dominick came in."

"The guy is a fucking bastard," he spat. "Part of me is glad you weren't there for his big announcement. You didn't see me lose it."

I cringed. "I'm so sorry, Derek. I couldn't believe it when Michael told me."

"Everything my dad built is dead. He's destroying what the Network stood for."

"So new recruits pay to play."

"That's why he didn't care if the parents knew and told all of their friends. He's bringing the Network public and using his money and wife's connections to turn it into an official organization. It's not a mentoring program anymore. If recruits or anyone else want access to the members, they pay through the nose.

"How much?" I asked. "Will there at least be tiers?"

"It's a flat thousand to apply. If you're accepted, it's five hundred a month to keep your membership. After all of that, if you want to get near the members you have to agree to whatever rate they choose."

"That's insane. No one will agree to that."

"People already have. The news is spreading through Evergreen fast. Most of them think it's a great idea. Parents around here spend thousands for tutors anyway. Why not skip the nobodies and just hire a top NBA champion?"

My new shirt wrinkled in my fist. "The Network becomes another exclusive club for the rich."

"Yes. It's open to men and women now, but all of those men and women will have trust funds. I've dropped out. So have Landon, Michael, Cole, and Hunter. The kid is a good friend," Derek added. "I should be nicer to him."

"I wish I could do something."

"You can do something," he continued. "We talked about meeting up over the break. Do you still want to?"

"The answer to that is a resounding yes. We've put this off long enough. We should have done it the first day of school."

Derek finally laughed—a full, rich sound that broke the lingering tension. "Think how much sweeter it'll be because we didn't rush."

I hummed. "I don't know. Our wild fumblings in the bathrooms and broom closets are plenty sweet. Or were you lying about my pussy tasting like honey?"

"You're so damn dirty, Zela," he growled, "and I love it. I'll pick you up tomorrow night. Tell your mom you'll be at Adam's or something because I will not have you back at a respectable hour."

"Don't worry. I have it covered."

"Bye, Zee. I love you... and I will get the truth out of you."

I shook my head. "I love you too."

We hung up and I went back to putting away my new clothes. I did have our night covered. I went to Mom and told her the truth. I said Derek was planning a special date night for us and I'd miss curfew. I didn't go into detail, but Mom was no dummy. She looked at me without speaking for so long that it grew uncomfortable, but she said yes.

My mom bought me birth control pills. She met all four of my outrageously hot boyfriends, and she's given me so many lectures on female sexuality being a natural thing that I lost count. In the end, the truth was best.

Mom and I counted down the final hours of Christmas reading our favorite books on the living room couch.

The next day, I got ready to meet Derek. I didn't know where he was taking me, but he was the kind of guy who thought of everything. I kept it simple and packed a toothbrush and a change of clothes for the morning.

"Zela?" Mom poked her head in. "Derek is downstairs."

"I'm ready."

"I want you back by ten a.m."

"Yes, Mom."

"And if there's a problem, call me."

"I will." I pecked her on the cheek. "But there won't be a problem."

Derek waited for me on the porch. I threw myself in his arms.

"Finally," I whispered. "When we get there, we're going straight to bed. I'll strap you to it if I have to."

He chuckled. "Looks like I'm getting a reputation of holding out, but trust me, it wasn't on purpose. We're on the same page, Zee. You'll be lucky if we make it to the bedroom."

We tried not to run to the car in case Mom was watching. Derek zipped out of the neighborhood and headed for the highway, blowing past the speed limit. It was pure luck that we didn't get pulled over.

Soon, anonymous highway was replaced with thick woods and tall pines that sweetened the air. I realized minutes away where we were going.

"The cabin?"

"Mom and Dad went out for a romantic night of their own. He changed the locks on this place, but I swiped the new one and made copies."

"You're so bad, Derek Grayson."

"That's a reputation I will hold on to."

The porch lit up when we pulled up the drive, revealing the secluded paradise. Changes were made since our last visit. Flowers lined the path to the door and comfy rocking chairs were on the porch.

"Wow," I said as I climbed out. "It's just as beautiful as I—"

Derek raced around the car and scooped me up.

"Admire the landscape later," he said over my yelp.

That was fine with me.

We stumbled into the house, mouths connected, and hands fumbling to tear off our clothes. Derek kicked the door shut with a slam that rattled the windows. His eagerness made my lower belly clench.

I ripped my bra off and flung it over my shoulder somewhere. I did the same with his belt. I broke our kiss, earning a growl, but I made up for it by dropping to my knees and dragging his pants down. His member sprang free, erect and desperate for me. I swallowed him to the hilt and bobbed my head.

He let out an almost primal groan. Derek tangled his fingers in my hair. "Come here."

I obeyed. We connected in a kiss that poured molten heat through my mouth and scorched me from the inside out. I broke away, gasping.

"Bedroom," I rasped.

"We're not going to make it."

I slipped out of his hold anyway and ran giggling for the room. I made it four steps before Derek wrapped his arms around my middle and carried me to the couch. I hitched my breath as he bent me over the arm of the chair.

"Der—"

He pushed my panties down and warm air hit my heated cheeks. He positioned himself at my entrance and stopped.

"Do it," I practically screamed. "Do it, Derek. I want you now. Just like this."

That was all the encouragement he needed. He pushed inside of me and a moan escaped my lips. He moved and I rocked against the couch. My nipples brushed against the leather as he pumped faster, deeper, harder.

Derek and I had done a lot of stupid things but waiting was at the top. That molten heat raged into an inferno that blotted out my mind and being. Nothing existed but Derek and the molding of our bodies in the place where we confessed our love. The place where he truly became mine.

The sensations surging through me collected in one spot. My orgasm crested, reaching a fever pitch, and then he struck that spot and I tipped over.

I buried my face in the leather as waves and waves of explosions burst in my mind. Derek collapsed on top of me. He cuddled me tight and whispered in my ear as I came down.

"I love you, Zee," he said. "I love you so much."

"I love you too."

He nipped the shell of my ear. "You know that one doesn't count though, right?"

My eyes snapped open. "What?"

"I got a little carried away. Believe it or not, I didn't picture bending you over a couch for our first time."

I giggled. "That's how I pictured it. The first time we were intimate was in the woods behind school. Also, do I need to get into how many times you've put me on my knees in the dirt?"

"So I guess I thought we'd try a bed for once." He dropped soft kisses on the back of my neck. "I've got dinner, candles, and music. Tonight is going to be perfect."

"It already is perfect," I murmured. My eyes fluttered shut under his ministrations. "But I love you for doing all of this for me."

"Are you hungry?"

"Only if we'll eat in bed."

"That's a given."

We took our night to the bedroom and everything Derek promised was waiting for me. Candlelight flickered over us as we fed each other and then made love again beneath the soft sheets. Derek took his time, torturing me with foreplay, and I soaked up his love, knowing we had all night.

Four in the morning, we laid in each other's arms completely spent. I nuzzled in the crook of his neck, so happy I couldn't pen in my smile.

"What time do I have to get you home?"

"Ten," I said. "Which means we'll get in a quick one before breakfast."

"I should set an alarm. I don't want to risk your mother's wrath."

I pointed over his chest. "My bag is by the nightstand. Use my phone."

Derek rolled away and rifled around until he got my cell.

"I love this picture," he said.

"Picture?"

He flashed me my background. "No one could do your beauty justice but Hunter came close. Those socks still look cute."

I hummed. "You're showing your soft, sweet center, Derek Grayson. And all it took was hours of hot sex."

He winked. "Another hour might soften me up even more."

OUR TIME IN THE CABIN was over in a blink. Hours later, I helped Derek remove every trace of our presence.

"I wished this break wouldn't end," I said. I bagged up the trash and placed it by the door to take out. Derek was in the kitchen washing up our dishes. "Detention is filled with lowerclassmen every day because the Bs, As, and Elites go after them relentlessly with challenges.

"Why are they allowed to do that?" I raged. "They're demanding battles for privileges they already have. They should have addressed this in freshmen year when the Elites came after me."

"It's rough on the boys' side. Security has broken up three fights already."

"The girls' side isn't much better. The Elite seniors aren't joining in on the targeting, but I put that down to Melody. She claims they don't take her seriously, but that girl doesn't see how popular she is, or that the girls in our class consider her a friend. It didn't help that she funded the spring break trip herself. Or I should say it *did* help.

"Except for Everly rolling her eyes every time I breathe; the senior girls stay out of it. I can't say the same for the other grades. Beth doesn't want to join in either, but her friends are pressuring her. Whittaker and Argyle have to give in."

"Whittaker just won't do it," Derek said. "He can't accept that after all these years, Breakbattle is falling apart under his watch."

"I understand that he believes in this system, but it's been weeks and Refuse is going stronger. Tanner says they're willing to hold out for the rest of the year."

"Parents leaned on him and Whittaker got rid of the ten-point penalty. He's listening to them. If they protested the system like this, this could be over in a week."

I shook my head. "The parents sent them to that school in the first place. If they didn't want their kids dealing with the battle system, they made a crap choice. Of course they flew in quick to stop their kids from flunking, but the chances of them getting as organized as us are slim."

"You have a point." Derek put away the last dish and met me by the door. "This might be all we can do, but we won't give up."

I kissed him. "No, we won't."

"Ready to go?"

"I wish we didn't have to."

"You won't feel that way when I tell you Michael is dropping by your place today to surprise you with a date to the skating rink."

"He is? But now you've ruined the surprise."

"Worth it to put the smile back on your face."

We gathered the rest of our things and left. Derek took the garbage and tossed me the keys. The chime for a text sounded in my pocket.

I pulled it out and read the message. I stopped dead.

"Oh my— No. No, it can't be true." My phone shook in my hands. "No."

"Zela? Zee, what's wrong?"

Raising my head, I looked at Derek through wide eyes.

"Derek, I know who For All is."

"ZEE, ARE YOU SURE?" asked Michael.

"I'm one hundred percent sure," I repeated for the hundredth time. I picked up the pace and so did the boys. They were basically chasing me down the hall.

The first day of the new term began tomorrow, but it wouldn't start until I confronted the shadow hanging over our school.

Cole grabbed my wrist. "What are you going to do?"

"I haven't gotten that far."

"At least stop and talk to us."

"We've talked all through break. The talking is done."

"You can't risk—"

I shook free and burst through the doors of the boys' campus. Move-in day was chaos. People were rushing around, too busy to notice me. Even if they did, I didn't care. I was ending this today.

I stalked down the passage for the dorm building. The boys were one step behind. A few guys gave me curious looks but they didn't say anything. I wasn't the only girl around. Mothers, aunts, and sisters were helping their boys unpack. This was my chance to corner him in the only place he could hide from me.

I didn't slow down until I saw his dorm. I was correct about many things. For All was a guy. He was smart. And he hated the battle system. If only I had put it together sooner.

"Stay here."

My order triggered a chorus of protests.

"We're not letting you face him alone," Landon said. "The guy is unhinged."

"If all five of us pound on his door, he'll feel ambushed. I want you all to wait in the staircase too."

"Fuck that," Derek stated firmly.

"I'm serious. You need to trust me."

"We're not—"

"Ten minutes." Michael pushed through the boys and grasped my chin. "We'll give you ten minutes. If you're not out by then, I'm breaking down the door."

"Okay."

"No," Cole snapped. "Not ten minutes or ten seconds."

"Zela can handle herself," Michael replied. "Landon taught her to fight."

"You throw out the fucking rule book if he comes at you," Landon said. "Don't even think the word pacifist."

"Okay."

Michael pulled the boys out of the hall. Only when the door shut on Cole's pissed off expression did I turn and approach For All's room. I knocked once. Then twice.

"One second!" he shouted.

The door flew open. He beamed at the sight of me.

"Hey, Zela. What's up?"

"Not much, Hunter. Just wondered if we could talk about you being For All."

Hunter's smile melted away. He took a step closer and I tensed. Hunter looked up and down the empty hall. The Elites were all moved in. My boys were outside. It was just us.

"Please don't insult me by denying it," I said.

Hunter's sweep of the space ended on me. The boyish grin and teasing glint in his eyes was gone. I wasn't looking at Hunter. This was For All.

"I wasn't going to," he said in a surprisingly calm voice. "Come in. Let's talk."

"After you."

Hunter stepped back inside without a fight. Slowly, I followed him in, closed the door, and leaned on it. I tracked him as he pulled out his desk chair and took a seat.

"So how did you know?" he asked.

"The picture you drew of me and Derek. I was stupid not to see it before. I'm putting it down to the fact that it's been a hard year."

The tiniest wrinkled appeared in his serene mask. "What about the drawing?"

"The socks, Hunter. You drew me in knee-high socks that have a stripe around the ankle. I've worn knee-high socks around you before but the one time I wore socks like that was at the beginning when I had to borrow a pair from Melody.

"That was fine until I finally asked myself when. When did you see me in those socks? I left campus to meet Derek at the exact moment the automatic doors unlocked. If you came outside at the same time, I would have seen you. Unless you were already outside and you saw me pass." I gave him a hard look. "That was the night the gyms were trashed. If you were out all night, there could only be one reason why."

Hunter pursed his lips, nodding. "I drew a stripe on your socks." He clicked his tongue. "That was stupid of me. I poked my head out of the natatorium and saw you walk past. You looked so cute, I couldn't help but draw you. How was I supposed to know that was the first time you wore them?"

"Why did you do this, Hunter? I was with you when it was just stink bombs and tablets, but the bloody message, destroyed gym, greased floors, and cyberattacks? Why?"

"Come on, Zela." The corner of his mouth tugged up into a grin. "You're a smart girl and you've gotten this far. You tell me why I did it."

I swallowed around the needles in my throat. Who is this guy? He wasn't the sweet, kind boy I knew. I had the feeling he was never that guy at all.

I gave in. "This is about Becca Taylor, but I don't know why. I've looked for a connection between you two. There's nothing."

"Oh, there's something," he said conversationally. "I think you'd agree it's one of the strongest connections of all. Rebecca was my sister."

"Your sister?"

"That's right," he sang. "I used to be Kevin Taylor. My adoptive parents changed my name. Should I get into the whole story? I bet you're dying to know." He swept out his hand. "Sit. Get comfortable."

I didn't move.

Hunter laughed. "I'm not going to hurt you, Zela. Violence isn't my thing, remember? We have that in common."

"I'm fine here."

He shrugged. "Suit yourself."

"What happened to you?" I asked. "What drove you to this?"

"My sister was killed." The grin was gone. "Make no mistake, the boys who hounded her and hounded her until she broke were murderers. Mom was pregnant with me when she died and Rebecca's death ripped my parents to shreds. They blamed themselves every day for not doing more. If only they transferred her out or forced the administration to listen.

"If onlys were Mom's daily mantra. The months passed and she sank further into depression. She didn't want to talk to anybody and refused to take medication. Then I was born."

"What happened?"

"Postpartum psychosis."

I clapped my hand over my mouth. "Oh my gosh. Did she...?"

"Hurt me? No. It wasn't me the voice said to hurt. It was everyone else. People were after her baby. They would kill me if she didn't protect me. Which is why she charged Dad with a knife and put him in the hospital for a week."

Hunter turned in his chair, shifting slightly away from me. "They put me in a temporary home while he recovered, but when Dad got out, he said I should stay. Both of them had serious issues they needed to work through and they couldn't be the parents they wanted to be.

"It wasn't supposed to be forever. He wanted me back. Mom wanted me back. But every time I returned home, I triggered Mom's demons. I was a constant reminder of her failure as a mother and what she'd done to Dad. My third return to my foster parents was my last. They made the open adoption official."

"I'm sure it was hard for all of you," I said. "I'm sorry."

His smile didn't reach his eyes. "Every villain has a tragic backstory."

"I don't think you're a villain. I understand why you hate Breakbattle. What I don't get is why you enrolled?"

Hunter looked around. "This place was the first domino to fall. The destruction of my family began here. And yet, it was open. People sent their kids here. They called it one of the best schools. They swore up and down that Breakbattle has changed. I wanted to see if it was true for myself."

"It wasn't true," I said.

"Of course it wasn't. Everyone knew the name Becca Taylor, but the changes made in her memory were laughable. They split the genders and that was supposed to solve everything? The year before I came, you were targeted, bullied, and framed, and the battle system helped the Elites do it.

"I became For All because people needed to wake up. This system is bullshit and they wanted to force it on every public school in the state. I had to make people see." He leaned forward. His eyes pierced me with an intensity I'd seen before—in my reflection. "I'm going to enact real change in Rebecca's name by making sure Whittaker does what should have been done after they killed her."

"End the battle system," I finished.

"Yes."

"Okay, Hunter." I went to him. Hunter stood to accept my hug. "I understand. Honestly, I do."

"If anyone could, I knew it would be you."

"Thank you for telling me about your family." I let him go. Moving back to the door, my mind spun with the truth of this boy's life. "I'm sorry for everything that happened. Breakbattle failed Rebecca in every way."

"Now I'll make it right."

"I don't approve of the things you've done but at least it's over."

"Over?" Hunter cocked his head. "What are you talking about? It's not over."

"I know, but students are protesting. They're awake. They're fighting back. Whittaker will give in eventually."

His brows drew together. "Eventually isn't good enough. I've waited and Whittaker let the protesting go on last semester and didn't do anything. I bet he's planning to do the same this semester."

"You've done all you can do."

Hunter laughed—a sharp, harsh sound that grated on me. "Are you sure about that? Because I've barely started." He yanked open his drawer and pulled out a notebook. "I've been working on these the entire break, and trust me, they're inspired. I thought I'd start with hacking into the system and deleting all the grades, and then I'll finish by burning these uniforms and their disgusting labels."

"Burning?" I croaked. I took a step back, and then another. I groped blindly for the knob. "Why?"

"A fire in the laundry room should do it."

"A fire? Are you insane?!"

"I thought we understood each other, Zela."

"Well, you were wrong! You said you weren't violent!"

"I'm not," Hunter replied evenly. "I'll make sure no one is around."

"The fuck you will. I'm giving you up to Whittaker. I could have let everything else slide, but starting a fire in a school full of kids is the stupidest, most dangerous thing I've ever heard and you're supposed to be a genius."

Hunter's expression remained neutral. "You won't tell Whittaker."

"Watch me." I gave him my back.

"You won't say anything because I'm going to make you a deal. You keep my secret and I'll tell you who killed Cameron Dupre."

My muscles went rigid. *What did he say?*

"You're thinking how could I possibly know you're looking for his killer?" Hunter went on. "Your boyfriends aren't as sly as you think. I thought it was strange when Derek started asking the recruits about the fundraiser and if Cameron was fighting with anyone. Then I overheard them questioning Santiago.

"One of you wants to know who killed Cameron, and if it's important to one of your guys, it's important to you. Or it could just be about you. Either way, I can tell you who I saw covered in blood the night he was killed."

I ripped open the door. The guys were coming down the hall.

"Ten more minutes," I shouted at them.

"Zela—"

"I said ten minutes."

I closed the door in their bewildered faces and locked it for good measure. I faced Hunter, breathing hard.

"Who was it?"

He stood. Hunter wasn't smiling or smirking now. "First, I want you to know I haven't been sitting on this the whole time and protecting a killer. I didn't realize what I saw was important until I heard Landon and Santiago talking about fights, blood, and the fundraiser."

"Tell me."

"I don't have proof," he said. "All I know is the night Cameron was killed, I was out prepping another strike against the system. The administration building is usually empty around that time. I overheard someone in the bathroom and cracked the door open. He was standing over the sink, cleaning a cut on his chest."

I advanced on him. "Who?"

"I really didn't think anything of it, Zela," Hunter plowed on like I hadn't spoken. "They said there must have been a fight. That Cameron was beaten and hit on the head. He didn't look like he just came from beating a guy to death. His cut wasn't even deep. But when he spoke about the fundraiser, I remembered. I saw who hit Cameron that night."

"Hunter! Tell me his name!"

"I will. I just need you to agree you won't tell anyone the truth about me." He held out his hand. "Deal?"

I slapped it away. "No, we're not agreed. You want a deal? Here's one. You're going to give me the fucking name of a killer, Hunter. A *killer*! This isn't a game. An actual life has been taken and he had friends and a family who loved him.

"You're going to tell me who did it because it's the right thing to do. And then we'll make another deal. You won't sabotage or set fire to *anything*. Melody and I made a list of safe, peaceful protests against the system and you won't do anything but what's on it. As long as you do, I won't tell Whittaker you're For All. That's it, Hunter. Tell me the name."

Hunter's skin flushed deathly pale. "But, Ze—"

"Tell me his name!" I screamed.

Violent pounding sounded on the wood. The boys went mad shouting for me to let them in.

"It's— It's Zach," he stuttered. "Zachary Fields."

I blew out of the room. Hunter was a fleeting niggle in my mind the second my eyes were off him. There was only one thing I cared about.

"Zela, are you okay? What did he do?"

I ducked their reaching hands. "He told me who killed Cameron. I have to go."

"Wait. What?" Derek said.

"He's downstairs. I'm getting the truth right now."

"Zela, slow down and tell us what's going on."

An emotion I'd never felt and therefore couldn't name squeezed me too tight to breathe. If I stopped, it would drag me under. "Zach killed my brother. I'm going to find out why."

Landon shot in front of the door.

"Let me go," I shouted.

"You're not going anywhere," said Derek.

He took hold of my wrist. I violently jerked away, but he came after me. He grabbed both of my hands and pushed me against the wall. I fought and the guys huddled in, blocking my escape.

"You told me that you'd come to us when it got too much. You promised, baby, that you'd let us take care of you."

I sobbed wretchedly.

"We'll do whatever you need us to do," Landon said. "Just talk to us."

I stopped fighting. Derek caught me as the strength leeched out of my body. They carried me to his room and put me on the bed. The four of them laid with me, crushing me in the middle and pouring their love and attention on me. Eventually, I calmed.

"What did Hunter say?" Michael asked. "Why does he think it's Zach?"

I took a shuddering breath and released it. "The night Cameron died..."

THE FIVE OF US WERE a silent troop marching through the hall. We talked for almost an hour going over how I would approach Zach. I suggested talking to him alone and that was rejected immediately, but I stuck to my point that he wasn't going to talk to all of us. Eventually, we agreed to a plan that we all liked.

It's possible Zach was innocent. I couldn't think of a motive he had for killing Cameron. Despite that, Hunter witnessed their fight, so there must be a reason they were once on the outs.

We reached the ground floor. The noise of unpacking, goodbyes, and last day off excitement floated out of the F dorm.

"Don't let him get between you and the door," Cole said. "Don't let him lock it and keep your phone on."

"I know the plan."

"We'll be right outside."

"Thank you."

I stepped into the madness and walked a familiar path to my old dorm. Zach opened on the third knock. His face crumpled into a scowl.

"What do you want?"

"I need to talk to you, Zach."

"Fuck off."

I jammed my foot in the way, stopping him from slamming the door in my face.

"You talk to me or you talk to the police," I hissed through the doorjamb. "Your choice."

He stilled. "The police?"

"Are you going to let me in or not?"

"Whatever. Come in."

Zach threw himself on Adam's old bed. He watched me close and lean against the door with eyes dripping with dislike.

He scoffed. "What the hell are you going on about? Why would you call the police?"

"Simple. A witness just told me you murdered Cameron Dupre. Don't you think the police would be interested in that information?"

I studied him for a reaction. His expression didn't change.

"I have no clue what you're talking about," he replied. "Get out."

"They saw you fight with Cameron at the fundraiser. And you were seen cleaning up blood in the administration bathroom the night he was killed."

He shrugged. "So? Cam and I got into an argument, but we made up later with no hard feelings. As for the blood, I got banged up at soccer practice and went to the administration bathroom for privacy. The only place I can get any since you stole my dorm."

I didn't rise to the bait. "Is that your story? Soccer practice and no hard feelings."

"It's not a story. It's the truth."

A smile stretched across my lips. "Great. I'm relieved we cleared that up."

"Great," he mocked in a high-pitched voice. "Now get your ass out."

"In a minute. Before I go, I'm going to call Detective Langman and tell him it was all a misunderstanding. He'll be relieved too."

Zach leaned up off the pillow. "Call who?"

"You don't mind, do you?"

"Why would I mind?" he snapped. "Call whoever you want."

"Good."

His eyes bore into me as I scrolled through my phone. I found the number and hit call. The room was silent except for the ring.

"What are you trying to prove?" Zach asked.

I put my finger over my lips. "Shh."

"Hello. This is Detective Langman. What can I do for you?"

"Hi, Detective," I greeted. "This is Zela Manning."

"Okay, you can hang up," Zach cut in.

"Miss Manning," said Langman. "Have you called to ask more questions about the case? Because I can't discuss it with you."

"I've called to give you some answers actually."

"Hang up the phone, Manning," Zach said, his voice getting louder.

"I found out who Cameron fought with at the fundraiser. And the night he was killed—"

"I get it. Hang up!" He jumped off the bed.

I threw up my hand and stopped him in his tracks. I pointed at the bed.

Zach got the hint and sat down.

"I have to call you back, Detective."

"Call me back? But you just—"

I hung up.

Zach's gaze locked onto mine. Dislike stoked into naked hatred. I could only imagine what he saw in my eyes.

"Talk, Zach."

"I didn't kill Cameron."

"Try again."

He bared his teeth. "I did *not* kill him!"

"So why did you hit him at the fundraiser?"

"None of your business."

"Wrong answer again." I hit redial.

"Stop it!"

"If you don't want to tell your story to the police, then you'd better tell me now. I won't ask again."

"Why do you even care?" he spat. "Cameron hated you."

The comment struck me but I didn't let on.

"Cameron may have hated me, but he didn't hate you. You were his friend. Why would you hurt him?"

Zach said nothing.

"What happened to you, Zach? Adam told me you used to be a great guy. Funny. Kind. Self-deprecating, but in a good way. You were one of his best friends and now look at you."

Color stained his cheeks. My words struck him too.

"You outed your friend to get into the Network. You bullied me, drugged me, and targeted me. You turned into this disgusting cockroach of a person and that was bad enough. Then you had to take it a step further and kill the only friend you had."

"He wasn't my friend," he forced through gritted teeth.

"You wouldn't let him be. He tried but you drove him away like you did everyone else."

"That's not true."

"It is true. He got you into the Network. He helped you and you thanked him by caving in his skull."

Zach smashed his fist on the nightstand. "He didn't help me!"

"Despite his faults, he was a good person and he didn't deserve—"

"Deserve!" Zach's shout blew me back. "You want to talk about what Cameron deserved? The answer is exactly what he fucking got!"

Bile burned my throat. What an awful thing to say. "Are you admitting what you did?"

"I didn't do anything."

"You attacked and threatened him at the fundraiser. You snuck off in the middle of the night covered in blood. I have a witness, Zach."

His throat bobbed.

"I'm giving you a chance to tell me your side," I said. "You get one more. Why did you kill him?"

My finger hovered over the phone.

"Who is this witness?" Sweat glistened on his lip. "Why didn't they come forward months ago? I don't think they exist."

I tapped my skull. "Think, Zach. How would I know about it if someone didn't see? Didn't you think you were alone both times?"

His eyes widened. How would he get around that one?

"I didn't—"

I turned around. "Goodbye, Zach. I have a call to make. I hoped you'd at least have an explanation for why you killed your friend—"

"He wasn't my friend!" Zach roared.

I spun just as he jumped up.

"Cameron Dupre wasn't anyone's friend. The guy was a selfish piece of shit!" Zach advanced on me. I didn't move as his hot breath hit my face. "Do you know what I went through because of him? He destroyed my life!"

"How did he do that, Zach?" I challenged. "You chose to do the Network's test. You lost the tournament and I was the only one who played fairly. You're the one who did those things."

"But he's the one who fucked my mom."

My comeback died on my tongue. "He what?"

"You heard me. Cameron came to my place before our junior year to convince me to challenge you to another tournament. That's when they met."

"Wait." My brain struggled to make sense of this. "Is your mom Em?"

"Crystal Emmeline Fields." His lips peeled back from his teeth. "They thought they were being so careful, then one day I came home early from tennis and found them on the couch. Mom asked me not to tell Dad. She promised it would never happen again, but she lied. I knew they hadn't stopped.

"I told Cameron to back off. I texted him. Called him. Tried to get him to listen. Their affair would ruin my family. Want to know what he finally said to me?"

I didn't. I already knew it wasn't what he should have said.

"He said it was none of my business and the two of them could do whatever they wanted."

Rage rolled off of Zach in waves. His fists were clenched so tightly his knuckles were white. He was reaching his boiling point and I feared what he'd do when he blew.

"Well guess what? Dad found out. Now they're going through a nasty divorce for the whole world to see!"

"What Cameron and your mom did was wrong, but they made a choice—"

"Choice! You keep saying that but when did I have a choice?" He thumped his chest. "Cameron hazed us and everyone went along with it. But I was the one who lost my friends! He ordered me to target you and the other Elites did it too, but you fuck all of them and look at me like I'm the trash.

"And you think I don't know Cameron sent my dick to the entire school! Where was my choice in that? Huh? Tell me!"

I trembled against the wood.

"My parents are getting divorced and my dad is moving out of Evergreen. That sure as fuck wasn't my choice." Zach shoved his face in mine. I could count the tiny teardrops clinging to his lashes. "Cameron hazed me, humiliated me, and then blew up my parents' marriage."

"So you killed him," I whispered.

"So I begged him to stop! I begged and I fought back and I shoved him off when he came at me with scissors!" A tear raced down his nose and splashed onto mine. "He wouldn't s-stop coming at me! He said he let me get two shots in but there wouldn't be a third. I punched him to end the fight and he hit his head on the bedpost! It was an accident!"

"Then why didn't you come forward?"

"Cameron ruined my life," he sobbed. Zach grew smaller—sinking, diminishing, folding in on himself like a man with nothing left inside. His head dropped onto my shoulder. "I lost everything because of him. I wasn't going to prison for him too."

"I don't want to be this guy, Zela." Zach hugged me tight. "I didn't have a choice, but Cameron did. His choices turned me into this. I'm sorry."

Shock dotted out my mind as Zach said the phrase I lost all hope I would hear.

"I'm sorry for everything. Please, tell me what to do," he cried. "I don't know what to do."

My arms rose inch by inch. I was unsure of myself even as I hugged him back, but I pushed it aside.

"Don't worry, Zach," I said gently. "I'll tell you what to do."

Chapter Nine

I went to bed that night with a single question on my mind. It plagued me through my first week of classes. I missed my morning meetups with Derek, my breakfasts with Michael, my study sessions with Cole, and my practice with Landon.

I knew who killed my brother. What did I do next?

I didn't make my decision until Friday morning. I stared at my reflection in the vanity and suddenly knew exactly what I would do.

Whatever it took.

I picked up my cell and made a call.

THE MANSION WAS JUST as magnificent in the daylight. I would say more so for the fact that you could see the beautiful flower gardens. I wouldn't be surprised if he paid a fortune for those. He paid a fortune for everything else.

"Thank you."

My driver honked a bye and drove off. Paying a driver to take me an hour to Evergreen on a Saturday morning wasn't ideal, but I couldn't ask the boys or Mom to take me here.

I passed the vintage cars and climbed the steps. The door opened after my first ring.

"Good morning," said the staff. "What can I do for you?"

"I'm here to see Dominick Dupre. Can you tell him Zela Manning is here?"

The man made no move to do so. "I'm sorry, Mr. Dupre is very busy today. He's not seeing anyone. In the future, please call ahead."

"Tell him I know who killed his son."

He blinked at me. "I see. Well... that is another matter entirely. Please come in. My name is Winston."

"Thank you."

Winston let me inside. "I'll let him know you're here."

I settled in to wait. My heels click-clacked on the marble as I admired the paintings.

"Miss Manning, follow me, please."

Winston and I walked the length of the front room and turned down a hall on the right. He pointed to the door at the far end. I thanked him again and went in.

Dominick Dupre's eyes were the first thing I saw. If I thought the reason for my visit would inject them with emotion, I was wrong.

"My butler says you have something to tell me."

"I do." I motioned to the chair in front of his desk. "May I sit?"

He nodded. Once.

I sat and got comfortable.

"What is their name?" asked Dominick.

I smiled at him. "I'll tell you... but I want something in exchange."

"Excuse me?"

"I'll give you what you want if you give me what *I* want."

"Is this a joke?"

I shook my head. "No joke. I know who killed your son. They confessed to me themselves."

Dominick folded his hands in front of him and gazed at me across the table. "Are you aware blackmail and obstructing justice are crimes, girl?"

"I don't want to do either of those things. I'm happy to tell you who did it. All I ask is that you give back control of the Network to Jonathan Grayson."

Dominick heaved himself out of the chair. "That's enough. Get out of here and don't come back."

"Cameron was sleeping with a married woman," I announced. "Someone found out and fought with him in his dorm room. They broke his alarm clock and at one point, Cameron slashed him with a pair of scissors. That's how his blood got on Cameron. In the struggle, Cameron hit his head on the post. He rushed out of there and took the scissors with him."

I gave him a hard look. "How did I know about the missing scissors when the police haven't released the information? I know because I found and spoke to him."

Dominick straightened to his full height. His eyes were a deep dark brown that bordered on black. They glittered as he towered over me. "You will tell me his name and I will give you nothing in return."

I looked back without flinching. "That hardly seems fair. I did what the police and your high-priced private investigators couldn't do. All I ask is that you give back what was never yours."

"All you ask?" Anger leeched into his voice. "I've drawn up papers, bought office space, lined up investors, and jumped through more hoops than you can imagine. You don't know what you're asking."

"I know that you loved your son more than anything. You're not a good man, but you were a good father, or as good as an awful man can be. You'll do the right thing and give back what you stole. You'll do it to get revenge for your son, and yes, I know it's revenge you want."

"I am not making myself clear." Dominick bent and put his hand on my shoulder. "I am the head of this organization. Grayson's time is done. That is all there is to it. You're beginning to make me angry, girl. If you know who killed my son, tell me *now*." His grip tightened on my shoulder. "He was murdered by a senseless coward and I will make them regret what they've done."

"I'm not telling you until you agree and put it in writing."

"You will tell me."

"No, I wo—"

Dominick seized my throat.

Gasping, my hands flew to my neck and scrabbled at his fingers.

"You come into my home, blackmail me, and use my son's murder as a bargaining chip?"

My eyes bugged out of my skull. Naked, raw fear flooded my mind and threw my plan out the window.

"Who killed my son?" he bellowed. Dominick shook me roughly. "Tell me, you stupid little bitch!"

I pounded on his arms. "N-no!"

He slammed my head on the desk. I screamed as pain exploded in my nose.

"You think I'm not a good man?"

Black spots danced in my vision.

"This is me being a good man and doing right by my son," he said. "You're not getting in my way."

I jabbed at his eyes as hard as I could.

"*Argh!*" His hand snapped to his face and I took my chance.

I ran for the door. "H-help!" I rasped.

Dominick grabbed me by the scruff of my neck, lifted, and threw. I sailed onto his desk. My head hit the surface hard and I saw stars. I rolled off and smacked into his chair. We both fell to the floor.

My entire body was pain. Warm blood gushed from my ruined nose and stained my dress. I struggled to push myself up.

Come on, Zela!

The floor thudded with heavy approaching footfalls. Agony ripped through my skull. Dominick yanked me to my feet by my hair, tearing out several strands.

"Give me his name."

He wrapped his hand around my neck again and I screamed, "Zach! Z-Zachary Fields!"

"How do I know you're telling the truth?" he growled in my ear.

"Ask him," I rasped. "He wants to confess. Zach's ready to tell the truth. It's him."

"We'll see."

Dominick marched to the door. I clawed at his hands. He didn't release his hold on my head or neck. The tips of my shoes skated over the tiles as I was dragged through the front room.

"Open it!" ordered Dominick.

He threw me out onto the driveway. I rolled a few feet and then smacked to a stop, not moving. The door slammed close.

I don't know how long I laid there. Consciousness drifted in and out, brought in on a haze and taken out by inky darkness. In a stream of lucidness, I took my phone out of my pocket. My hand shook so hard it took several tries to dial.

"Hello?"

"Zachary Fields," I forced out. "Dominick D-Dupre's house. Help."

I dropped my head on the pavement. The darkness came for me once more.

"WHAT IS THAT? WHAT are you giving her?"

I slowly came to.

"You didn't give her that yesterday. I want to know everything you're doing."

"Yes, ma'am."

I cracked open an eyelid and groaned. The light was a nail through my brain.

"Zela? You're awake." A gentle hand stroked my forehead. "Can you open your eyes?"

I tried again. Blinking blearily, Mom came into focus.

"Hi," I croaked.

One word and Mom burst into tears.

"Oh, my only one."

I took stock while Mom cried and a nurse stepped up to poke and prod me.

"Zela, what were you doing at that man's house?" asked Mom. "What did he do to you?"

Langman emerged from the bathroom. "I'm sure we would all appreciate a deeper explanation. I wasn't expecting this when you phoned and said you'd call me back the next day with the name of someone I needed to protect and the name of a killer in that order. I'd love to know how we arrived here."

I nodded. "One sec."

The nurse helped me sit up and sip some water. When I felt human, I began.

"It started with the car that almost hit me at the park. It didn't make sense to me that the driver was sharp enough to stop for the woman and her dog, but right after was suddenly too drunk to see me standing still. The next thought was that someone tried to kill me."

Mom sucked in a sharp breath.

"The only reason someone would have wanted me dead back then was if they believed I killed Cameron. The list of people who would avenge Cameron was small, and his dad was at the top of my list. He confirmed it at the party. The way he spoke about getting him justice scared me."

My voice was rough and scratchy. I plowed on anyway. "The problem was I couldn't prove it. When I found out the truth about Zach, I bet that Dominick would go after him too, so I wanted you there waiting, Detective. He tried to have me killed and now he'll be charged for attempted murder. Also, assault."

"Did you go there knowing he would do this?" Mom asked, horrified.

"No. I thought he might shout or threaten me. I never thought this would happen. He flipped so quickly I didn't know what to do."

"You were right about him if that's a comfort," Langman said. "That night, he sent a hitman to kill Zach. We caught him putting a bomb under his car and he told us everything. But my biggest surprise of the night was a full confession from Zachary Fields."

"Zach broke down. He asked me what to do to make things right and I realized his confession could be used to get a dangerous man behind bars. I told him a detective named Langman would come for him and he needed to tell you the truth."

He scrubbed his face. "What you did was incredibly foolish. You should have told me everything from the beginning and let me handle it. I have weapons, training, and backup."

I glanced down at myself and my hospital bed. "Trust me, I have learned my lesson."

"I hope so. Dupre will serve time for what he's done, and we'll help Fields the best we can. This case is officially put to bed." He patted a bit of me that wasn't sore. "Good luck, Zela. Feel better."

It was just me and Mom—and the nurse.

"How long have I been out?" I asked.

"Two days. And they were the worst two days of my life."
She took my hand. "Don't ever do this again."

"I won't.

"About that man…"

"I know he's my father," I finished.

An unhealthy, sallow sheen took over her face. "How?"
she whispered.

"The cops did a blood test and they matched it with
Cameron's."

She dropped her head in her hands. Mom was quiet for
a long time.

"I hope you see why I did what I did."

"I do," I replied. "He wasn't a man I needed to know."

"How could he hurt you? His own daughter."

"I didn't tell him the truth and I never will. As far as I'm
concerned, I don't have a father."

"Are you truly okay with this?"

"Yes." I smiled and it tugged uncomfortably on my ban-
daged nose. "My mom raised me to be a strong, independent
woman who doesn't rely on a man for her identity."

She kissed my forehead. "That's my girl."

"Mom, one more thing," I began. "I've thought about
the money for the plane ticket and I decided I want to buy
two."

"Two?"

"One for me and you. It's been a long time since the
Manning women explored the world together. Plus, if you
come, Adam's parents will definitely say yes. What do you
think?"

"I'd love to, Zela. We'll buy them as soon as we get back home. We might even stretch it to four tickets and get all the Manning women on board."

"IT LOOKS WORSE THAN it is."

"It looks terrible," said Derek.

The five of us were in my bedroom at home. I got out of the hospital a few days ago and was taking some time off from school.

"This shouldn't have happened," said Cole.

Derek added, "You promised we would do this together."

"I broke my promise," I said, "but I plan on spending the rest of my life making it up to all of you."

His gaze softened. "You didn't really go through this to get the Network back, did you?"

"No. I only said that because Dupre wouldn't have believed I was giving him the name out of the goodness of my heart. He thought Cameron and I hated each other."

"It doesn't matter now. The Network is dead. Dominick made it so public that the entire world found out when he was arrested. All of the members dropped out to avoid the bad publicity. There's nothing for my dad left to save."

"Are you guys disappointed?"

The four of them shook their heads.

"We have everything we want," said Cole.

"Zela," Mom called. "You have another visitor."

"Send him up."

"Who is it?" Michael asked me.

"You'll see."

The door creaked open and Hunter stepped inside. The four boys jumped to their feet.

"What are you doing here?" Derek demanded.

"Zela asked me to come."

Derek turned on me. "Why?"

"Because I had an idea while I was cooped up in the hospital. It's gotten crazy over the years, but we all want the same thing. The end of the battle system. I think I have a way we can make it happen."

Hunter surged forward. "I'm listening."

"Remember the video you sent to the school? We need to do that again, but I want to add one more name to the list..."

Final Chapter

Of all my semesters at Breakbattle, my final one won favorite by a mile. At the start, Hunter and I recorded a video of me sans hood. In it, I talked about my life at the school since my first night. I spoke about the Network, the hazing, the targeting, the fights, the Battle Doctor, and all of the things in between.

Hunter sent it to everyone at school including one addition: Ezra Lennox.

Number one on our list of peaceful protests was contact the media and I can't believe we didn't do it sooner. Ezra ran my video for four weeks in a row. The principal was inundated with so many calls from parents, mental health specialists, and members of the school board that he had to disconnect his line.

Halfway through February, he announced the battle system was no longer a part of the curriculum. In the years to come, they would determine what kind of school Breakbattle would be, but it wouldn't be one that separated kids by class and gender.

Without the battles, there were no more assigned privileges. Students went where they wanted, hung out with everyone, and learned that helping someone become better was not cheating. With everyone having an equal chance, we turned our sights to the spring break trip.

Melody proved her fierceness by organizing the biggest bake sale the school had ever seen. We raised more than double the money we needed to send all of the seniors on the trip.

My boys and I had an amazing time in New York making memories—some naughty—all over the city. They loved it so much that when we got back home, they announced they were coming to Europe with us too.

"Can't leave you alone with Moon," Landon reminded me.

Our last semester was perfect in every way.

"And now we have the next four years at university," I said. I smoothed down Landon's lapel.

"Do I pass?" he asked. He did a little spin in his cap and gown.

"Don't you always?"

He kissed me. "Yes."

Together, we joined the graduates in the front rows. Parents hooted and hollered behind us—Andronika, Aunt Bev, and Naomi Grayson loudest of all.

"Good morning, students, staff, families, and honored guests," Whittaker began. "Join me in celebrating the class of 2020."

We stomped and cheered our heads off.

"The last four years with this class have been the most challenging in my career."

That earned a few chuckles.

"But challenges aren't to be feared, they're to be faced. Without life's challenges we cannot grow. Our valedictorian is a young lady who embodies the spirit of that message. Ladies and gentlemen, Zela Rae Manning."

I jogged onto the stage in a shower of applause. Whittaker shook my hand warmly. "Congratulations, Zela."

"Thank you, sir."

Taking his place at the podium, I looked out at the sea of faces and smiled.

"Hello, everyone," I began. "A lot of you know my story thanks to a certain trending video. I am the girl who dressed as a boy and got into all sorts of trouble. That message was great and important, but it was about what I lost, not what Breakbattle has given me. I once said that there were pieces of me out there that I needed to get back. Well I found those pieces right here at Breakbattle.

"The first piece, education and a strong mind, I owe to my teachers, Mr. Dawson, Dr. O'Quinn, Mrs. Peterson, Mrs. Munoz, and my mom. She taught me everything from math to conquering the world.

"The second piece, integrity, I owe to the people who stood for what they believed in even when it wasn't easy. You inspire me always.

"The third, friendship, meant more to a girl who moved around her whole life than my friends will ever know.

"And the final piece, love, I owe to a few people. Love isn't kind. Sometimes it steals your dessert and tells you to F off."

Titters broke out in the space.

"Love isn't patient," I continued. "It leaves without you when you take too long. And love isn't perfect. It's messy and frustrating and wonderful and most days, perfect."

The audience clapped.

"I found all my pieces at Breakbattle," I said, "and maybe you did too. All I know for sure is Class of 2020 is going to be the one to spread education, integrity, friendship, and love into the world." I lifted my hands. "We're the class that changed Breakbattle. After that, the world is easy."

"Yeah!" They stomped and cheered.

"Good luck, 2020!" I shouted. "We did it!"

Fifteen Years Later

"WHERE IS THE POTATO salad? Noah? Noah!"

The ten-year-old skidded to a stop and gave his mom a wide-eyed 'what now' look.

"Where did you put the potato salad?" Jordan asked.

He shrugged and then went back to running around with his cousin.

She sighed. "Well, this barbeque is off to a great start. Food is missing and most of the guests are late."

"It is great, baby." Her husband tugged her onto his lap and wrapped his arms around her swollen belly. Adam nuzzled her neck until she sighed with pleasure. "Just relax. Everything is perfect."

"Mom and Aunt Bev are running late," I said. "Their flight was delayed."

"I still can't believe those two travel and run a blog together," Jordan said. "Remember when they couldn't stand each other?"

"Yeah. That was like... last week."

We burst out laughing. The absolute best thing about the home we bought next to the Moon mansion was having Jordan five minutes away.

"Baby bump," she chirped.

I heaved myself off the patio chair and bumped my seven-months pregnant belly with hers. I swear we didn't plan their synchronized birth dates.

"So how's work, Zee?" Adam asked. "Last week at lunch, we spent so much time talking about the kids we didn't get to it."

"Work is great. A new semester is always hectic but my Partial Differential Equations class is a great bunch. We're going to have a lot of fun this year."

"I need to update you on what fun is," Jordan said.

"Oh Zela knows how to have fun," Derek cut in. His words were laced with so much suggestion you couldn't mistake his meaning. Thirty-three years old and he couldn't shake that bad boy streak.

Derek dropped a kiss on the sleeping three-year-old's head. Noelle's favorite nap spot was her daddy's chest and he made sure he was here to provide it even if he had to leave set early. It helped that his boss/director was his dad.

He'll never lose that great dad streak either.

Michael stepped onto the patio bearing gifts. "Found the potato salad."

Our son followed him out. "And I've got the forks," he said happily, waving them in the air.

Six years old, Michael Junior was a bundle of energy. Michael Senior liked to joke that he finished med school early because MJ demanded to be played with.

"Alright," said Jordan. "We can get this party started."

"Gotta find Cole first," Michael said.

Derek pointed across the lawn. "He'll be at home."

Our second house is where I left my love while our ten-year-old daughter, Kadence played with Noah. People found our setup strange, but they also found our relationships strange so who cared what they thought. We bought a huge, grand manor and chopped it up into three sections and homes.

Each one had a kitchen, a master bedroom, rooms for our kids, and a living space. Doors between the section gave us the chance to connect as a family and maintain our privacy as four couples. Michael, Landon, Derek and our kids loved living in the big house. And Cole had his peace in the converted pool house in the back.

It was wonderful because the kids loved that too. They got ridiculously excited for their sleepovers at Daddy Cole's house.

"And where's Landon?"

"I've got to drag him out of the nursery," I said. "He's in there obsessing over color treatments."

"You remember how he was with Henry," Jordan teased. "Just be happy he isn't ordering another three-thousand-dollar crib from Switzerland."

I chuckled. Daddy Landon was super protective, but he made sure I didn't lift a finger when I was pregnant with our son seven years ago, and he didn't let me lift one with our daughter now.

As if they knew we were talking about them, Cole and Landon rounded the house, deep in conversation.

"—have people come in and talk to the students," said Cole. "They'd get a lot from it."

"I already have people in mind."

I love seeing these two join forces.

Landon as the lawyer and owner of the best LGBT youth shelter in three counties, and Cole as the new principal of Breakbattle.

"The main crew is all here," Adam said. "How about a toast?"

We all gathered around the table and lifted our glasses.

"What should we toast to?" Jordan asked. She patted her belly. "New additions?"

"New opportunities?" Michael put in.

I looked around at the people I loved and the family we made.

"How about we toast to finding our missing pieces and becoming whole?" I asked.

We raised our glasses high.

"Becoming whole."

Mailing List

1

---

1. https://dl.bookfunnel.com/f959ie6xk0

The Angels

My parents forgot something when they ran... me.
After scamming most of our town out of their life savings,
my folks disappeared in the middle of the night.
Forced to take me in, my estranged aunt and uncle shipped
me off to Raven River Academy the first chance they got.
In my town, the line between the haves and the have-nots is
actually a twelve-foot gate that keep the unwanted where
they belong. Nothing could unite the two factions until I
set foot on campus.
For the first time in our history, they all agree on one thing:
I must pay for my father's sins.
But why should I care?
The joke is on them because I have nothing left inside. No
part of me that isn't already broken. I invite them to do
their worst.
Until the Angels enter the game.
The most dangerous gang in town has a score to settle with
my family, and Cassius, Clay, Hiro, and Royal are here to
collect.
Raven River soon becomes a battleground of lies, deceit,
and violence, and I stand at the heart of it.

The gorgeous otherworldly Angels will remind me that there is one thing left that I care about... and they'll destroy it in heavenly fire.

If you'd like to read The Angels click here.[1]

---

1. *http://mybook.to/TheAngels*

ABOUT THE AUTHOR

Ruby Vincent is a published author with many novels under her belt but now she's taking a fun foray into contemporary romance. She loves saucy heroines, bold alpha males, and weaving a tale where both get their happy ever after.

www.ingramcontent.com/pod-product-compliance
Lightning Source LLC
Chambersburg PA
CBHW032012310726
48972CB00002B/375